This book is dedicated to my parents.
Antonio, whose Italian ancestry inspired both my pen name and Detective Inspector Paolo Storey's lineage, and Elizabeth Rose (1934-2011), who would have been thrilled to see this novel published.

Frances di Plino is the pen name of Lorraine Mace, humour columnist for Writing Magazine.

She is also a deputy editor of Words with JAM, writes fiction for the women's magazine market, features and photo-features for monthly glossy magazines, and is a writing competition judge for Writers' Forum. Winner of a Petra Kenney International Poetry Award, she has been placed in numerous creative writing and poetry competitions.

Lorraine, a tutor for Writers Bureau, is the author of the Writers Bureau course, Marketing Your Book, and the co-author, with Maureen Vincent-Northam, of the Writer's ABC Checklist (Accent Press).

Also featuring Det. Insp. Paolo Storey

Someday Never Comes

Bad Moon Rising

CHAPTER ONE

"Please, no. Oh God. No more. Please."

Excited by her pleading, he pounded his fists into her face. He craved release, but couldn't give in. Not yet. Not while she could defile him. Only when her swollen lids meant she could no longer see did he allow himself to take her throat between his hands and free her soul.

He waited for her death throes to pass, then relaxed his grip and moved down the bed to suck and caress her breasts. His heart pounded. Now. He had to move now before it was too late. Shifting position, he straddled her body. Arching his back, he emptied his hatred onto her breasts.

Shuddering, he slid from the bed and fell to the floor.

"I'm sorry," he whispered. "So sorry, so sorry, so…"

His throat constricted. As tears flowed, he screamed. Thrashing wildly, he knocked against the chair holding the woman's clothes. Her tights fell across his neck and he panicked, clawing himself free.

Fucking whore!

"God forgive me," he sobbed. "She made me. Forgive me, God. Forgive me."

Crawling to the corner cupboard, he opened the door and reached for the scourge. He braced himself, then flicked the nine-tailed lash, the tiny spiked ends digging into his flesh.

Each strike lifted him closer to purity, until he collapsed. Exhausted, he slept.

He woke at first light, ready for the next stage. Filling a bowl with water, he brought it to the bed, then scraped under each of the woman's nails before washing most of her body in the warm water. He swabbed above and below her breasts, careful not to disturb his gift, the sign of her salvation. From under the bed he brought out a small black leather casket. He removed a fine-toothed comb and ran it through her pubic hair, placing the loose hairs in the envelope he'd already marked with a number four.

***

Detective Inspector Paolo Storey hunched deeper into his sheepskin. The cold suited his mood. A biting wind, typical for the dying days of February, gusted across the front of the criminal courts and played havoc with the press microphones. One of the reporters dropped his dictaphone. It bounced once before landing in the gutter. A spasm of disgust crossed his face as he reached down and brought it up, dripping with sludge. For the first time that day, Paolo felt like smiling. He didn't like reporters, and that one in particular enjoyed knocking the police.

He couldn't understand why the press considered it was okay to have a go at the people trying to put criminals away. Lowlife cons had more rights than their victims. He tried to contain his anger but he was too mad at the world in general, and justice in particular.

Paolo and his Detective Sergeant, Dave Johnson, stepped back to allow the solicitor and Frank Azzopardi to pass. The reporters began yelling questions, each determined to be heard. Matthew Roberts stood beside his client, waiting for the noise to abate.

"Seems the bastard's got away with it, sir," Dave whispered.

Paolo turned his head slightly to answer; the icy wind was making his eyes water. "Yeah, that tends to happen when the only witness disappears, particularly when she's also the victim. Ssh, let's hear what Roberts has to say."

"My client, Frank Azzopardi, a well-respected businessman, has been the victim of yet another effort by the police to improve their conviction rates. He has been unfairly targeted, accused of attempted murder and grievous bodily harm, yet not one witness to the alleged attack has come forward. Even the supposed victim hasn't felt it worth her while to follow up on her original statement. We have been told today that the Crown Prosecution Service cannot find sufficient evidence to bring the case to trial and that all charges against Mr Azzopardi have been dropped. We shall be making a complaint about the harassment he has suffered at the hands of an overzealous police force. Depending on the outcome of that complaint, we will consider our legal options. That is all, we have no further comment."

Paolo knew they were most probably too far away for Roberts and the reporters to hear him, but he lowered his voice just in case.

"I could've written that speech for him," he said. "He's like Pavlov's bloody dog. See a camera – badmouth the police."

They made an incongruous pair, the Maltese pimp and his legal representative. Matthew Roberts dressed with a quiet elegance at complete odds with his client's flamboyant attire. It was easy to see why Roberts made female heads turn: tall and good-looking, he exuded confidence and charm. Azzopardi was only a few inches shorter, but a swarthy complexion, shiny black hair and flashy designer clothes made him look almost a caricature of his companion.

Roberts and Azzopardi had a close friendship that went all the way back to their shared schooldays. As a teenager in the same school, Paolo had once wanted to be part of Matthew Roberts' inner circle, but even back then he'd loathed Azzopardi. Now the less he had to do with his former classmates the better, but with Roberts representing Azzopardi it was impossible not to run up against both of them.

The two walked away, the reporters at their heels still calling out questions.

Paolo sighed as they passed. "I'll get that bastard one day. We'd best try and track down our missing witness."

They walked towards Dave's car, Paolo silently running through the possibilities of what might have happened to Lisa Boxer, until Dave interrupted his thoughts.

"Do you reckon Roberts believes all that guff he spouts?" he asked, patting his pockets until he located his car keys. "I mean he can't really be stupid enough to think you'd try to frame Azzopardi just to get a conviction, can he?"

Paolo wondered if Dave was questioning his integrity. They hadn't been partners long enough to establish any kind of rapport yet, so he wasn't sure what the younger man thought, especially as the case predated Dave joining the team.

"I don't know what goes through his head. Maybe he just likes being on the box. I feel as though I can't switch the set on without Mr Smooth spouting police corruption." Paolo changed his voice to imitate the cultured tones of Matthew Roberts. "It is my belief the police couldn't find their own stations without a map. They are incompetent."

He waited until Dave stopped laughing. "All I know is, I had Azzopardi this time and I let him slip away. I should've insisted on protection for Lisa Boxer, but I didn't. On the other hand, she might have done a runner. Prostitutes don't like dealing with the police, not even when we're on the same side."

They got in the car and Dave manoeuvred it away from the kerb, edging smoothly into the Bradchester traffic.

"How come you never clean this garbage heap?" Paolo asked, kicking around to move empty Coke cans, burger wrappings and newspapers so that he had somewhere to put his feet.

"I never have time, sir. Maybe I should get myself a girlfriend."

Paolo grunted. "Fat chance of that. You know what they call you back at the station?"

"Of course. Tomcat. I love 'em and I leave 'em. But I bet I could still get one of them to clean the car if I put my mind to it."

"Sorry to ruin your daydreams, but we're living in the twenty-first century, not the dark ages, or haven't you noticed?"

"No! Are we really?" Dave asked, laughing in a way that irritated Paolo even more than his crass comments.

Paolo allowed his mind to wander until Dave's next question caught his attention.

"So you believe Azzopardi did it, sir? I mean he says he didn't, and his alibi seems pretty good. The girlfriend's not budging, and we don't have anything on him other than the prostitute's story." He paused. "What made you believe her, anyway?

Paolo fumbled in his pocket, bringing out his cigarettes. He shook one out and held it halfway to his lips. "I saw her in hospital after she'd been beaten," he said, his voice hardened as he remembered. "There wasn't a part of her that wasn't bruised."

Paolo fell silent, remembering the way Lisa had barely been able to move without crying out.

"You really think the girlfriend was ready to perjure herself?"

Paolo sighed. "Maria Vassallo has been Azzopardi's girlfriend since she was fifteen. She'd say the sky was black at midday if he wanted her to, then hotfoot it to confession straight afterwards to wash her soul clean."

"So why did he do it? I mean, why would he get his own hands dirty?"

"I think it was meant as a warning to the Albanians to stay off his turf." He raised his lighter and lit the cigarette, then dragged the smoke deep into his lungs. "Azzopardi only took over his uncle's empire a few years back; he's got no intention of letting anyone else in. As for why he did it himself, I know for a fact he likes to slap the girls around. His Maria has carried the odd bruise."

"Then why has Lisa Boxer disappeared just when we needed

her to convince the CPS? D'you have to smoke? The car stinks for days afterwards," Dave said, opening the car window.

The sudden rush of cold air hit Paolo like a physical blow. "Christ, you trying to give us both pneumonia? Close the window, for God's sake. This car stinks whether I smoke or not." He took another drag on his cigarette, then opened his window just enough to let the smoke out. "I agree with you, it doesn't add up, which is why we're going to pay a visit to Miss Boxer."

The car moved steadily through the Bradchester streets. Paolo closed his eyes, uninterested in the change of scenery as they travelled away from the affluent detached properties that ringed the centre of town and headed towards the council estates on the outskirts. The thought of a man like Frank Azzopardi getting away with anything stuck in his gullet, but his real contempt he kept for Matthew Roberts. How Roberts could bring himself to represent someone like Azzopardi was beyond him. Even though he'd known both men for more than twenty-five years, he still didn't get it. Strange how just recently he'd been running into people he'd gone to school with...

Paolo's phone rang, bringing him back to the present.

"Storey. Okay, where? Right, about fifteen minutes. Yep, we're on our way."

He put the phone back in his pocket. "Seems like our chat with Lisa Boxer will have to wait. Turn around when you can; we're heading to Gallows Heath. Remember just after you'd joined the team, they found a woman's body that looked like a lump of butcher's meat?" At Dave's nod, Paolo continued. "They've found another one."

Chapter Two

He switched on the laptop and waited for it to power up. Taking the memory stick from the table, he tried to fit it into the USB port. Anticipation made his hands shake and he had difficulty fitting the flash drive into the opening. Breathing deeply, he forced himself to calm down and eventually succeeded in slotting it home. Turning off the table lamp, he sat in the dark and waited for the images to appear.

Even though the camera angle still wasn't exactly right, he could see more of this one's face as she thrashed from side to side trying, and failing, to avoid his fists. As he watched his onscreen self, his hand slipped under his cassock, moving in time with each punch.

Now, as he saw himself spurting over her dead body, the heat rose, higher, tighter, throbbing, spurting. Dead... fucking... filthy... whore. He fell forward, body jerking in ecstasy, until the last exquisite twitch.

Sated for the moment, he lolled back in the chair, heart pounding, thinking of the great gift God had bestowed on him. It meant he'd never be caught.

You can't catch someone who doesn't exist.

***

Gallows Heath formed a green barrier between the haves and have-nots of Bradchester. The wide expanse of common was the only place where the two sectors of society almost met. Council estates bordered the south and east sides, private housing overlooked the heath from the other two boundaries.

The car park on the southern border, providing parking for two nearby tower blocks, was already cordoned off. The blue and white tape, fluttering in the howling wind, looked almost festive.

A crowd had gathered, and a chorus of whispered horror battled against the sound of the rising storm. Paolo shook his head.

"I'd pray for rain to drive this lot indoors, but that would make our job even harder," he muttered.

A constable came over as they approached the cordoned-off area. Flashing his warrant card, Paolo smiled at the uniformed man.

"PC Gibson, sir," the young man said. "The schoolboys who discovered the body are over there with WPC Start. Their names are Patrick Kilbride and Freddy Samson."

Paolo looked across to where a couple of lads were being reassured by a policewoman. "What do you know so far?"

"The boys were playing football on the heath and kicked the ball into the car park. They saw an arm and panicked. Fortunately that chap over there, a Mr James Smedley," he said, pointing to a man sitting on a nearby bench, "was passing and had a mobile. He called the emergency services and stayed with the lads until we arrived."

"Right, let's have a look, shall we?" Paolo saw the young man's face blanch and took pity on him. "You wait here, Gibson. Keep the vultures at bay."

A look of relief flooded the constable's face. Paolo guessed it had probably been the young policeman's first corpse.

As Paolo and Dave approached the body the stench of decay made them gag. The top half of the corpse had been dragged from its black plastic shroud. It looked likely that an animal had ripped through the bag. Teeth marks showed where chunks of flesh had been torn off. At first glance it was barely recognisable as human, apart from the bleached hair and painted fingernails.

"Jesus!" Paolo looked up to see that the SOCOs had arrived and walked back to the tape to meet them.

"Dr Royston," he said, nodding in greeting.

Paolo kept his expression neutral, aware of Dave watching for any possible interplay between him and Barbara Royston. There'd been some talk at Christmas after the party, which he was sure would have been repeated when Dave joined the team, even though no one had actually asked him face to face if there was anything going on. His thoughts drifted back to that night and he wondered if Barbara would ever forgive him. Sighing, he shoved the question to the back of his mind.

Barbara held his gaze, almost challenging him to say something, but he had no idea what. The forensic pathologist's thick blonde hair was held back in a ponytail, emphasizing her pale complexion and dark blue eyes. The livid birthmark staining her neck was on show for all to see. A flicker of emotion passed across her face, but Paolo couldn't read it. When he didn't speak, she gave a half shrug and turned away. As she walked towards the body, Paolo watched her rigid back. He had to clear the air, but now wasn't the time.

Leaving Barbara and her team to their examination, he turned to Dave.

"Come on, let's go and talk to the kids who found the body."

WPC Start was smiling and chatting to the two lads. Paolo looked over at Dave and could see him eyeing up the policewoman in terms of a future conquest. Coffee-coloured skin and almond-shaped brown eyes hinted at an ethnic mix. Pretty without being striking, she gave Dave a look that seemed to sum up his interest and reject it. Paolo took a silent bet with himself that Dave would see that as a challenge.

Patrick Kilbride and Freddy Samson looked to be in their early teens; both had short cropped hair, one dark and the other ginger. They were wearing the hoodies and oversized jeans that comprised the uniform of Bradchester youth and both looked terrified. They squared up to him as he approached, trying to give the impression that finding a dead body and dealing with the police was no big deal. An impression that disappeared as soon as they had to describe what had happened.

"It were just lying there, like. All bloody," Patrick said in answer to Paolo's question about finding the body. He shuddered. "The ball went in the car park, dinnit? An' we ran after it. It rolled up against the… you know… the…"

Paolo waited, but Patrick swallowed and shook his head. "What happened after you found the body? Did you touch anything?"

"No way," Freddy jumped in when his friend didn't answer. "We ran. He was screaming like a girl," he said, giving Patrick a disparaging look.

"I was not," spat his friend. "What about you then? You puked your guts up. You wasn't so tough, was you?"

"Well it stank, an' I nearly fell on it when I went to get the ball."

Paolo was put in mind of his daughters, when they used to bicker. His throat closed with the old familiar ache and his guts tightened. His skin suddenly felt clammy.

"Okay, lads, that's enough," he said in a harsher tone than he'd intended.

Forcing himself to concentrate, he continued to question the friends for a little longer, but it was clear they couldn't tell him anything else. Paolo asked WPC Start to see them home and make sure there was someone to take care of them.

He left Dave to question James Smedley, who looked even more shaken than the boys, and headed back to Barbara.

"First impressions?" he asked.

"You know I hate it when you do that," she answered. "This is science, not some guessing game."

"I wasn't asking for details, Barbara, just your impressions."

"Ja, well, you always want answers before I've even had time to decide what the questions are." As always when she was upset he could hear a slight South African twang in her voice.

Paolo watched as she debated with herself whether or not to answer him. Professional pride won.

"Initial impressions? Cause of death appears to be strangulation. The way the body was left and the black plastic bag used, I'd say we were looking at a repeat of last month's murder." She looked up at him, her full lips curved, not quite smiling. "But don't quote me on that until after the autopsy."

She turned back to the body, dismissing him. As Paolo walked away, his mobile phone rang. The display showed his ex-wife's number and his stomach churned. That was all he needed to make his day complete.

"Hi, Lydia. Nice to hear..."

"Don't forget Katy's prize giving. It starts at 7.30, so don't be late."

She was gone before he could reply. Paolo sighed. How had he screwed up his life so much that Lydia now hated him? Shaking off the familiar despair, he sighed and continued over to where Dave was standing, grinning broadly.

"What have you got to smile about?"

"I've got a date tonight. WPC Rebecca Start is about to find out what a lucky girl she is," Dave answered.

Paolo glared at his Detective Sergeant. "Let me tell you something right now," he hissed so that no one else could hear, "you need to change your ways. When you're on the job, that's all you think about. Got that?"

Dave nodded, but the smirk playing around the corners of his mouth riled Paolo.

"Don't think being related to the Chief Constable earns you any special treatment in my eyes, because it doesn't. So stop using my crime scene as a fucking dating agency. And keep your conquests to yourself." He waited to make sure the message had got through. "Right, drop me off back at the nick. You go over to Lisa Boxer's place and see what you can find out about our missing witness. I'm going to read through the reports on the last girl who ended up looking like this."

Paolo looked up as Dave entered his office.
"Any joy?"
"None, sir," Dave answered making himself comfortable in the chair opposite Paolo. "Looks like Lisa Boxer has done a bunk. Her neighbours claim they haven't seen her for over a week. Not that I'd take their word for anything. Definitely a bit dodgy, the residents of that house. I got the impression they wouldn't let on even if they had something to tell."
"Were you able to get into her place and look around?"
"Yeah, the old bag who runs the rooms let me in. She swore she hadn't seen Lisa since she last paid her rent. What a dump. I feel as if I need a long hot shower, which I'm now going home to have. Aren't you supposed to be somewhere, sir? I didn't expect you to still be here."
"Shit!" Paolo grabbed his jacket. "I'm off. Call me tomorrow if anything comes up."

***

Paolo searched frantically for a place to park. Finally he found a spot, streets away from the school. Parking the Ford Focus, he slammed the door and ran.
Sidling into the back of the hall, he was relieved to see Katy still at the side of the stage waiting for her name to be called. As she walked forward, she scanned the rows for him. Her face lit up when she spotted him at the back; the fingers of her right hand wiggled in acknowledgement. His heart contracted at the sight of her. Dark hair and eyes, olive skin and delicate features, she had his mother's beauty and grace. Katy was a true Italian – petite in stature, but powerful beyond her size when her temper flared. So unlike Sarah who'd been tall for her age; fair-haired

with striking hazel eyes – his eyes...

Paolo shook off the memories.

Katy rushed up and hugged him as soon as the ceremony ended. Following close behind came Father Gregory, her English teacher, yet another ex-classmate from Paolo's schooldays. It was turning out to be a day for meeting people he would rather not have to deal with.

"Pizza Hut, Dad?" she asked, eyes shining.

"Why not, unless your mother minds?" he said, turning to Lydia.

Father Gregory spoke, distracting Katy's attention and Lydia moved towards Paolo.

"We can go," she said, "but I need to get home early."

Paolo took in Lydia's expression. *And you don't want to spend time with me, do you?* He wanted to say something, anything to take that look off her face, but Katy had finished speaking to Father Gregory and turned back to them. The moment was lost.

"Please say we can go," she begged her mother.

Lydia smiled. "I've just told your father we can. Come on, I'm starving."

As they turned towards the exit, Paolo felt a hand on his arm.

"Paolo, could I have a word?" Father Gregory said, his usually open face clouded.

"Yes, of course. You two go on ahead, I'll meet you inside Pizza Hut," Paolo said, then turned back to the priest. "You look solemn, something up?"

"Nothing serious at this stage, but it could develop into a problem. I need to talk to you about Katy's religious beliefs."

"Me? Why? She's free to believe what she wants," Paolo said.

"Well, no, she isn't, I'm afraid. Not in *this* school, Paolo, you know that as well as I do. The school board's views were made clear before we accepted her. I'd hate Katy to be suspended from St Ursula's, but unless she keeps her disturbing views to herself, that might happen."

Sending his girls to St Ursula's Convent School had been his only concession to his own catholic upbringing – and he wouldn't have done that if his mother hadn't left him money and a guilt-ridden obligation in her will. He'd stopped believing in God when he was about Katy's age.

"What disturbing views?" he asked, trying not to lose his temper.

"She told her class today that there was no such thing as life after death. She refused to accept the resurrection of our Lord and tried to hold a poll on the subject. Sister Mercy had to remove her from the class."

Paolo tried hard not to laugh, but a chuckle got through.

"It's no laughing matter. She's also insinuating that all priests are paedophiles."

Losing all urge to laugh, Paolo glared at Father Greg. "She actually said that?"

"Not in so many words, no. But it was clear that's what she meant. Please speak to her, Paolo. She's too good a student to risk losing her place here."

They'd found a table and ordered by the time Paolo arrived. He didn't want to question Katy tonight about what Father Gregory had said, but knew he couldn't put it off for long.

"I thought I'd come over tomorrow, do those jobs around the house I've been meaning to get round to," he suggested with a smile in Lydia's direction.

"Not tomorrow, Paolo. Maybe next weekend."

"Oh, Mum, why not? Dad never gets to come over when he wants to. You always make him wait."

Lydia sighed. "Katy, that's not true. Your dad never thinks about my life. He feels he can just turn up whenever he wants."

"Well maybe he should be able to. What's wrong with that?"

"Katy, don't speak to your mother like that." He smiled at Lydia. "Next Saturday will be fine, but maybe Katy and I could do something together tomorrow, what do you say?"

"Great," Katy said. "Say yes, Mum."

"Why not?"

Lydia smiled at him, but without warmth. Even now, it seemed she couldn't forgive him for leaving her to deal with her pain alone.

Chapter Three

He carefully placed his beloved scourge back in the cupboard, locking the door to keep it safe. He pitied the child he'd been before it came into his life. How old had he been? Six? Nearly seven? It was hard to remember his exact age, but he'd never forget the day he'd been introduced to its exquisite pain.

"You promised me. You promised!"

He stood outside his parents' bedroom, ear pressed to the door. His mother's voice screeched, but his father spoke so quietly it was hard to pick out the words. He loved his father, nothing ever made him angry. His mother was different, nothing ever made her happy. Not even when he did really, really well in his spelling tests or mental arithmetic.

"You promised me no more whoring. You stink of that slut's perfume."

"What do you expect? I'm a man, not a monk. I have needs."

"You disgust me."

He jumped as something smashed against the inside of the door and he stepped back, ready to run if one of his parents came out.

Now his father raised his voice.

"My desires are natural. You're the one with a problem. If you allowed me into your bed I wouldn't need to go elsewhere to—"

"I can't," his mother yelled. "You know that. I can't. It's a sin."

"No, it isn't. How do you think I feel, knowing you whip yourself with that disgusting thing rather than sleep with me? Just

because you're frigid, don't expect me to stay celibate."

"It's a sin unless it's to procreate."

"Oh, for God's sake, don't start on that again. I'm as good a catholic as you are, but—"

"No you're not," his mother yelled. *"If you were, you wouldn't run around with dirty whores."*

"I don't run around with them. I pay because you—"

"Don't say it. Don't say it," she screeched.

"Don't say what? That you would rather whip your own back until it bleeds than do what comes naturally?"

"Get out. Get out."

Footsteps approached. He fled to his room, shutting the door as quietly as he could. Flinging himself on his bed, he reached for Mr Sam, the best teddy in the world. Mr Sam would make him feel better. Tears dripped onto the teddy's head. He tried not to make a noise, but the sobs rose in his throat and he couldn't hold them back.

He heard his father stomping down the stairs and then the front door slammed. Using his sleeve, he wiped his eyes and prayed his mother wouldn't be in one of her moods when he went downstairs. Maybe he shouldn't go down. Maybe he could hide up here until his father came home. Maybe...

The door crashed open and his mother stood in the opening.

"Are you snivelling again, boy? Are you like your weak-willed father?"

The question was always the same and he could never work out what the right answer was. When he said no, she beat him for lying. If he said yes, she beat him to make him stronger willed. This time he stayed silent and it seemed to work because she came to the bed and sat down on the edge, drawing him into an embrace.

"Poor baby, it isn't your fault," she whispered.

He allowed himself to be held, but it felt awkward. He wasn't used to being crushed against her like this. He didn't know what to do with his arms, so left them hanging limply at his side. She pulled him in even more and he found it hard to breathe. The tighter she hugged, the more he struggled for breath. Suffocating, he finally lifted his hands to push against her, desperate to drag air into his lungs.

His hands connected with the softest flesh he'd ever felt. They seemed to sink deep into her chest. She pulled away and threw him back against the bed. Standing up, she towered over him.

"I knew it! You dirty little bastard! Just like your father."

Not knowing what he'd done wrong, he stayed silent, cowering away from her.

"Did you enjoy touching my breasts?" She smacked his head. "Answer me. Did you enjoy it? Did you? Did you? Did you?"

Each question was accompanied by a blow, each one harder than the one before. Then she stopped hitting him and took hold of his hair, dragging him from the bed and throwing him to the floor.

"Do you know what happens when you touch a woman?"

He had no idea if it was safe to speak, so shook his head.

"You burn in hellfire, that's what happens to dirty little bastards who can't keep their hands to themselves."

She grabbed his hair once more and dragged him from his bedroom. His legs scraped against the doorframe and bounced along the hallway to his parents' room. She let go of his hair and he fell in a heap at the foot of his parents' bed. Leaving him sobbing on the carpet amidst shards of broken porcelain, she crossed to the door and locked it.

"I'm going to teach you a lesson you'll never forget," she said as she turned back into the room.

She took off her blouse and he watched, mesmerised, as the dark blue silk fell to the floor. Then she removed the lacy thing she had on underneath. Coming over to him, she pulled him up by his hair.

"Touch them. Go on, it's what you want to do. Touch them," she whispered.

He'd never heard her speak so gently. She almost sounded as if she cared about him. He reached up with one hand and stroked the soft flesh. She groaned and he snatched his hand away, terrified that he'd upset her again, but she took both of his hands in hers and guided them to her body.

"Feel them," she said. "It's what men want to do. It's what you'll want to do when you grow up. I have to teach you right from wrong. It's my duty."

As he touched her, she groaned again, but kept tight hold of his hands, so that he couldn't move them away.

"Kiss them," she said, dropping to her knees. "Kiss my breasts."

Her voice sounded funny, but she'd never been so gentle with him before, so he knew it was okay. He leaned forward to do as she'd asked. The next moment he flew backwards as she let go of his hands and smacked him across the face. He sprawled on the floor, scrabbling to get away as she came after him.

"Dirty little bastard. You enjoyed that, didn't you? Well, now you get to find out what the price is for touching a woman's body."

Glaring at him, she moved to the small cupboard at the side of her bed. As she knelt down to open the door, he saw that her back was covered in cuts and scars. She reached into the cupboard and pulled out a thing he'd never seen before. It looked like a handle with lots of thin strips hanging from it.

"Get up," she demanded. "Take your shirt off and come here."

His hands shook, but he did as she ordered. When he stood in front of her, she grabbed his hand and forced the handle into it. Still gripping his hand tightly, she flicked her wrist and the thin strips flew over his shoulder and cut into his back. She flicked again and the thongs cut into his back over the other shoulder. He cried out with pain and she smiled.

"Good boy," she said. "It has to hurt. You have to learn right from wrong."

She let go of his hand and the lash fell to the floor.

"Pick it up," she said. "Ten lashes this time. Five over each shoulder."

When he didn't move, she leant forward and gently stroked his cheek.

"Don't cry. This is for your own good. You must do it or I'll have to whip you and that will hurt much more."

He reached down. The handle was too big for his small hands, so he was forced to use both to make the lashes fly over his shoulders. As the spurs bit into his flesh, he cried out, but with each lash he could see his mother's smile become more tender.

"You won't grow up to be like your father. You won't try to force any woman to defile her body. I'll make sure of that."

When he'd whipped his back for the tenth time he dropped the scourge, tears coursing down his cheeks. She knelt in front of him and drew his body in close against hers.

"It's okay. Don't cry, Mummy's here. This will be our secret. Our special times together. Just the two of us."

She did love him, after all.

***

Barbara Royston and her assistant, Chris, had already started the autopsy when Paolo and Dave arrived.

She looked up and nodded in acknowledgement, but didn't pause in her examination. Why the hell Paolo could never be on time for anything was beyond her. She wondered if he'd arrived late deliberately so he'd miss most of it. She knew he wasn't particularly squeamish, but he'd told her he felt there was something obscene about watching another person being picked apart.

She murmured into the dictaphone, recording the trauma the victim had suffered. Only when she'd finished the post-mortem did she again glance up at Paolo and Dave.

"She was about seventeen or eighteen. I'd say she's been dead for approximately ten days. The injuries are consistent with those suffered by the victim last month. She's undergone the same degree of violence to the upper body and head, but no trauma from the waist down. It's almost as if he hates the upper part of the woman's body."

She gestured to the girl's breasts.

"There's something odd about the way both bodies were

treated. They were washed from top to toe, had under their nails cleaned and all stray hairs removed from the pubic region, but were left with semen on their breasts. Now why would someone go to all that trouble to clean the corpse, but leave DNA behind?"

Barbara was speaking rhetorically and didn't expect an answer, but Dave spoke up.

"What if it isn't the killer's? Maybe he got hold of a batch from somewhere and squirted it on after he'd killed them. Maybe he can't get it up and uses some other poor sod's semen instead of doing it himself."

Barbara despised Dave's crudity, but had to concede that he might have a point.

"It's a possibility, but there are others. The semen could belong to an earlier sexual partner. When the DNA sample gets back from profiling we'll at least know if we have a match for the two killings, although I don't know how far that's going to take us. The semen is the only forensic evidence available. He's been very careful not to leave us anything else."

Paolo frowned and the crescent-shaped scar on his cheek showed vividly as his face muscles tightened. He'd told Barbara he'd got it as the result of a thug smashing a full beer can in his face. She thought it added character, but he'd laughed when she said so. Trying not to think about how nice his laugh was, she turned back to the body.

"It seems the best chance we have to identify her is through her fingerprints," Paolo said. "Let's hope they're on record. Last month's was an Albanian prostitute who'd been booked a few times. If he's targeting prostitutes there's a possibility we might at least be able to put a name to her. Okay, come on, Dave, we've got work to do. We'll leave you to it, Dr Royston."

Barbara's eyes lingered on Paolo's back as he and Dave left. They'd only spent one night together, and most of that he'd spent talking about his ex-wife. Silently cursing herself for her stupidity in wanting someone who didn't want her, she turned back to the autopsy table.

"Okay, let's get her stitched up, Chris," she said. "It seems she has nothing more to tell us."

***

Paolo couldn't stop thinking about the girl's battered face as he and Dave walked back. She was little more than a child, only three or four years older than Katy. How the hell had she fallen into the hands of this madman? She hadn't been wearing a scrap of clothing when she'd been dumped in the car park.

"We've got to get this bastard, before he does it again."

Paolo realised it was possible he'd been sitting at home feeling sorry for himself, wondering where Lydia was, while the young woman was being beaten to death by a sicko who either couldn't get it up, or… ? At this point his reasoning broke down. It must be as Dave suggested, or why leave the semen there, but clean every other trace? At his office door he turned back to Dave.

"Get on to the fingerprint match straight away, will you? Also find out who Lisa Boxer's working friends are. Some of the girls on the street must know where she's hiding. That is, if she is hiding and Azzopardi hasn't done anything to her. She might be in real trouble if that's the case."

***

When the phone in Barbara's office rang an hour later her thoughts were still on Paolo, so it spooked her to hear his voice asking about the autopsy report. Consequently, when she answered, her own voice carried more than a little irritation, as much at herself as at him.

"Jesus, Paolo, you haven't even given me time to write a report yet. What is it with you? You think the world revolves around what you want?"

"Hey, calm down, Barbara. I was only asking when it would be ready. Not asking for it this second."

"Ja well, that makes a change. It'll be ready when it's ready. Okay?"

Paolo lowered his voice and Barbara knew it was so that his team in the outer office wouldn't be able to hear.

"Look, Barbara, we have to talk."

"We are talking."

"No, I don't mean like this. We have to talk about what happened over Christmas."

"Did something happen?" she asked. "I don't recall anything happening that needs to be discussed two months after the event, do you?"

"Barbara, I…"

"My report will be with you as soon as possible. That's assuming I'm allowed to get on with it instead of dealing with your problems. Is there anything else?"

Putting the phone down without waiting for Paolo's reply, Barbara took a deep breath. This was ridiculous. She wasn't some stupid teenager with a crush; she was thirty years old, for Chrissakes.

She needed to get out and have some fun for a change. Leanna would help her get things into perspective. She was the only one Barbara had confided in about her infatuation with Paolo. She lifted the receiver again and dialled. Her friend's message service kicked in.

"Leanna, it's Barbara. If you're free tonight, do you fancy going to the Nag for a drink? I need to talk." She paused. "Actually, I need to get drunk. It's a pity I never touch alcohol. Call me, hey?"

The Horse and Panniers was one of Bradchester's best-kept secrets. It was a secret too well-kept according to Larry Harper, who wanted to update the place. But the regulars loved the pub and hated the idea that the 'Nag and Bag' might get dragged into the modern age of fruit machines and electronic quiz technology. Even the subject of introducing a pool table had met with fierce opposition and that was hardly cutting edge. The only concession to the present century was the small flat-screen television fixed on the wall over the bar permanently on either a news channel or one of the more serious talk shows.

Barbara walked across the main square, past the Law Courts and turned right into a narrow walkway. The Horse and Panniers was tucked away at the end. Light spilling from the pub's tiny lead-lined windows gave the alley a Dickensian feel. About three-hundred years old, low ceilings and dark beams in the two tiny bars created an intimacy lacking in the larger pubs that littered Bradchester.

Larry's wife, Sharon, also South African and long-time friend of Barbara's, served great food, which was another good reason for going there.

Leanna, a solicitor, had come straight from court and was already seated at one of the side tables, gin and tonic in front of her, when Barbara arrived. Larry brought over a diet Coke for Barbara.

"Sharon's done a lamb curry as the special tonight," he said, smiling at the two women.

"Sounds good to me," said Leanna. Barbara nodded her agreement and Larry went off to shout the order to his wife.

"I always feel that creep's imagining what I look like naked," Barbara whispered. "If he was anyone other than Sharon's husband I'd have thrown a drink over him by now."

"I know," Leanna said with a mock shudder. "He does it to every female who comes in. Why can't Sharon see what an arsehole he is?"

Barbara smiled. "He reminds me of Paolo's sidekick. He can't see a woman without mentally undressing her either." She took a sip of her diet Coke. "Leanna, what the hell am I going to do about Paolo? I know I'm being stupid, but I'm obsessed with him and it's driving me nuts."

"He's still in love with his wife, so you're going to have to let it go, sweetie. There's no point waiting around for someone who's pining for someone else. Now, is there?" Leanna softened her bracing words by squeezing Barbara's arm.

"Ja, I know. You're right." She grinned at Leanna. "You're always bloody right. Don't the other solicitors hate you for it?"

Leanna deepened her voice. "Frankly, my dear, I don't give a damn."

Larry interrupted their laughter by bringing over two steaming platefuls of his wife's curry. "Here you are, girls, always a pleasure to serve you two."

"Wow, this smells good. It reminds me of the Malay curry I used to get back home. This is the only place I know where the food is like a taste of South African heaven."

Barbara waited for her friend's response, but Leanna's attention was fixed on the television screen. Matthew Roberts was the guest on one of the political talk shows. Leanna looked shaken and close to tears.

"What is it?" Barbara asked.

"Nothing," Leanna replied, shifting her gaze to her food. "Let's eat."

"Come on, tell me."

"Damn it, I said there was nothing wrong. Just leave it, will you."

Her outburst was so out of character that Barbara was more concerned than ever. Leanna took a sip of her gin, her hands were shaking and she was clearly distressed. After a few deep breaths she seemed to get herself back under control.

"Sorry. We knew each other at uni, the great Matthew Roberts and I. The ending wasn't good and I'd prefer not to talk about it. Okay?"

"Sure, as long as you're all right now. What shall we talk about instead? How I can get Paolo's Lydia on my autopsy table?"

Leanna laughed. "What do you see in him?"

"Hmm, would you like a detailed list, or just the potted version?"

"You've really got it bad, haven't you? Maybe if you give him time to get over his marriage breaking up..."

Barbara forced herself to smile and hoped Leanna wouldn't realise how much it cost her to do so. "It might be too late by then. I've never been good at coming off second-best."

Chapter Four

The smack of his fist connecting with her skull reverberated around the cottage. When he'd found the place the previous year, he'd had little idea of how useful it was going to be. The old shepherd's hut had been added to and modernised over the decades, but, for him, its best feature was a complete absence of neighbours. Only half an hour's drive from Bradchester, yet surrounded by fields, its isolation was perfect.

The woman sobbed, huddled on the bed, trying to protect her face. He stopped punching, grabbed her arms, dragged her up.

"Come to me. I'm sorry, I'm sorry. I didn't mean to hurt you," he crooned. She pulled away and he slapped her face.

"I want you to dance with me."

The first one he'd killed had enticed him with her dance. He'd almost enjoyed how his body felt, swaying in time to the music in her arms. This whore should have done as she was told. He sang along to *Bad Moon Rising*, knowing the words off by heart. Murmuring against her ear, he held her close.

"You want to dance now?"

When she shook her head, he threw her back onto the bed and straddled her, using one hand to slap her face in time with the beat. The other strayed towards his erection.

Anger erupted. The filthy whore was trying to tempt him. Trying to make him defile his body. He climbed off and dragged her arm until she fell to the floor.

"Beg. Kneel before me and beg."

Her lips moved, but her words were muffled by sobs.

"What? What did you say? I can't hear you." He leaned down to catch the whispered words.

"Please," she said again, louder this time. "Please no hurt. No more hit."

Tears and blood obscured her features, but he could still see the soul in her eyes.

"Say it again," he said.

"Please, no more hit. Dance, I dance."

"Thank you," he said. "Thank you." He reached forward and caressed her battered face. "Now," he breathed. "Now I'm going to save you. God chose you, did you know that? He chose you to be one of his lambs and you repaid him by allowing filth inside the temple of your body. But don't worry, I'm here now. I'm here for you."

Drawing back his fist, he punched her full in the face, then reached down and lifted her tenderly onto the bed.

***

Paolo sat at his desk, stunned. The identity of the latest victim had taken his breath away. He'd not recognised his missing witness from the bloody mess on Barbara's autopsy table, so when Dave said the prints were a match for Lisa Boxer, Paolo felt as though he'd failed her all over again. Damn Frank Azzopardi, what was his connection?

He looked out of his office into the open plan area and stared across at the Perspex board on which the photographs of the two victims were displayed, disgust gagging in his throat.

His team were waiting for him. Apart from Dave Johnson, he'd known most of them for years. He finished the last of his coffee and went out.

"Right, everyone, listen up. As Dave has no doubt told you, the victim was Lisë Bojaxhiu, an Albanian working the streets as

Lisa Boxer. None other than the missing witness from the Azzopardi fiasco two weeks back."

"Still, at least that explains why she didn't turn up to give evidence," Dave said before adding something Paolo couldn't quite catch.

"Judging by the grin, you must have told yourself one hell of a joke, DS Johnson. You want to share it with the rest of us?"

Dave flushed. "I don't think so, sir," he said, looking around, glancing over at the only female team member. "It wouldn't be appreciated by everyone here."

Detective Sergeant Cathy Connor, Irish temper flaring as usual whenever Dave made one of his comments, glared at him, but before she could speak Paolo stepped in.

"CC, whatever it is you were going to say, don't."

Cathy's eyes flashed, but she nodded.

He turned to Dave. "I have no idea what you said, but you seem to find this girl's death amusing and that's something I won't allow in my office. Any more inappropriate humour and you'll find yourself walking a beat. Understood?"

He turned back to his team.

"CC, I want a second questioning of all those with a view of the car park from their windows. I know uniform has already asked, but her body didn't arrive there by magic. Maybe one or two of the residents will have remembered seeing something. Even if we can't find out what type of vehicle we're looking for, one of them might have spotted what they thought was rubbish being dumped. George, you go too."

"Right you are, sir," Cathy said, waiting while Detective George Stone gathered his belongings.

Paolo held his temper in check until he and Dave were alone. "You really shouldn't rile CC, you know. She'd make mincemeat of you."

"She's a dyke, that doesn't make her superwoman," Dave said with a shrug.

"Jesus, Dave, are you stupid, or just pushing me to see how

far you can go? Don't ever use that word in front of me again or I'll make sure you end up in front of a disciplinary panel. Cathy's preferences are nothing to do with you or anyone else. She's a bloody good copper and you'd do well to remember that. As for her not being superwoman, she comes damn close. She's a judo black belt. The last time I saw her in action, the idiot who tried to molest her ended up with a broken wrist."

He wondered if Dave would have a comeback on that, but it seemed he'd given the younger man something to think about.

"Right, you and I are going to pay a visit to my old friend Frank Azzopardi. It's too convenient for him that Lisa disappeared when she did. Let's find out what he was up to the night she died, shall we?"

As Dave started the car and pulled away Paolo opened the window and lit a Camel. Everything pointed to Azzopardi. Could it be that simple? And if it were, would he be able to prove it?

"You still pissed off with me, sir?"

"Why?"

"You're quiet. I wondered if you were still mad at me, that's all."

Paolo shrugged. "No, just thinking about this case. I can see Frank going after Lisa, but what reason would he have for killing the first girl?"

"Enjoyment? From what you've said, he seems to like slapping women. Maybe it's the way he spends his leisure hours."

Paolo thought he could hear a note of approval in Dave's voice. He hoped he was wrong, but now seemed as good a time as any to try to find out what was going on in his head.

"So, what is it with you, Dave? What have you got against women?"

"Me? Nothing. I love them."

"You've got a funny way of showing it," Paolo said. "The way you've been talking about our vics, it sounds like you despise them."

"They're prostitutes, not women. Well, yeah, they're women, but ... oh shit. I can't explain it."

"Try."

Dave flicked the indicator and turned into Connaught Way. "They've decided to sell their bodies. You know? Put a price on it."

"You think they're doing it from choice? Most of them have been forced into it one way or another. I don't suppose there are many women who go on the game because they want to." Feeling he'd said enough for now, Paolo changed the subject. "Anyway, how did it go with Rebecca?"

"Rebecca? Who's Rebecca?"

"The WPC you made a date with on Gallows Heath. Remember?"

Dave laughed. "I'm not likely to forget her, she was quite something."

"But you couldn't remember her name?"

Dave didn't answer and Paolo gave up. He had enough on his mind without trying to solve Dave's problems.

The car pulled to a halt outside the gates of Azzopardi's mansion. Dave let down his window and pressed the intercom.

Through the ornamental ironwork, a wide tarmac drive curved away from the gates and disappeared into trees and shrubs. Nothing could be seen of the house.

A scratchy static voice sounded from the intercom. "Who is it?"

"Police."

"What do you want?"

"We're here to chat to Mr Azzopardi. Open up," Dave said.

"You got a warrant?"

Paolo leant across and called out through Dave's open window. "Now why would we need one? You just run off and tell Frank we only want to have a nice friendly chat. Ask him if we need to come back with a warrant."

"Wait," the voice ordered.

The intercom fell silent. Just as Paolo was about to tell Dave to press the buzzer again, the gates slowly opened. They moved through and followed the drive as it zigzagged upwards through a tunnel of greenery.

"This is like driving through Bradchester Park," Dave said, clearly impressed.

As they rounded the final bend, Azzopardi's house came into view.

"Bloody hell! I thought crime didn't pay?" Dave breathed.

Paolo had been to the mansion before, but even so, he could see why Dave was knocked out by it. The house had all the class Azzopardi lacked. A Georgian three-storey building covered in ivy stood in isolated splendour at the top of the driveway. Two men, who Paolo knew carried their brains in their muscles, came towards the car as it stopped.

Paolo and Dave got out and walked towards the men.

"We're here to see your boss," Paolo said.

Without a word, they both nodded and turned back to the house.

"Not great on dialogue, those two, are they?" Dave said.

"They don't need a large vocabulary for what they do."

They followed the two men up the broad steps leading into the entrance hall and along a wide corridor to the back of the house. It didn't matter how many times Paolo saw the mansion, he was stunned by its beauty. Dave had it wrong; crime definitely paid; there was no legal way Azzopardi could afford to live as he did. Paolo wondered how Frank slept at night, knowing that misery paid for all this luxury. They reached the end of the long passage and entered a massive conservatory. Palm trees in gigantic planters fringed an indoor pool where Azzopardi was swimming laps. Maria Vassallo, costume partially covered by a multicoloured wrap, stood to one side of the pool, clutching a towel. She glanced over at Paolo and Dave before switching her gaze back to the swimmer.

"It's like a sauna in here," Dave said. "You'd think it was the middle of summer instead of the beginning of a miserable March."

Paolo kept quiet and waited for Azzopardi to reach their end of the pool and hoist himself on to the side. As he stood up, water cascading from his torso, Maria Vassallo rushed forward to wrap the towel around him. He didn't so much as acknowledge her presence, simply stared at Paolo and Dave.

"What's this, Paolo, police harassment? You plods too thick to know when to give up? Maria, get me a drink."

"Campari?"

"What else?" Azzopardi said, turning away from Paolo to watch Maria as she walked over to the bar.

Paolo could see ownership in the man's stance. Maria belonged to Azzopardi, body and soul. Paolo wondered if she knew it, or if she even cared. She returned, handed Azzopardi his drink and sat down on a wicker couch, never once taking her eyes off his face, as if trying to gauge his mood. Azzopardi took a sip of his Campari and soda, then looked at Paolo and grinned, completely relaxed.

"So, are you going to tell me why you're here this time, or are you going to stand there playing statues? Don't think I don't appreciate your company, but I've worked up an appetite with my swim and right now you aren't what I fancy."

He winked and then looked over at Maria as he spoke. Paolo saw a flush deepen under her olive skin. Maybe she was embarrassed about the way Azzopardi treated her after all. She kept her eyes down, but began to fidget, crossing and uncrossing her arms. Her nervous mood must have been pleasing to Azzopardi because he laughed.

"I'd say she's about ready for me. You've got five minutes to say your piece, then you can fuck off."

Paolo handed over a photo of the dead woman. "You might not recognise her from this, but that's Lisa Boxer. She didn't turn up to give evidence against you because she was already dead. Bit convenient for you, don't you think?"

Azzopardi took a cursory look and passed the photo back. "Very convenient. Tell whoever did that to her I said thanks."

Paolo forced himself not to rise to the bait. "So you didn't do it yourself, Frank? What happened, did you get one of your boys to work her over? Can't you do a man's job anymore?"

"You keep on and on about this Albanian whore. I didn't beat her up and I didn't kill her. I want the fucking Albanians wiped off the face of the earth. I'd like them all to disappear, not just one of their cunts, that don't mean you can pin her murder on me. Whatever happened to that cow she had it coming, but I didn't do it. Why don't you ask her pimp? Slags like her need a smack now and again. Keeps their mouths shut and their legs open. Not that I'd fuck her, she's Albanian."

He ran his hand under his chin in the age-old Maltese gesture of disgust. "Scum," he said. "They're all scum. But at least she's dead, so that's one less to deal with. Besides, I'm a respectable businessman. I shouldn't have to put up with this shit, not even from you."

Paolo laughed. "Respectable? Are you seriously trying to tell me your business is respectable? Pull the other one, Frank. We know all about your *little dealings*. You should be careful, there's more than one way to bring you down. Don't forget the taxman is watching you, not just us."

"I pay my taxes. What's more, I bet I'm better regarded than most with all the dough I give to charity and the church. You've got nothing on me or my business, so fuck off. You tell me the whore is dead? So what? Is that the only reason you're here, to bring me the good news?"

"No, we're here to find out where you were when Lisa Boxer went missing."

"I was with Maria. Just like I was when the stupid bitch got herself worked over before."

Dave took a step forward. "We haven't told you the date

yet."

"Calm down, sonny. You don't need to," Azzopardi said. "Whatever date you spout, I was with Maria. She'll tell you, she never leaves my side, do you, sweetheart?"

Maria kept her gaze fixed on her hands as she answered. "Frank's right. I'm always with him. We never spend a moment apart."

"What about when she goes shopping for clothes and suchlike?" Dave persisted. "I can't picture you hanging around outside the changing rooms while she tries on hundreds of dresses. Not your style at all."

Azzopardi grinned. "Sonny, you have such a lot to learn. Maria doesn't go out to shop. The shops who want my custom come to me. Maria wears what I like to see her in and right now I'd like to see her in nothing. If you boys have nothing else to say, it's time for my massage. Unless you want to watch? Is that what gets you going these days, Paolo?"

Chapter Five

He peered through the car's windscreen and smacked his fist against the steering wheel. None of the girls strolling up and down the street matched his ideal. After a while the windscreen misted over, so he wiped away the condensation with a gloved hand. As a gap cleared he saw a newcomer join the procession and his heart raced. Snapping down the sunshield, he took the photo from its hiding place and compared the features and colouring of the young woman on the other side of the road. She moved under the street light, and he realised she was perfect. She was everything the Lord demanded. He started his car, ready to edge over to her side of the road.

At that moment, a car came round the corner and crawled to a halt. The girl sauntered over. Within seconds, she'd climbed in. He burned with rage as his prize was driven away.

Waves of nausea flowed over him as he fought to control his fury. Eventually he was able to breathe again. Reaching up, he replaced the photo and flipped the sunshield back. At least now he knew where to find her. He'd come back tomorrow and the next night, every night until he could pick her up.

He had to save her – he had no choice but to relive his first killing again and again until the Lord told him to stop.

Music blared from the room, drowning out the sound of his tentative knocking. The rooms on either side seemed to be taking part in some sort of noise competition. No wonder she couldn't hear his knocks. It would be a miracle if his hearing wasn't permanently impaired just from standing in the hallway. Not that he was sure he even wanted the door to open. Maybe he should leave. Go home and forget he'd ever been given her address. Did he really want to confront her?

Just as he'd convinced himself to give up, the door opened. A raddled face topped by bleached straw peered out at him through eyes that struggled to focus. Blinking, the woman held onto the doorframe as if it was the only way she could remain upright. Before he could speak, she staggered back and waved him into the room.

He stepped through the opening and entered a place from his childhood nightmares. It was everything Mama had said a whore's lair would be. The bed, dominating the small room, was unmade and clothes littered every surface of the floor. To one side of the room a tiny table held a CD player, the source of the deafening music. But even so, the competing tunes from either side added to the discordant din.

He didn't hear her stagger up behind him and jumped back as she clutched at his arm.

"Blow?" she slurred, "or fuck?"

He turned to face her, throat closing as words refused to come. Shaking his head, he took another step back to break free from her grasp.

She fell into an armchair next to the table. "Wha' sor' fuck you wan' then?"

"None," he said, finally finding his voice.

"You wan' blow? Shit, they all wan' blow," she said staggering to her feet and coming at him again. "'s more if I swaller. You wan' swaller or spit?"

He put his hands out to hold her off. "I just want to talk to you, ask you some questions."

She somehow managed to avoid his barricades and threw her scrawny arms round his neck.

"You wanna dance instead? I like dancing."

He tried to drag her arms from his neck, but she held on tight and rubbed her groin into his. Bad Moon Rising *came on the CD player as she gyrated. He took hold of her wrists and forced them down.*

"I just want to talk to you," he yelled over the music.

She wrenched her wrists free and came at him again, grabbing between his legs and rubbing. "You wanna fuck, dontcha."

He tried to get free, but in his efforts to get away, he lost his footing and fell back onto the bed. She fell on top of him, still rubbing between his legs.

For a brief dreadful moment he responded, desperate to give in to the need. Forcing himself to resist, he pulled her hand away and shoved her to the floor. Scrambling up from the bed, he looked down on her. Her nightgown had fallen open, displaying her naked breasts. He fell to his knees. Of their own volition, his hands reached out to caress her. She opened her legs and a rage such as he'd never known filled him as he remembered who and what this whore was to him.

He snatched his hands away as if burnt.

"Whore," he sobbed. "Fucking, fucking, dirty whore."

Fighting against his desire, he began to pummel her with his fists. Choking with tears, he gasped for breath and let his hands fall by his sides. Then he realised what he had to do. Taking her throat in his hands, he squeezed. He could feel her scrawny body under his, fighting against his weight. Her fingers clawed at his hands, but she was no match for him. He squeezed harder and harder, wanting to break her neck. Needing to rip her head from her shoulders. The bitch, the fucking bitch, how dare she come on to him like that.

Finally, the life left her body and he felt a moment of absolute peace. No more whoring for her.

But the moment passed all too quickly. Realisation flooded in. He couldn't be found like this. He got to his feet and forced himself to think. She was dead, for God's sake. Clean up, he thought. Leave no traces. Looking around, he found a plastic supermarket bag in the tiny kitchenette area behind the dirty curtain next to the armchair. He stripped her gown and shoved it in the bag. Then he took the sheet from the bed and put that in too.

Going back to the kitchenette, he found a bowl and filled it with warm water and a squirt of washing up liquid. By the time he threw away the dirty water and rinsed the bowl, he was sure he hadn't left any traces of himself behind, either on her or in the rest of the room. He unravelled a roll of black bin bags he'd found under the sink. Folding in her limbs, he wrapped her body in as small a parcel as he could.

He needed something to seal it and went to rummage in the telephone table drawer. He found half a roll of sellotape – perfect! Above the phone was a photo pinned to the wall. The prostitute as a young woman, still in her teens, blonde, smiling and carefree looked back at him. She held a baby on her lap and had one arm draped around a small dark-haired child. How old was the child, he wondered? Two? Three at most.

He slipped the photo into his pocket and returned to seal his package.

Satisfied he hadn't left any evidence behind, he lifted the black plastic bundle. Fortunately she barely weighed anything and he wondered when she'd last had a proper meal. Not that he could afford to think about her as a person. Right now she was simply garbage he had to get rid of.

Leaning forward, he picked up the bag containing her nightgown and sheet.

The music moved onto yet another track as he quietly closed the door, but the people on either side wouldn't have noticed. Their music was winning the battle of the bands.

***

Paolo pressed buttons on the remote and the screen flickered between channels. He didn't care what was on, but needed the background noise to keep him company. He settled for a talk show and chucked the remote down next to him on the almost threadbare couch.

Looking around the bedsit, he forced himself to take stock of his surroundings. Living here had only been a temporary option while he and Lydia sorted out their problems, and now they were barely on speaking terms – problem solved. Ha, bloody, ha.

Somehow he'd never found time to look for anywhere better. Anywhere *permanent* a voice insisted. As long as he stayed in the bedsit he could convince himself he was just marking time until... until what? Until Lydia decided to take him back? That didn't look like it was going to happen any time soon. He needed to find a proper home. Somewhere with a spare bedroom so Katy could stay over during the weekends.

Decision made, he felt almost cheerful and was about to reach for the newspaper to check the classified ads when a new interviewee was announced by the talk show host.

"We're fortunate to have the benefit of Matthew Roberts' expertise. Matthew, welcome to—"

Paolo snatched up the remote and switched off the set. The last thing he needed was to listen to Matthew Roberts droning on about police brutality and human rights. Human rights for garbage like Azzopardi, but no human rights for his victims. And the media believed Roberts was one of the good guys. How sick was that?

He tried to recapture his earlier moment of good humour, but it had evaporated as rapidly as it had arrived. Ignoring the newspaper, he stood up and walked to the unmade bed. Throwing himself down, he stared up at the myriad cracks running across the ceiling. He lit a Camel and watched the smoke spiral above his head. It would be nice to live somewhere he could take pride in. The surrounding walls, from what he could see under the grime, must once have been painted pale beige. They still had the remnants of Blu-Tack the previous tenant had used to fix posters over every inch of space.

When he'd taken the place, sight unseen, he wouldn't have cared if cockroaches had been partying on the coffee table. He hadn't even put up any pictures; nothing that would make the dump look lived in. He'd definitely look for a new place tomorrow.

He closed his eyes and drifted towards sleep. Just as he was dropping off he remembered Father Gregory's words. He hadn't spoken to Katy yet. Damn! That was a problem for his next weekend visit.

Paolo looked up from the papers on his desk as his team filed in to the main office. He picked up his coffee mug and joined them in front of the crime board.

"Right, what have you got to tell us, CC?"

Cathy opened her notebook. "Main points or full detail?"

"Main points for now," Paolo answered. He knew how she worked. She'd give all the information they needed without wasting time on the insignificant.

Paolo caught sight of Dave staring out the window. He had his feet up on his desk, with his chair leaning back on two legs. His whole attention seemed to be on the view outside. His eyes flicked back to the room briefly, then he yawned before turning his head away again.

"We boring you, Dave?" Paolo barked. "If so, why don't you go and get us all a coffee? Do something useful."

Paolo was pleased to see Dave's face flush as he allowed the chair to drop back into place. He waited for him to leave the room before nodding to CC to start her report. It was about time Dave realised this was a team effort.

"One of the neighbours, a Mrs Fulbright, thinks she remembers seeing a large dark car when she got up to visit the bathroom at about three in the morning. Apparently she doesn't switch a light on at night, so was startled when the room suddenly lit up. She peered out and saw someone dumping garbage and was going to report it to the council. Only problem was, she didn't have her glasses on, so couldn't make out the number plate. By the time she'd found her way to the bedroom and back again, the car had gone. I asked her if she could identify the make and she said no, just that it looked posh. Also, she's not sure which night it was, so it might not even be our perp."

CC grinned at Paolo. "So that makes our job nice and easy, doesn't it? We're probably looking for a posh, dark car that might, or might not have been the one used to dump the body." She looked at her notes again. "No joy with a description of the man. It was too far away for her to see him clearly, even if she'd had her glasses on, but she was sure it was a man. None of the other neighbours saw or heard anything."

Paolo added the information, such as it was, to the board. While he was writing, Dave came back in with mugs of coffee and handed them round.

"Thanks for that, Dave. Pity we don't have time to drink them, but as you didn't have any joy in finding one of Lisa's street buddies, we'll go together to chat to the girls on her beat. Maybe I can find one of them who can tell us something useful. CC, you and George can watch Azzopardi for a while. Let's see what he gets up to when he thinks I'm not keeping an eye on him."

Dave drove into Granger Street and manoeuvred the car onto the tarmac area behind the bingo hall. It was the nearest car park to the red-light area of town.

"Bit early in the day for the girls to be at work, isn't it?"

Paolo smiled. "You think the punters only have sex at night?"

"No, but..."

"No buts about it, the girls work long hours and cater for daylight customers who can't get away from the wife to come over at night. Besides, I thought you said you'd checked this area? You should already know they're on call during the day."

Dave mumbled something and Paolo opened his mouth to have yet another go at him, but decided it wasn't worth the effort. He'd speak to the Chief Constable and see if he could get his golden boy nephew moved to a different station. Clearly he and Dave would never end up on the same wavelength.

They strolled towards Beacon Street, passing girls who suddenly seemed to be really interested in the derelict shop windows. Paolo had never figured out how the working girls knew he was a copper.

"The Maltese run the far end of this district, the Albanians this end. I'd like the girls to feel free to speak, which means you keeping your misogynist mouth shut. Okay?"

When Dave didn't answer, Paolo stopped and grabbed his arm. "Did you hear me?"

"I heard you."

"Then next time answer me. I don't know what your problem is, but if you want to stay on my team, you'd better try a bit harder to do things my way."

He walked away without waiting to see Dave's reaction and reached the corner just in time to see a young girl wearing a black leather skirt short enough to be a belt duck into the first shop doorway. He walked up to the opening, but made no attempt to get close to the girl. He stood back and called out to her.

"I'm looking for someone who knew Lisa Boxer."

The girl kept her back to him and pretended interest in the dirt-streaked glass of the disused shop. The area was a slum, but the council wasn't interested in encouraging shopkeepers back. The streets had long been abandoned to drug dealers, prostitutes and their pimps. The turf wars between the Albanians and the Maltese seemed to be beyond the force's powers to end. Paolo knew Azzopardi controlled the Maltese girls, but couldn't prove it.

"Lisa Boxer – did you know her?"

The girl turned her face towards Paolo and shook her head.

"You wan' fuck?"

Paolo felt sick. She looked about Katy's age, but could be even younger, it was hard to tell. Life on the streets, probably with a drug habit, had taken away any hint of youth. He heard footsteps and looked back. Dave came and stood next to him.

The girl looked at Dave. "I no do two fuck. One fuck then one fuck more. No two fuck."

"It's okay," Paolo said. "We don't want to hurt you. We're police."

The girl put her hand in her skirt pocket and Paolo wondered if she was going to pull a knife. Turning to Dave he signalled for the two of them to take a step back so as not to spook her any more than they already had. Her eyes darted from side to side and she shook.

"Look at her," Paolo whispered. "She's a child. Call in for a WPC and we'll get her to social services."

Dave took out his phone, but before he could dial, a car screeched around the corner. As it slowed, the rear door opened and a man's voice yelled in rapid Albanian. The girl had started running towards the car as soon as it came into view and hands dragged her inside as she reached it. The car accelerated away. Paolo took off after it, but the door was pulled closed and it disappeared down a side street. Out of breath, he retraced his steps to where Dave was still standing, phone pressed to his ear.

"Damn," Paolo said. "She must have had a phone in her pocket with their number on speed dial. Did you call in the number plate?"

Dave nodded. "Just waiting."

"I want someone watching this street. If whoever was in that car puts her out to work again, I want her taken in and given over to social. I can't bear to think of a kid like that being used." He kicked the shop door. "Fucking bastards!"

Dave held up one hand and Paolo fell silent.

"Okay," Dave said into the handset. "Thanks." He put his phone in his jacket pocket. "Plates are false."

"Why am I not surprised?"

"I've given CC the car's description and she's checking it out against the stolen list."

Paolo sighed. "Come on; there must be someone who's heard of Lisa Boxer."

They walked to the end of the street, but it had turned into a ghost town. There wasn't a soul to be seen and not even a curtain twitched in any of the windows of rundown flats above the shops. They turned and headed back towards the car. As they entered the street where the girl had been, a woman stepped out of an alleyway. Bleached hair topped a haggard over made-up face. She was dressed in a red halter neck top nowhere near warm enough for the chilly March afternoon and a black short skirt meant for a woman at least twenty years younger.

"You police, no?" she asked.

When Paolo nodded, she ducked back into the alley and signalled for them to follow her.

"Dave, stay there and keep an eye on the street. Give us a warning if anyone comes."

When Paolo entered the alley, the woman had moved behind some garbage bins so she was hidden from the road. Paolo offered her a cigarette. At least that would help to mask the smell of piss and rotten garbage. She took the cigarette with shaking hands. He held his lighter out for her, then lit his own, giving her the chance to speak first.

"You want know 'bout Lisa?" she asked. "You give money. I tell you what happen. What I see. Need money. You pay?"

"That depends," Paolo answered, "on what you have to tell me." He could see the track marks on her arms. By the way she was shaking, her fix was already overdue. "What's your name?

"Alice."

Paolo raised his eyebrows. Her accent wasn't as strong as the child's, but no way had she been christened Alice.

"You want to try again?"

"You no able make my name. Is too hard. Alice good. I be

Alice for you."

"Okay, Alice, why don't you go to the local clinic? Get on a rehab programme. I'll help you, if you like."

"No. Need money, not programme. You pay. I tell what I see. No programme."

He pulled out his wallet and took out some notes. "Okay, Alice, this had better be good. What can you tell me?"

She snatched the money and stuffed it in the black bra on show under the halter top. "You know bad man, Maltese? The one she say beat her? He no do it. Lisa, she tell me. She lie to police."

"Are you saying Azzopardi didn't beat her? Why did she say it was him if he hadn't done it?"

"You want find out? Ask pimp. He tell you plenty."

"Where can I find him?"

"I no know."

"What's his name?"

"I no know."

"You sure about that? Isn't he your pimp, too?"

The woman stayed silent, eyes fixed on the alley opening. She looked ready to make a run for it. Paolo decided to back off a bit. "Okay, I'll find out myself. What else can you tell me?"

"The last night she here, I see her, she go with new man. I no see him, but I see car. Big. Dark. Maybe blue, maybe black."

"Anything else?"

She shook her head, but stopped when Paolo took out his wallet again. She hugged her body, tremors coursing through her. He held out another note. "What do you know about the child working this area? She went off with someone in a dark car. Was it the same car that Lisa got into?"

The woman shook her head, reached out and snatched the money before Paolo could take it back.

"No, not same car. Bad. I no talk 'bout them."

She took off and ran out of the alley, shoving Dave to one side and trying to force her way past him. He grabbed her arm, but released it on a shout from Paolo. As the woman ran, Dave stood looking after her until Paolo joined him back on the street.

"Why'd you let her go, sir?"

"Because I don't think she knows anything else about Lisa's disappearance. Besides, we can pick her up whenever we need to. Interesting, though. She's more scared of whoever is running that girl than she is of us."

Chapter Six

How long had he been praying? Two hours? Three? His knees burned with pain, but he would not stand. He kept his head bowed and whispered words of supplication. He needed the strength only God could give. The strength to stay pure, to remain clean. He couldn't give in. Had to force mind and body to obey him. As he prayed, hands clasped together so tightly his fingers ached, images of the woman's battered face danced before his closed eyes. She looked beautiful in death. Women only looked beautiful when God took their souls so that the shells remained to be used by the weak. Mama had said he was weak. But how could it be a sin when the soul had already gone? His erection grew and throbbed.

Don't think of how it feels to slide inside. Don't remember their naked bodies.

Even as he tried to control his thoughts, heat coursed through his groin and he rose from the *prie dieu*. His vision misted over as he shook.

He woke several hours later, prostrate on the floor next to the scourge. Drenched in sweat, he felt as though his heart would burst if he tried to stand. Moving onto his side to ease the pain in his lacerated back, he forced himself to confront the truth. No matter how many he killed, it would never be enough to help *her*. He'd never be able to save *her* soul. By the time he'd killed her, it had already been too late, she'd given in to the devil. But he'd prayed and God had answered his prayer. If he saved enough souls then *hers* would be redeemed.

He reached across to the bedside table and lifted the photograph, picturing in his mind once more the mess she had become. How she'd looked before he'd ended her miserable life.

It was his duty, his sacred duty to save the souls of those who would take her path. The first one he'd chosen had been close to the older version in age, but then the Lord had appeared and shown him his mistake. It was too late for the older ones; he had to pick them while they were still young enough to have a soul worth salvaging. He chose younger whores, ones who looked like the woman in the photograph.

But it still wasn't enough, night after night the line of those who needed his touch stretched into eternity. He would never be able to save them all – and if he couldn't do that, then he could never save his mother's soul.

***

Paolo wondered if he'd ever get used to ringing the doorbell instead of letting himself into the house he used to call home. He'd had long enough to adjust, so the answer was probably no. After a few moments the door flew open and Katy launched herself at him.

"Dad! I thought you weren't coming."

"Sorry, Katy. I got tied up this morning. Had to go into the office to finish off some paperwork, but I'm here now, so what would you rather do – go out somewhere or play this?"

He held up the video game she'd asked him for on his last visit and watched her face light up.

"You got it. I can't believe you got it." She turned and went into the house, dragging Paolo with her into the kitchen. "Mum, look what Dad's brought over."

Lydia was perched at the breakfast bar, drinking coffee from one of the cups they'd received as a wedding present so many years earlier.

"Video games *again*?"

Paolo remembered how much he'd put her back up the last time they'd met and tried hard to swallow his annoyance when she poured cold water over Katy's enthusiasm.

"You're planning to stay indoors on a lovely day like today?"

"Mum, it's freezing out there. You said yourself it was miserable."

"That was early this morning. The sun's shining now."

"But it's still freezing. Besides, I like playing games. I don't see why I should—"

"We can play for an hour or so and then I'll take you out for a burger." Paolo thought it best to step in before yet another war broke out. "How's that?" He turned to Lydia, but he could have saved his breath.

"Do what you like. You always do," she said, getting down from the stool and leaving the room.

Katy pulled a face at Lydia's back as she left and Paolo knew he should tell her off for it, but he just wanted to enjoy a couple of hours with his daughter. If he started in on Katy's behaviour the visit would turn out to be yet another disaster and that he couldn't face, so he pretended he hadn't seen. He still had to tackle her over Father Gregory's concerns. That would be fraught enough without putting extra tension on the table.

"Shall we go and set this up?" he said with a smile.

The game was noisy and fun, but at the back of Paolo's mind Father Gregory's words stopped him from letting go and just enjoying himself. He put down his control.

"Katy, I need to chat to you about school."

"Oh Dad, not you, too. Mum's already being a pain about it. Why can't I ask questions if I don't think what they're saying is right? You don't believe in all that guff anyway, so if you tell me you do I know you're lying."

"I'm not going to tell you I believe in anything, but I am going to tell you to keep your thoughts to yourself. That's a good school. If you get kicked out of there, where do you think you'll end up? Would you want to go to Kettlefields?"

"Don't be daft; no one *wants* to go to Kettlefields, not even the kids who live near there."

"Well, if you get expelled, that's the only school open to you around here. Father Gregory says... don't roll your eyes up like that."

"Father Gregory is a perve. None of us like him."

"What do you mean, a perve? Has he said or done anything to you?"

"No. It's the way he looks at us. All pervy and creepy. He's a sad sicko. Gloria says he hangs around with prostitutes."

"Who's Gloria? And how would she know any such thing?"

"She's a mate of mine in school and her dad is part of some group or other wanting to clean up the streets. Gloria says her dad doesn't like Father Gregory because he says the women need help, not whatever it is Gloria's dad's lot are doing."

"Katy, that's second-hand gossip at best. I'm surprised at you."

"Why? Gloria wouldn't say it if it wasn't true. Besides, I told you, he looks at us funny."

"You can't accuse someone of being a pervert because you don't like the way he looks at you."

"Why not?"

Before Paolo could answer his mobile rang.

"Don't answer it. Don't. If you go, I'll never forgive you," Katy said. "This is our time."

Paolo's stomach turned over. He'd given strict instructions, no calls unless it was absolutely necessary, which meant this wasn't going to be good news.

"Storey," he said.

CC's voice told him all he didn't want to know. Another body had been found and it was almost certainly the work of their killer.

He put the phone in his pocket and turned to his daughter who was glaring at him. "Katy..."

"Don't say it, Dad. Don't say you have to go. You were going to take me for a burger. You promised."

As he reached out for her, she picked up one of the controls and threw on to the couch.

"I hate you," she yelled and ran from the room.

He heard her sob as she fled upstairs. Seconds later the slamming of her bedroom door reverberated through the house. As he gathered his belongings together, a shadow fell across the sitting room. He looked up to see Lydia leaning against the doorframe.

"I take it from Katy's yelling and door slamming that you've done what you do best, let down the women in your life."

"Give it a rest, Lydia. I have to go. It's work and…"

"And what? And you can't wait to run away? Isn't that what you always do? Give up on trying to make things work?"

He stood up and walked towards the doorway. Lydia moved to one side to let him through.

"I tried to make our marriage work," he said as he passed her. "Then I found out that you were having an affair. There didn't seem to be much point in trying after that."

She shot him a look of pure loathing. "And who drove me to it? Who made me so desperate for affection that anyone would do?"

"But it wasn't just anyone, was it?"

She shook her head and pushed him to one side, then turned and headed into the kitchen. Paolo let himself out. He had never felt more alone.

***

Barbara was exhausted after a heavy bout of retail therapy. She didn't usually come into town on a Saturday, but had woken feeling as though she needed a treat. She walked into the Nag and Bag ravenously hungry. Whatever Sharon had on as special was going to go down well. Unusually, she was behind the bar and there was no wonderful aroma wafting through from the kitchen.

Dropping the bags at her feet, Barbara smiled across the counter at Sharon.

"I decided to treat myself to one of your wonderful meals. I don't often see you serving the drinks, Sharon. Is this a regular Saturday thing?"

"Larry's out, so I'm having to cover. There are no specials on today though, Barbara, sorry," Sharon answered without turning her head in Barbara's direction. "What can I get you to drink?"

"Diet Coke, please. Is there something wrong with your neck?"

"No, why?"

"You seem to be holding it at a funny angle."

Sharon turned to face Barbara and revealed something more serious than a stiff neck. The right side of her face was swollen and she had a painful looking black eye.

"What happened to you? That looks really bad."

Sharon shrugged and winced as if the slightest movement hurt. "I fell down the stairs." She moved away to serve another customer and then came back to Barbara. When she spoke again, her voice was barely audible and Barbara could hear she was close to tears. "Go and sit at your usual table. I can get one of the kitchen girls to make you something from our bar menu."

Barbara made sure no one was within hearing distance. "Come on, Sharon, what happened really?" she whispered. "You didn't get that falling down stairs. Is Larry up to his old tricks?"

Sharon's lip trembled and she nodded. When she spoke her words were barely audible. Barbara leaned forward as Sharon answered.

"We had a fight and Larry got mad at me. I think he's having an affair, Barbara. He's always going out without telling me where he's going and leaving me to cash up. I got fed up last night and when he came back I told him I wasn't going to take it anymore and he freaked. Started chucking stuff around upstairs in the flat and when I tried to leave... well, you can see what happened when I tried to leave."

"You can't stay with him, Sharon. Not if he's hitting you again."

"I drove him to it. He didn't mean it. He's a good man really, Barbara. I know you don't think so, but he is. He wouldn't have hit me if I hadn't kept on at him. He was so sorry this morning when he woke up and realised what he'd done."

Barbara was furious, but before she could say anything more a customer on the other side of the bar called for a refill. By the time Sharon came back Barbara had an argument well prepared. Sharon could stay with her for as long as she needed to. No way would she let Larry anywhere near Sharon, but she never got a chance to outline her plans for Sharon's future because the door opened and Larry came in, peering out from behind a massive bouquet of roses. He walked up to the bar and handed them over to Sharon with a flourish.

"These are for my special girl." He turned to Barbara. "Did she tell you about her fall? Frightened me half to death, it did, seeing her lying at the bottom of the stairs. Still, she seems to be okay now. We don't usually see you in here at the weekend. You want something to eat? Now I'm back Sharon can rustle you up something, no problem."

Barbara's phone rang, saving her from having to answer Larry, which was just as well because he wouldn't have liked what she had to say. More to the point, she might make things worse for Sharon. She sighed, snapped open her phone and turned away from Larry to take the call.

"What? It's the weekend. Why me? Oh, okay. Ja, I'll get there as soon as I can."

She slipped the phone into her handbag and gathered up her shopping.

"I have to go," she said, "but I'll be back later. Chat then."

Barbara could only hope that Sharon realised the last bit was aimed at her. She had to find a way to help Sharon stand up to Larry and stop being his punch bag.

***

The illegal dump site was on the western boundary of Bradchester; right next to the open countryside. The view of rolling hills and trees was marred by only one thing, the mountain of black bags, rotting mattresses, broken televisions, fridges and computers. The pile was finished off with an assortment of plastic garden furniture, which looked as if it could come toppling down if the swirling gusts battering the garbage heap were any stronger. Paolo stood upwind, away from the stench, to question the council worker who'd found the dead woman, while Barbara and her team worked with the body.

"How long has this been here?" he asked, pointing to the mass of refuse.

"The council have known about it for six months or more, but we only started clearing this week. People have been complaining, but you know what the council's like, never do nuffink if they can get away with it. They said with the budget cuts, there was no money to pay us lot overtime. That's what they always say. No money, no overtime. Simple as that."

"If that's the case, how come you're working today? Why not send you out during the week?"

"They did," the man said with a grin, "the pile was twice as high a few days back. It's been classified as a health hazard, so now the tight bastards at the top have to pay us to work non-stop until it's cleared. Good for us, this is. I'm putting the extra towards a nice holiday for me family."

Paolo took the man's details and moved over to where Dave was chatting to the young WPC who'd been first on the scene. Paolo smiled. From the look on Dave's face, it didn't appear as if this was one of his partner's easy conquests. It looked more like a full-scale argument had erupted, so Paolo stopped to enjoy the sight of Dave being given a tongue lashing by a slight figure who barely reached his shoulder. Maybe the idiot would learn that not all women would fall at his feet. This one looked like she'd rather chop them off. The wind changed direction and a few words drifted across, just on the edge of Paolo's hearing.

"...she lied. I never did..." Dave said, sounding really pissed off.

"That's exactly right, *Mr I'm an important policeman*, she said you couldn't..."

"... fuck you..."

"Rebecca says... can't... up," the WPC said, grinning at Dave who'd flushed a vivid fiery red.

Paolo decided it was time to step in. He pulled his phone out and opened it. Holding it to his ear, he spoke loudly enough for Dave and the WPC to look up.

"Hmm, yes, that's right. Thanks for the call."

The WPC glared at Dave and moved away. Paolo walked over and stood next to his partner, waiting until the WPC was out of earshot.

"This is your last warning, Dave. I catch you using a crime scene as a dating agency just one more time and you are off my team. Do I make myself clear?"

Dave nodded and turned away, but Paolo thought he saw a tear fall down the man's face. Considering how insensitive Dave usually was, that seemed really out of character and Paolo regretted speaking as harshly as he had.

Dave turned back, wiping away the tear. "Bloody wind makes my eyes water every time."

"Here comes Dr Royston," Paolo said, glad of the chance to change the subject. "Shall we find out what she's got to say about our latest victim?"

Paolo waited for the pathologist to reach him. Remembering their last encounter, he prayed she would give him a break. He didn't think he could cope with any more disapproving looks today.

"What can you tell us?" he asked, determined to keep his voice light and friendly.

"Not much until I get her back to the lab." As Paolo opened his mouth, she continued. "No! Don't ask. I don't have any instant answers and I don't want to start making guesses just to give you something to write in your report. The only thing I'm sure of is that this body has been here for quite some time. Weeks, possibly longer, which means she was killed before the other two. Make of that whatever you want. I was hoping to have some time to myself this weekend and I'm not in the best of moods, so unless you really want me to let rip at you, it might be best to stop asking bloody silly questions that you know as well as I do I can't answer."

As she stormed off Dave's mouth dropped open. "Blimey, what rattled her cage?"

Paolo sighed. "I have no idea, but right now a monastery with really high walls and padlocked gates sounds like the safest place for me to be. Have I got *hate me* written across my forehead?"

CHAPTER SEVEN

After a weekend spent alone, despite several ineffective calls trying to make it up with Katy, Paolo was relieved when Monday finally came round and he was able to go to the station without anyone asking him why he was working when he should have been enjoying his time off. His tiny bedsit felt more like a prison cell than the cells in the nick, so he'd escaped the place on Sunday by going to work. Maybe he should just move into the station and be done with it.

He walked along the corridor leading to his section, wondering if he'd ever get his problems with Lydia sorted out. Surely, to remain so angry with him after all this time must mean she still had feelings for him?

He stopped dead as he reached his office. Bloody hell, this was just what he needed on a Monday morning. Talk about the worst possible start to the week! Leaning against the wall was Matthew Roberts.

Matthew smiled at Paolo as if they were friends, making Paolo's head throb with anger.

"What the bloody hell are you doing in here? Who let you in?"

Matthew laughed. "Which question would you like me to answer first, Paolo? I'm here to stop you from harassing my client. Your desk sergeant let me in to wait for you. Aren't you going to invite me inside, or do you chat to all your visitors in the corridor?"

Paolo unlocked his office door and gestured for Matthew to go ahead.

"Where would you like me to sit? Your chair looks more comfortable than that rickety old thing," he said, pointing to the visitor's chair.

Paolo didn't bother to reply. He moved behind the desk and sat down. "Well, I haven't got all day. Why are you here?"

Matthew sauntered over. "Hmm, I hope the stains on the seat aren't fresh," he said as he sat down. "Paolo, we've known each other for too long to play games. Let's not mess around with the niceties. Either you leave my client alone, or I'm going to go after you with everything I've got. Frank Azzopardi has many, shall we say, less than savoury activities, but that doesn't mean you can drop in and threaten him whenever the mood takes you. He tells me you and your latest sidekick accused him of murder. I was under the impression no charges had been brought against him involving the Albanian prostitute – and also that the CPS didn't intend to bring charges in the near future. But maybe I was hallucinating that day."

"She's dead, Matthew. That's why she disappeared and her disappearance meant the CPS had no case to bring. Now, if you take into account the fact that she died before she could testify against Azzopardi, doesn't that seem a little suspect to you? It did to me, so I thought I'd have a nice, friendly chat with him to ask about his movements."

Matthew stood up. "Now that you've had your chat, just bear in mind that the next time you visit Frank at home, or at any of his businesses, you'd better come armed with a warrant, because he isn't going to let you in to have, as you put it, a nice, friendly chat without one. Now that we've got that over and done with, how's Katy doing? I hear she's causing a few raised eyebrows at school."

"How do you know about that? Don't tell me it's got as far as the school board?"

"No, it hasn't, not yet at any rate, but Father Gregory

mentioned her behaviour to me privately. He seems to think it might become a school board matter and, as chairman, I would have a strong voice in any decision that was made."

"Are you threatening me through my family?"

"Don't be ridiculous, Paolo. It was a genuine desire on my part to let you know that Katy's place at the school is in danger unless she changes her attitude. You need to talk to her. Don't let your approach to God cause Katy to lose her way. That's meant as a friendly warning. Telling you to stay away from my client is a non-friendly warning."

Matthew smiled and walked to the open door just as Dave arrived. Matthew stood to one side to let the other man pass into Paolo's office, then he turned back.

"See you at the next fund raiser," he said, smiling in a way that made Paolo's hands itch to punch him right between the eyes.

"I didn't know you two were on social terms, sir," Dave said as Matthew strolled away.

"We're not," Paolo snapped. "He's on the board of my daughter's school. We bump into each other occasionally and it's always too often for me."

"Apart from the fact that he represents Azzopardi, what have you got against him? He sounded friendly enough towards you."

"You don't think his dealing with that piece of shit is reason enough for me to dislike him? It's his hypocrisy that gets to me. Mr Perfect. He dresses right, says all the right things, and yet he is happy in the company of trash like Azzopardi."

Paolo knew he was irrational when it came to Matthew Roberts. The man was everything Paolo wasn't – successful, in control of his life, admired. He made Paolo feel like a complete failure by comparison – and, if he was honest with himself, always had done.

Dave shifted across from the doorway and sat down. "He has a point about Azzopardi, though, sir. That prostitute you spoke to said Lisa Boxer might have been lying about who attacked her."

"She might have been lying and so might that prostitute who was ready to say anything to get her next fix. One way to find out is to lean on Lisa's pimp. We didn't need to look for him while Lisa was alive, but if she was put up to making a false claim, and I'm not convinced yet that she was, then finding her pimp is a priority now. Get on to it, Dave. When you find him, invite him down here to chat."

Dave nodded, but didn't move. He opened his mouth as if he had something to say, then closed it again. Paolo waited.

"Sir, I, er, do you mind if I have a word?"

Paolo nodded. Now what?

"Look, I know we didn't get off on quite the right foot. You think I'm being looked after by my uncle, but I'm not. I'm here on merit, sir."

For the first time that morning Paolo felt like smiling. At last, a breakthrough. "I've never doubted that, Dave. If I'd thought otherwise, I wouldn't have taken you on my team."

"But you don't like me."

"I don't need to like you. I need to be able to trust you to do your job. I don't like your attitude at times, or the way you treat women, and I don't like the way you use crime scenes to find new conquests. Other than that, you're a good copper. So, if you keep your personal life out of the job, we'll get on better. Okay?"

Dave looked relieved. "Okay, sir," he said, standing up. "I'll go and find the pimp. I don't suppose anyone is up and about yet over in that part of town, but I can hammer on a few doors."

"You can swap places with me if you don't want that job. I'm off to the autopsy of our fragrant corpse." Paolo laughed at the expression of horror on Dave's face. "Don't fancy that?"

"Christ, no! Good luck with that one."

***

Barbara spoke into her dictaphone machine, recording the minute details of the victim's death and only glanced across at Paolo when she'd finished. She signalled to her team to tidy up and pulled off her gloves. As she walked towards the door, she nodded to Paolo to follow her. There was no need to stay with the body; they could talk outside where the air was fresher.

She led the way to her office and moved behind the wide mahogany desk. Every inch of it was covered with paperwork. Folders stacked on top of each other made a paper leaning tower of Pisa. They looked as if the slightest nudge would send them toppling to the ground, but Barbara knew from experience that they were safer than they looked.

She flopped into her chair and motioned for Paolo to sit opposite. She deserved some eye candy after what she'd seen this morning and looking at Paolo was no penance, that was for sure.

"This one was older than the other two, by quite a bit. I'd estimate her age to be at about fifty-one, fifty-two – early fifties anyway. But that's the only significant difference between her and the others."

Paolo nodded. He was writing as she spoke and she watched his hands, allowing herself to remember how they good they'd felt on her skin. He looked up and she flushed at the questioning look on his face. Damn it, she'd been so engrossed in her memories, she'd stopped speaking.

"Sorry," she said, "I was miles away. Thinking of something else. From the point of view of when this occurred, I'd say three months ago, give or take a few days. She'd been there quite some time, but the long hard winter we've had, plus the fact that this month has been bitter, has helped to preserve her remains. Such as they are. You need to catch this one pretty quick, Paolo. He's really sick the way he goes at these women."

He nodded. "I know that. He'll be working on another one

soon unless we can find him first. Trouble is, if it isn't Azzopardi, I have no idea where to even start looking."

Barbara wanted to reach across the desk and wipe the frown from his brow. Instead she gripped her hands tightly together in her lap, where Paolo couldn't see them.

"... and so I'll be off."

"Sorry, what did you say?" Barbara asked. "I missed that last part."

"Are you okay, Barbs?"

"Don't call me that. I've told you often enough I don't like it."

"Barbara, please, let's clear the air once and for all. I..."

Barbara forced herself to smile. "Paolo, if I'm honest, I read more into our night together than you did. I don't usually sleep with someone I'm not romantically involved with and, I don't know, I suppose I just wanted it to mean more than it did."

Paolo reached forward and took her hand. Why the bloody hell couldn't her heart beat normally? Surely he could hear it pounding? Just to make matters worse, he smiled. He had the most gorgeous smile.

"Barbara, it meant something to me, don't think it didn't, but you knew how I felt about Lydia. We'd spent most of that night talking about her. It's not as if I pretended I was over my marriage. I know you most probably won't believe this, but you are the only woman I've slept with since I first met Lydia – and I've known her since my teen years. I'm sorry, Barbara, really sorry. I should never have let it happen, but I don't regret that night, apart from hurting you, of course."

She pulled her hand away, but gently so that he wouldn't think she was still mad at him. "It's okay. But you behaved like a jerk afterwards. That was the problem; you avoided me and I felt like I'd been used. That's a crap feeling for any woman."

"Jesus, Barbara, I'm sorry. The next day I was called out first thing to work the Standerton case. Remember how bad that was? The entire force was working flat out for a month. I barely slept for the first three weeks and then, when I had time and tried to call you, you wouldn't take my calls."

Barbara sighed. "I know. I wanted to speak to you and I didn't want to speak to you. It was easier to think of you as a bastard than to hear you say what you've just said. I knew how you felt about Lydia. I just didn't want to hear it. Sorry, Paolo. Pax?"

Paolo stood and walked around to her side of the desk. "Is it okay to hug you?"

Barbara smiled; trust him to ask such a stupid question. "Sure, why not?" She stood up and leaned into his open arms.

"I'm sorry, Barbara. Friends?" he said.

She hugged him back and tried not to want more, but it wasn't working. "Ja, of course we're friends. Go on, get back to work. We're fine."

She felt his arms tighten around her briefly and then he moved away with a look suspiciously like relief on his face. Bloody men. She forced a smile onto her own face. Her features felt like lead, but she managed it. As the door closed behind him, her phone rang. Work calling. Thank God.

Barbara picked up the receiver and hoped her voice didn't crack, but she doubted it would even have been noticed. Sharon's sobs were loud enough to drown out any other noise.

"Barbara, I... didn't know who to... I can't believe... it's..."

"Sharon, hang on, honey. Take a deep breath. What's wrong? Has he hit you again?"

"No, I'm sorry. I... I shouldn't have called you. I didn't know who... you are a doctor, though, aren't you?"

What on earth was going on? Barbara concentrated on calming the other woman down and eventually Sharon seemed to get her emotions under control.

"Barbara, I need your help. Can you meet me tonight after Larry goes out?"

***

Paolo stared at the ceiling of his office. At least the one at work wasn't crisscrossed with cracks. He hadn't had a spare moment to look for somewhere else to rent. Getting a home sorted out needed to become a priority.

He thought back to his conversation with Barbara and felt relief, but also another emotion which nagged at the back of his mind. He recognised it as guilt – what else? His old friend guilt was always there in the background, a lasting product of his Catholic upbringing, but right now it was tap-dancing and pushing its way to the foreground. He'd treated Barbara badly, no two ways about that. Even if he hadn't meant to, he'd still hurt her. All he could hope for now was that she'd find someone nice to ... to what? Take her mind off what an arse he'd been?

He looked down at the papers littering his desk and picked up the file on Azzopardi. His DNA wasn't a match to that found on the dead women, but that didn't necessarily put him in the clear. Azzopardi rarely did the dirty work himself, unless roughing up Maria counted as work. If he'd targeted the Albanian network then he'd have sent a few of his thugs round to work the girls over. It was always possible one of them had a taste for murder.

On the other hand, the latest find didn't quite fit the profile. The woman was much older than the other two. What the hell did that mean? If it was the same killer, why switch from an older woman to girls barely out of their teens? One thing at least was clear now – the murders had started much earlier than they'd first realised.

His thoughts were interrupted by his mobile ringing. He picked it up and saw it was a call from his daughter.

"Hi, Katy, what's up? Shouldn't you be in class?"

"Nah, it's break, so it's okay. Dad, I'm sorry I wouldn't speak to you when you rang, but..."

"I know, kiddo, you were mad at me – and you were right to be. I'm just sorry I had to leave when I did."

"Anyway, I just wanted to make sure – you are still coming

this Saturday, aren't you?"

"Of course I am. Why?"

"No reason."

"Come on, Katy, spit it out. I can hear there's something you're not telling me."

"Is it that you are, 'ow you say, detecting, Inspector?" she said in a terrible impersonation of Inspector Clouseau.

Even though they were ancient films, Katy loved Peter Sellers in all of the *Pink Panther* releases. She always claimed that's what Paolo did when he went to work, acted like the mad inspector.

In spite of himself, Paolo laughed. "Yes, very good, Katy, but don't think you'll put me off. What's up? You wouldn't call from school unless there was a problem, so what is it?"

Katy didn't answer and Paolo remembered Matthew Roberts' parting shot earlier that day.

"Come on, Katy, spit it out. What's wrong?"

"I need you to calm Mum down."

"What? I'm more likely to do the exact opposite and that's without even trying. Katy, unless you tell me what the hell's going on, I can't help you. Now, for the last time, what's wrong?"

He heard Katy draw in her breath. It was an old trick of hers when she needed to say something that she knew Paolo wasn't going to like. He had a vision of her looking down at the ground, knuckles white from holding the phone so tight. She'd count to three under her breath, not realising Paolo could hear her.

"One, two, three," she whispered. Then there was another long pause before she spoke again. "Father Gregory's trying to have me expelled."

CHAPTER EIGHT

Thank God he had this cottage. He'd go insane if there wasn't a safe place for him to let go of all inhibitions and be free to please God. Day after day he suffered, allowing the other one to take centre stage, but here he could give God his due. Whores spread their filth over the town and he couldn't do a thing about it. At least in the safety of his special place he could punish those he caught and deliver their souls to God wiped clean of sin.

The number of whores plying their trade grew daily; he couldn't deal with them all. And now the Albanians were taking over many of the streets, introducing more corruptors. They were being sent out younger, too. Far too young to match His chosen ones. Was this God's way of telling him he had failed?

He shrugged his habit from his shoulders and bared his back. The whip's spikes drove deep into his scarred flesh, slicing through his skin. He gritted his teeth to prevent himself from crying out. He deserved to burn for letting so many whores live. Flicking the lash over each shoulder in turn, he begged for release from his guilt.

"*Mea culpa*, my fault, Lord. *Mea culpa*. Forgive me, Lord, for I have sinned. In my weakness, I have sinned. I have let you down, but I promise to make your beautiful world clean again."

Blood splattered on to the walls from the open wounds on his back, but still he continued to wield the whip. He could take the pain of any number of lashes, but not the pain of disappointing his God.

Eventually he fell to the floor, too exhausted to move his arms or drag himself to the bed. He lay prostrate, tears falling unchecked.

"Tomorrow, Lord, I swear. There will be one less in the cesspit tomorrow."

***

Barbara checked her watch yet again. After an hour sitting on the padded seat of the coffee bar's most secluded alcove, her backside had almost gone numb. She shifted her position to try to get some feeling back and then had another look at the time. It was just after ten and she'd arranged to meet Sharon for coffee at nine. She'd already called twice, but both times Sharon's phone had gone straight to voicemail. She'd give her ten more minutes and then go home. Barbara's caffeine level was already sky-high. If she drank just one more cup she'd probably bounce all the way to her front door. She tried not to imagine why Sharon had failed to show up, but couldn't stop the mental images of Larry using his fists as a battering ram.

Interfering in a marriage wasn't something Barbara believed anyone had the right to do, but if Sharon was being knocked about then she needed someone safe to speak to – and also someone to give her a way to protect herself. Barbara's hand rested on the pamphlets she'd picked up at the women's refuge advice centre. She knew from the voluntary work she did there that more women stayed in abusive relationships than left them. She just wished Sharon was a leaver and not a stayer.

She signalled to the waitress to bring over the bill. As she rummaged in her bag for her purse, the phone resting on the table next to her empty cup sang out the opening bars of *Nkosi Sikelel' iAfrika*. She smiled. No matter how many times she heard it, the South African anthem reminded her of home. One day she'd go back, but for now she was happy in her life in the

UK, even if her love life sucked.

She saw Sharon's name on the display as she picked up the phone.

"Hi, where are you? Are you on your way?"

"Yes, sorry. I had to wait until Larry went out, but I'll be there in a few minutes. I've asked Gareth our barman to handle things until I get back, but I won't be able to stay long as Gareth likes to get off as soon as possible after closing time. I just wanted to make sure you hadn't given up on me and gone home."

"I'm still here. I'll order you some coffee," Barbara said, waving at the waitress again.

Five minutes later Sharon was facing Barbara in the alcove, but seemed unable to unload her problems. Barbara silently pushed the leaflets over to Sharon's side of the table. Sharon flicked through them.

"I've read all this stuff before, you know that," she said. "Larry hasn't hit me for months. I thought we'd found a way to live without him getting so angry all the time. It's my fault—"

"Crap!" Barbara cut Sharon short. "Sorry, Sharon, but it isn't your fault. I'm not saying you're perfect or don't do things to make him mad, but if he hits you, that isn't your fault, it's his."

She could see by the look on Sharon's face that she wasn't getting through to her. Bloody Larry had her so downtrodden she believed every word he said.

"I can't bear to see you so unhappy. Let me help you. Please."

Sharon shook her head. "No one can help me. I need to stop being so stupid. Larry wouldn't act as he does if I didn't keep messing things up."

Barbara forced herself to wait before speaking. Pouring out how she felt about Larry wasn't going to help Sharon.

"You know I counsel battered women here? Well, that's something I began when I still lived in Cape Town.

"I've heard some horrific stories, seen some distressing sights, but you know what every single woman had in common?" She sighed, remembering some of the really bad injuries she'd seen. "They all said it was their fault. No matter how badly abused they were, they all said the same thing. That if they hadn't upset their husbands or partners they wouldn't have been burnt with cigarettes, had bones broken, been beaten almost to death and other crap like that. It doesn't matter what any of them did, no one deserves to have that sort of treatment handed out. So, no more nonsense from you about poor Larry being driven to it. He chooses to hit you, Sharon, because he knows he can control you that way."

As tears streamed down Sharon's face, Barbara reached out and put her hand on her friend's.

"Honey, I'm sorry. It's no good me lying to you. You need a friend, not someone who'll tell you it'll all get better if only you learn to be the perfect wife. That's not going to happen."

Sharon pushed the leaflets back towards Barbara. "I know you want to help, but that's not why I'm here. I need ... I need to ask you something as a doctor, not a friend." She inhaled deeply, her eyes flicking across the room, and then let the words out in a rush of air. "How can I tell if I've got syphilis?"

Whatever Barbara had been expecting, that wasn't it. She tried to frame an answer, but words just wouldn't come.

Sharon shrugged. "You look shocked. Sorry."

"What makes you think you might have syphilis, Sharon? Forgive me for asking, but have you slept with someone other than Larry?"

"No, boot's on the other foot. I've had... let's just say unpleasant symptoms for a while. Last night, when Larry went out, I asked Gareth to watch the bar for me. I followed Larry. I thought if I knew who he's sleeping with I could find out why he wanted to stray, you know? Why he needed someone else as well as me."

She stopped. Silent tears flowed down her cheeks, forming black rivulets as they mixed with her mascara.

Barbara reached across squeezed her hand. "And did you find

out who the other woman is?"

Sharon laughed. A harsh bitter sound that seemed to come from deep within. "Oh yes, I found out more than I wanted to know. He's not having an affair, Barbara. He's going with prostitutes. It seems I'm a failure in bed, too. He has to pay to get what he wants."

***

Paolo looked at his mobile as it vibrated on the bedside table. Lydia's name flashed on the caller display. God, he really didn't want to deal with her right now. He'd stayed at the station until the desk sergeant, passing on his way to the canteen, had asked him if he had a home to go to. He looked around at his scruffy bedsit. Yeah, right, some home this was and he still hadn't found time to even look in the classifieds. He took his notebook out and scribbled a message to himself to call an estate agent tomorrow.

His damn phone stopped vibrating only to start again immediately. Lydia would be breathing fire whether he answered it or not. He'd deal with Katy's rebellion tomorrow. How serious could it be, for Christ's sake? It was only a classroom argument between Father Gregory and Katy and, from what he could make out, it sounded like Katy had probably misunderstood Father Gregory anyway. No way could he have her expelled. It was more likely that he'd threatened her with expulsion just to frighten her into toeing the line a bit.

He switched his phone off and closed his eyes. God, he needed to rest. When was the last time he slept properly? His head felt light. It was so nice just to relax for a few minutes.

He woke up to a furious hammering on his door and wondered where the hell he was. Barely awake, he staggered to the door and opened it. Lydia pushed her way in.

"This place is a tip. Don't you ever tidy up?"

Paolo peered at his watch. "Yep, good idea. Tell you what, I'll do that tomorrow, but right now I'd rather know what the hell you mean by waking me up. It's gone eleven!"

"Since when do you go to bed this early? Besides, you're still dressed, so it's as well I woke you."

"And now that you have, why are you here? Sorry, sit down. I'll just move that stuff," he said, pointing to a battered armchair hiding under a heap of papers and clothes. "If it's about Katy's row with Father Gregory, don't worry about it. I promised Katy I'd go and smooth things over tomorrow."

Lydia crossed to the armchair, but stopped at Paolo's words. She looked at him, eyebrows almost disappearing into her hairline.

"You think you can smooth this over? You must be joking."

"No, why would I joke about that? I know Katy was in the wrong for yelling at Father Gregory in front of the class, but I bet you've already dished out masses of punishment. Where is she, by the way?"

"She's at home. In her room in disgrace. I called my sister and she came over to stay with Katy until I get back. If you'd answered your phone I wouldn't have needed to make the trip, would I?"

Paolo sat down at the tiny kitchen table's only chair and faced Lydia. "Okay, I should have answered the phone, but I was tired, Lydia, and needed some sleep. We could have dealt with this tomorrow."

"No, we have to deal with it now." She stopped speaking as a look of understanding swept across her face. "Katy didn't tell you, did she?"

"Tell me what?"

"What she actually said to Father Gregory. No way would you be so calm about it if she'd told you the truth. I had to force it out of her, but I assumed she'd at least been honest with you."

"Lydia, just get to the point, will you. Stop being so bloody dramatic."

She laughed. "You think I'm being dramatic? Katy has me beat hands down in the drama stakes. She said, in front of her entire class no less, that Father Gregory was a sexual pervert and probably the person the newspapers are featuring in their lurid headlines. In short, *dear* Paolo, *your* daughter accused a priest of being the murderer of those dead prostitutes." She smiled, but there was no humour in it. "Still think you can smooth it all over tomorrow?"

Paolo sat at his desk, head pounding from yet another night with not enough sleep. After Lydia had left the night before he'd found it impossible to relax enough to drop off again. What the hell was Katy up to? Fair enough if she wanted to question God and religion, but to accuse Father Gregory of being a sexual pervert and a killer? That was just asking to be expelled. He sighed and checked his watch – still too early to phone the school and try to fix things. Lydia was keeping Katy home from school today. They both thought Paolo stood more chance of sorting out the mess if Katy wasn't there to make it worse.

As for Katy herself, she was going to find out that even though Paolo no longer lived at home, he and Lydia still stood together as parents where her misbehaviour was concerned. He smiled grimly, Katy might wish he and Lydia didn't stand as one by the end of the weekend. Thank God it was Friday and he had the weekend to find out what was really bugging his daughter.

A light rap on the door broke his reverie. He yelled for whoever it was to come in, pleased to have something else to think about. The door opened and CC stuck her head round.

"We might have caught a bit of a break, sir. I've just heard from Liverpool. They have an unsolved up there with a similar feel to our killer's. All details are the same except for one."

"Okay, CC, I can see by your face that the one is a biggie, so come on, what's the missing detail?"

"No DNA."

"Fuck, that's a major missing detail. What makes you think it's our man?"

"It's not that I think it *definitely* is, but I do think there's a strong chance, sir. The body was wrapped in black plastic and found dumped in with garbage, just like ours. She'd been beaten from the waist up and died as a result of strangulation. As I say, sir, all the details fit except for that one."

"And this happened in Liverpool?"

CC nodded.

"When?"

"Ten months ago, sir. That's earlier than our three down here by a long way. I'm wondering if he started up there and worked his way down."

Ten months! If it was the same man, that meant the bastard was much further along on his killing spree than they'd realised – and there was always the chance that he'd started even before the Liverpool unsolved.

"Have they sent all the facts down?"

"Yes, sir, but there isn't much. The victim was a prostitute, so no surprise there, in her fifties, so similar in age to the last one found down here. But our older vic was killed before the younger two, so that makes sense in a way. Clearly, unless there are bodies we don't know about, he switched from older women to younger ones. Why do you think he did that, sir? Or is it just a male thing. You know, time to move on to the younger model?"

Paolo looked up into CC's grinning pixie face. Thank God there were officers like her around. Bloody good at their job, but with a sense of humour too.

"Do you think it's worth you making a trip up to Liverpool, CC?"

"It might be, sir. I'd like to look into the background of this victim. If she was the first... shit, I hope she was, then we might be able to get a lead on where and why our man chose her. It could help us down here."

Paolo mentally reviewed the cases he was working on and the officers involved with them. "I think you're right. You and George should go."

"Right you are, sir. I'll go and let him know we're off on a trip and to sort out his bucket and spade. I believe there's some nice coastline up that way."

Paolo laughed. "Yeah, right, and the two of you can build sandcastles in the middle of the coldest bloody March in years. Have fun and don't forget to pack a picnic."

As the door closed behind her Paolo checked his watch again. Still too early to call the school. He got up and walked across to the window separating his office from the main room. He tapped on the glass partition to get Dave's attention and signalled for him to come in.

Dave didn't look anywhere near his normal self. His face was drawn and showed the signs of sleep deprivation that Paolo was feeling.

"Rough night, Dave?"

The younger man scowled. "You could say that, sir. You wanted me?"

"Yes, I take it CC shared the news? I want you to run checks on every one of Azzopardi's businesses. See if you can uncover any connection with Liverpool, no matter how slight. If there's anything, anything at all, that would take him or one of his thugs up there, then I want to know about it."

Dave nodded and turned to leave. As he did so Paolo spotted blood on Dave's collar.

"Cut yourself shaving?"

Dave put his hand directly on a graze above the bloodstain. "No," he said. "Shall I get on with what you've asked me to do, or would you like to know what I had for breakfast?"

"Whoa, Dave, what's up with you? I only asked if you'd cut yourself."

"And you asked if I'd had a rough night. Either you want to hear about my conquests or you don't. Make up your mind," he said and walked out.

Bloody hell, Paolo thought. I must have really touched a nerve there. Five minutes later CC came back to say she and George were ready to set out on their way north.

"CC, come in a minute will you. Shut the door." Paolo waited until he was sure they couldn't be overheard. "Have you noticed anything odd about Dave this morning?"

"You mean odder than usual?"

Paolo laughed. "Yes, a bit. He seemed to be really touchy this morning. Was he off with you?"

"He always is, sir. He can't seem to get his head round the fact that I prefer my own sex. Anyway, yes, he is acting a bit odd, but I put that down to the fact that the girls have been talking."

"Don't tell me they are still falling over themselves to go out with him?"

"Nope," CC answered with a grin. "That's not it. What they're saying is that there isn't much point in going out with someone who can't get it up."

"CC!"

She laughed again as she got up and headed for the door. "Well, you did ask and now you know. See you in a few days, sir."

Okay, that really wasn't a situation he could do anything about. Dave would have to find his own way to deal with the consequences of upsetting so many WPCs that they'd joined forces against him.

He checked the time again. The school would be open now. Sighing, he picked up his phone. This was one call he really didn't want to make. He listened to the ringing tone and his stomach felt like it had been invaded by squirming centipedes. It reminded him of being ten years old and waiting outside the headmaster's door. He couldn't even remember now what he'd done wrong, but he sure as hell remembered the waiting time.

A female voice answered and Paolo recognised the homely

tone of Mrs Pearson, the school secretary. He asked to be put through to the headmistress and could hear in the way that Mrs Pearson responded that she knew why he was calling. It seemed he would have a fight on his hands if he wanted to secure Katy's future at the school.

CHAPTER NINE

He sang softly as he cruised. Friday nights in this part of town never changed, thank God. It made his work easier. The whores plied their trade in streets where no respectable people came; only those who used their services knew where to find them. As he edged the car around into Beacon Street for the fifth time he finally saw the whore he'd been searching for. She was leaning against the wall, eyes closed as if in prayer. He hoped she prayed. If she did God might save her. Almost as if she knew he was there, she opened her eyes and looked over towards the car. She was perfect for his needs. Almost the image of the girl in his precious photograph. If God approved of his choice, he'd make sure that she'd never turn into the hag that girl became.

He slowed the car. It crawled forward a few yards and then stopped. He touched the button to lower the window on the passenger side. She stood up straight and smiled, a look of interrogation on her face. Why did they all look like that, as if they really *wanted* to get in the car and open their legs? His heart pounded and his hands felt slippery on the steering wheel. He could barely swallow. It was always like this when he came to collect one of God's chosen.

If she turned and walked away that would mean God didn't want him to take her. *It's up to you, Lord.* She moved towards him, and he waited, shivering with anticipation. If she got in, then God had spoken and he would do His work. She reached the car and leaned in through the open window. He almost gagged as a cloying sweet scent filled his nostrils. Forcing himself to smile back at her, he nodded in the direction of the dashboard where a wad of twenty pound notes were resting on the leather in front of the steering wheel.

"Fancy a drive?"

She nodded and opened the door, slipping into the passenger side of the car.

"Like car," she said.

He didn't answer as he eased the vehicle forward and drove away. He didn't need to make conversation.

***

Paolo climbed out of bed on Saturday morning feeling as if he needed to sleep for a month. Yet another night had seemed to go on forever while his brain refused to shut down. Images of dead women had swapped places with Katy and Lydia in a macabre kaleidoscope until he'd given in and switched the light back on at three in the morning. He'd read a few chapters of Terry Pratchett's *Night Watch*, but even that man's brilliant humour had failed to hold his attention and he'd found his mind running in pointless circles. Desperate to sleep, he'd switched the light off again but had then lain in the dark until it was time to get up.

After his call to the school he'd realised his chances of getting Katy off with nothing more than a reprimand was optimistic at best. Now all he could hope for was to get to the bottom of Katy's sudden bizarre behaviour and find a way for her to put things right with Father Gregory. Failing that, the school board would be meeting next week to discuss expelling her.

By the time he'd showered and shaved he felt able to cope with the day ahead. Swallowing a mouthful of coffee, he switched on the television to see what was going on in the world. The BBC had a panel discussing human rights and Paolo's least favourite solicitor was spouting his usual politically correct garbage. He felt like chucking his mug at the screen. Bloody Matthew Roberts. The man made him sick. But Paolo knew he had to get beyond personal emotions. Matthew was chairman of Katy's school board and Paolo couldn't afford to upset him. At least, he couldn't do so before he'd resolved Katy's issues with Father Gregory.

Bloody hell, Katy, what sort of nonsense is going on in your head?

As he pulled up outside his old house the front door opened before he'd even switched the engine off. Lydia stood on the step, foot tapping. She looked as lovely as ever and Paolo wondered yet again if it might not be too late to save their marriage. He didn't wonder for long.

"It's about time, Paolo. Don't you care?"

"Good morning, Lydia, it's good to see you, too."

"Don't start with the sarcasm," she said, turning to go back into the house.

Paolo followed her and closed the door behind him. "Where is Katy?"

"She's up in her room and hasn't eaten anything since yesterday. Says she's on hunger strike until someone listens to the truth."

Paolo laughed, but stopped as Lydia rounded on him.

"That's right, you laugh. You couldn't give a shit about what happens to Katy."

Paolo was about to yell back when he realised tears were streaming down Lydia's face. He opened his arms and she walked into them, sobbing against his shoulder. He held her close, breathing in the familiar scent of her and wishing the moment would go on forever. Eventually the sobs stopped and she pulled away, furiously rubbing at her eyes with a soggy tissue.

"I'm sorry. I didn't mean to break down. She won't speak to me, Paolo. Please, find out what's wrong. She's always been closest to you. She'll tell you."

He squeezed her arm and headed for the stairs. "I'll do my best," he said, then turned back to face Lydia. "I'm not sure if my best is going to be good enough though. As I told you yesterday, the school aren't going to let her comments pass without some sort of action." He smiled and hoped it looked more reassuring than he felt. "Don't worry, Lyds, we'll get to the bottom of this."

He climbed the stairs and knocked on Katy's door. When no one answered he tried the handle, but the door was locked on the inside.

"Katy, it's Dad. Come on, open up."

Silence. He waited a few seconds more and then tried a different approach. "This is the police. Open up in there. We have the place surrounded. You can't escape, so give yourself up and I'll make sure the courts go easy on you."

Before he'd even finished, he heard footsteps approaching.

"Yeah, yeah. Very funny, Dad. I'm not going to apologise to that creep if I come out. You can't make me," Katy called through the door.

"Just open up and let's talk about it, okay? I don't even know what you said or why you said it. How am I supposed to argue your case with that very scary woman downstairs if I don't know what really happened? Huh? Come on, master criminal and scourge of the world, open the door."

He thought his humour hadn't worked because nothing happened for several seconds, but then he heard the key turn in the lock. The door swung inwards and Katy stood in the opening.

"Shall I come in, or are you coming out?"

"Is Mum still downstairs?"

Paolo nodded.

"I don't want to listen to her going on at me again. I know I've messed up. I don't need another lecture."

"You hungry?" Paolo asked. "Want to go somewhere for a brunch?"

"Can we go for a Big Mac?"

"It's too early for that," he said, hoping his thought that any time of the day was too early for MacDonald's didn't show on his face.

"You don't have to have one, Dad. You could have a MacMuffin. That's sort of breakfast, isn't it?"

"If I knew what one was I might agree with you. No, don't explain, I'll take my chances and find out when I'm eating it. And you can have whatever you want as long as I don't have to have the same."

She smiled, but it was a woeful effort. "Is that bribery? Should I be reporting you to the police complaints people?"

"You can if you want, but it's not a bribe as such, more a sweetener to get you talking. That's allowed. You get yourself ready and I'll go and put myself on lookout duty to see if the coast is clear." He stopped joking and took her hand. "Look, Katy, I'll make sure you don't even have to wave at your mum in passing on the way out, but you have to promise me that you'll speak to her when we get back. Okay?"

"Okay," she said. "But I'll need dessert too if I'm going to have to listen to a catalogue of all the things that I'm guilty of doing to ruin her life."

"Katy, your mum's never said any such thing."

"She doesn't need to," she said, snatching her hand back. "It's in her face every time she looks at me. Sometimes I think she wishes I'd got knocked down instead of Sarah."

He wanted to argue with her, tell her she was talking nonsense, but as usual thoughts of Sarah lying bloodied and battered in the road robbed him of speech.

Katy must have realised, because she gave him a half smile as she closed the door.

"No, don't try to say anything, Dad. Not now. I'll see you downstairs."

Paolo looked at the strange concoction on the tray in front

of him and tried to convince himself it was exactly what he wanted to eat, but his mind was fighting back. He picked it up, took a bite and was surprised to find it tasted much better than it looked.

He waited until Katy had devoured half of her Big Mac and fries and then asked her whether she wanted to go home to talk, or chat in the car.

"We can talk here as far as I'm concerned. I'm sorry, Dad, I get that you see him differently to me, seeing as you've known him for, like, forever, but I know for a fact that Father Gregory is evil. He's always going on about God and doing what's right, but he's just a pervert."

Paolo looked around, but no one seemed to be interested in Katy's outburst. "That's the second time you've said that to me. Has he...?" He stopped and shook his head, unable to put his revolting thought into words. If Father Gregory had touched Katy he'd ... he'd what? He pushed his tray to one side.

"This isn't the place to talk, Katy. It's too public. Let's finish eating and go for a drive."

As they walked out to the car park Paolo's thoughts were in still in turmoil. If Father Gregory was abusing Katy would she have attacked him in class like that? It wasn't usual for a victim to confront their abuser in public, but clearly something was going on for Katy to act as she did.

He pressed the button on his key to release the car's internal locking mechanism and opened the passenger door. Katy climbed in and smiled up at him. God, she was so young, he'd have trouble keeping his fists to himself if he found out that Father Gregory had laid a finger on her.

Walking round to the driver's side he took a deep breath. He had to stay calm. If he showed any anger Katy might clam up. He opened the door and slid behind the wheel.

"You want to go to the park, drive around a bit, or go home?"

"I don't mind."

"Okay," he said, "let's sit here and chat. It's as good a place as any. Has Father Gregory done anything to you, Katy? I mean..."

"I know exactly what you mean, Dad. I'm fourteen, not four! No, he hasn't done anything to *me*."

Waves of relief rushed through Paolo, but then her emphasis on the *me* registered.

"Has he abused someone else?"

She nodded.

"Who?"

"I can't tell you. I promised I wouldn't."

"Katy, if I don't know who it is how can I do anything about it?"

"Who asked you to? You don't need to do anything. I'm dealing with it."

"By getting yourself expelled? How is that dealing with it? Come on, Katy. Tell me. Let me help."

She sighed and turned her head away. They sat in silence for what seemed like eternity to Paolo, but finally she looked back at him and nodded.

"Okay, Dad, I'll tell you what I know, but you have to promise to do something about it without... without the girl being named. She's not to know I broke my word, okay?"

"Katy, I'm a policeman, I can't make that sort of promise, you know that. If I'm going to investigate..."

"You have to promise or I'm not telling you anything," she said, her eyes filling. "Dad, she told me in confidence. I can't tell you unless you promise."

He groaned – she'd left him with no choice. "Okay. I promise not to mention your friend's name, but you have to give me enough to start an investigation, Katy. This isn't like in a novel or on TV. I can't go off and arrest him with no proof. What do you know for a fact?"

"Well, I know he's got a creepy way of looking at us."

He shifted in the car seat. "Katy, that isn't fact, that's what you feel, but I can't accuse him of creepy looks, now can I?"

"I don't see why not, I did," she shot back.

"Yes, I know, and look at the result. Unless we can find a way round what you said to Father Gregory you'll most probably end up being expelled." She opened her mouth to speak, but Paolo continued before she could argue her case. "And do you know what would happen then? If your friend is being abused, or any of the other girls are, we won't be able to do a damn thing about it because we won't be able to prove it. If you get chucked out, Katy, do you think any of your classmates will speak out against Father Gregory?"

"No, but—"

"There are no buts, Katy. You can't accuse someone in public unless you can back up what you've said with proof. Now, tell me what you know, not the stuff about how Father Gregory looks at people. The facts, Katy, and then maybe I can help."

"Okay, Dad, but I can't tell you the girl's name. I'll tell you all the rest, but not her name."

Paolo realised he wasn't going to be able to push her on that, not at the moment anyway. He nodded for her to go ahead.

"A couple of weeks ago we had hockey practice after school and I'd almost reached home when I realised I'd left my hockey stick back in the changing rooms. You know the old ones next to the playing fields, not the new ones inside the gym?"

Paolo pictured the changing rooms. They were on the far side of the school grounds, a long way from any of the buildings – a long way from anyone hearing if something was going on in there. He nodded for Katy to continue.

"I went back for it and found... someone... crying. She's not in my class, she's a year younger than me, but I know her quite well because our class practises with hers. Anyway, she was all on her own in there and sobbing her heart out. I asked... her... what was wrong and she went mental, saying she couldn't tell me, she couldn't tell anyone or he'd kill her. All that sort of stuff. Anyway, I calmed her down and just sat there with her, you know? Just talking crap, sorry, talking about this and that.

Anyway, it turns out she's had sex. And she'd been forced, Dad. Not just once, either, loads of times by someone much older, but even though she told me that, she still wouldn't tell me who'd done it because he'd kill her. She was hiding out so he wouldn't find her."

Paolo waited for Katy to continue, but she was looking at him as if she'd reached the end of her story.

"But what happened next, Katy? How does Father Gregory come into it? Did she tell you it was him?"

"Not exactly, Dad, but I know it was."

He kept his irritation under control, but it was getting harder. "How can you know if she didn't tell you?"

"Because he came in. How could he even know she was in there if he hadn't been following... her?"

"He might have seen a light on, or even heard your voices if he'd been checking the school buildings; it could have been for any reason."

"Yeah, he tried to make out it was all innocent, but I saw how V... she reacted to him. She was terrified! And he offered to take her home and speak to her mother without even asking what was wrong with her. Of course he didn't need to ask because he already knew and no way was he really going to speak to her mother."

"Katy! I can't believe you've built this entire story around Father Gregory without any proof."

"But, Dad, listen to me. When he tried to make her go with him she begged him to leave her alone. Said she'd kill herself if he didn't."

"So then what happened?"

"The creep acted all concerned and asked me to walk home with V... her." She glared at Paolo. "I know what you're going to say, but it *wasn't* normal behaviour, Dad. You've got to believe me. There was something weird going on between them, I could see it. And, what's more," she continued on a note of triumph, "you know I said it was really obvious that he knew why she'd been crying? Well, when he went to take hold of her arm, she went absolutely mental, screaming at him to keep away and not touch her. Now why would she do that if *he* wasn't the one she was scared of?"

"I don't know, Katy, but surely that isn't all you have to go on? There must be more. Have you spoken to the girl since?"

Katy shook her head. "No, she's avoiding me. But not only me, she's avoiding the creep, too."

"Don't call him that! Not yet anyway. How do you know she's avoiding him?"

"Because I was walking behind her the next day and she saw Father Gregory and ducked behind a bush until he'd gone past. Now, you tell me, Dad, why would she do that if she wasn't scared of him?"

"Okay, let's say you're right. I can't do anything without proof or a complaint from the girl herself. Here's what I want you to do. Apologise to Father Gregory..."

"You must be joking."

"Just listen to me, will you. You apologise to Father Gregory. With a bit of luck that will satisfy the school and your case won't come up before the board." He smiled at the furious look on her face. "Cheer up, I haven't finished yet. Once we know you won't have to worry about getting expelled, I want you to get friendly with the girl and see if you can talk her into making an official complaint. If she does that then I can step in."

"But what if she won't? She's really scared of him, Dad."

"Don't worry; I'm going to keep an eye on Father Gregory without him knowing. If you watch out for your friend and I keep tabs on him, between us we should find a way to discover the truth. Okay?"

CHAPTER TEN

Paolo stood opposite Chief Constable Willows and wondered how the first good Monday morning he'd had in months had turned into a nightmare. He should have seen it coming after the weekend he'd had, but no, he'd believed his luck had changed at last and life was finally looking up. When he'd taken Katy home on Saturday to work out how they should handle her apology to the school, Lydia had been so relieved at Katy's change of heart that she'd actually thrown her arms round Paolo and kissed him. He'd been floating on air ever since – until now.

He looked around the chief's office, hoping to find something he could comment on to stop the flow of angry words firing at him from across Willows' incredibly neat desk. There was nothing. The man didn't have so much as a photograph Paolo could ask about. Everything was rigidly in its place; even the coat hanging on the rack next to the door had been smoothed into a neat shape. Willows was known to be anally tidy and compulsively private. Paolo doubted that many, apart from him, knew that Dave was the man's nephew. In Willows' eyes, the biggest sin a copper could make was to allow private lives to impact on cases. And now he seemed to think that Paolo was guilty of that particular crime.

"You have a grudge against Matthew Roberts, Paolo, and it's affecting your judgement."

"That's not the case at all, sir. I think his client is a piece of scum, that's all."

"That isn't all, damn it! Matthew Roberts tells me that you

have been questioning Azzopardi again, Paolo. He's complained that you are conducting a vendetta against his client. We've discussed this, Paolo. You have no proof of Azzopardi's involvement in any of these recent killings. If you can get the man on something concrete I'll be the first to back you, but right now it looks as though Roberts has right on his side. You're hounding Azzopardi on a hunch and Roberts believes it's to get at him rather than his client. You'd better have solid proof before you go within yards of Azzopardi. Roberts has promised to take action against you personally if you step over the line."

Well of course I'm pissed at Roberts, Paolo thought. The man has an above reproach persona and yet he works for scum. He forced himself to keep quiet, to stop the words from spilling out of his mouth. He wasn't after Azzopardi to get at Roberts, he was after Azzopardi because the bastard was evil through and through. Telling Willows that he knew how Azzopardi operated because he'd known him for years wouldn't cut any ice. Bradchester was too small for crooks on a national scale, but it was plenty big enough for Azzopardi's set up. The problem was proving his crimes. Anyone who could testify against him was either too scared to do so or already dead.

Maybe he wasn't directly involved in killing the prostitutes, but it certainly benefitted him that his opposition's girls were dropping out of sight. Paolo wondered if Dave had been able to establish a connection between Azzopardi and Liverpool. Unfortunately he'd been hauled up to Willows' office before he'd had a chance to ask.

"Sir, I promise I'll keep my distance and not give Roberts any ammunition he can use against me."

"Good. I'm sure you have your reasons for believing Azzopardi has a hand in these murders, Paolo, and I'd love to see the man behind bars where he belongs, but you need to move very carefully. Roberts is extremely well connected, nationally, not just locally, as you know only too well. He appears on just about every talk show up and down the country.

Heed my warning on this and keep me up to date on your progress. Good day."

Paolo heard the words of dismissal with relief and left the room. First things first, find out if Azzopardi had any Liverpool connections.

He entered the main office expecting to see Dave sitting at his desk, but his chair was empty.

"Anyone seen Dave?" he asked of the room generally, but only received negative responses.

Paolo recognised a WPC who was dropping papers on one of the desks. She was the girl Dave had chatted up on Gallows Heath. He was about to ask her if she had any idea where Dave was, but spotted the blush that had crept up from her neck and suffused her face. Maybe asking her about Dave wouldn't be the most tactful thing to do.

He was glad he hadn't when Dave walked in a few seconds later. The young WPC glared at Dave and walked out. Paolo was almost certain he heard the word bastard directed at Dave, but the WPC had spoken so softly, he couldn't be sure.

"Dave, in my office. Now," Paolo ordered and carried on walking, not waiting to see if Dave was behind him.

He threw his newspaper on his desk to join the mass of paperwork covering every inch of it, walked behind the desk and sat down. He waited until Dave had closed the door before speaking.

"Did I hear that WPC calling you a bastard?"

"I don't know. Did you, sir?"

"Don't get funny with me, Dave. That's the girl you took out after we found the body on Gallows Heath. Rebecca, I think her name is. Why is she swearing at you?"

"No idea, sir. I didn't hear her say anything."

Paolo could see from the look on Dave's face that he didn't want to talk about whatever was going on between him and Rebecca. Paolo didn't particularly want to know, but he agreed with Willows, you couldn't allow your personal life to overlap with the job. It would lead to problems they could do without right now.

"Okay, must have been my imagination," Paolo said. "But I don't want any more opportunities for my imagination to see or hear anything else. Understood?"

Dave nodded, but kept quiet.

"Right, moving on. Tell me what you've found out about Azzopardi. Any business connections in Liverpool?"

"Not as far as I've been able to ascertain so far, sir, but he does have family in the area. His sister married a Scouser and moved up there some years back. I don't know how close they are, but Azzopardi might have been up there visiting."

Paolo smiled. "Good work, Dave. Get on to CC and fill her in. She and George can do some sniffing around while they're up there. They might be able to find out if the sister's husband is in the same line of business as her brother. If he is, what's the betting they are on visiting terms?"

"I wouldn't give you odds, sir. If it's in the blood then she's sure to be as bad as Azzopardi."

Paolo nodded, although it didn't always follow that just because one part of a family was as crooked as forked lightning that all the rest were. Maybe this sister wasn't part of the criminal world, but her living in Liverpool pointed the investigation straight to Azzopardi yet again.

"Any news on the Albanian pimp?"

Dave shrugged his shoulders. "According to the girls I've managed to speak to, none of them have a pimp. They don't know what one is. Don't want to know what one is. And wouldn't tell me even if they suddenly remembered. Only one thing I know for sure. Whoever is running those girls has them too terrified to say a word to us. Every one of them sweated buckets trying to come up with lies to cover up for the pimp who doesn't exist. They are shit scared of him and I don't think it's just the normal pimp and prostitute power thing. I got the impression he, whoever he may be, has a greater hold over them than that.

"One thing they did tell me about was a priest who hangs around there most nights. It seems he's trying to get them to turn to God instead of turning tricks. They look on him as a bit of joke, but he might be worth investigating. They call him Father Gregory."

Paolo looked up in surprise. "Do they indeed? Hmm, I think I know who that is. Leave it with me."

"Right, you are, sir. I'll call CC and fill her in on the Azzopardi family connection."

The phone rang, so he nodded to Dave to carry on. The caller display showed Lydia's name. Heart beating just that bit faster, he flipped it open.

"Paolo here."

"Hi. I've just left the school. They've agreed to let Katy back from tomorrow, but she has to make a public apology to Father Gregory. I'm not sure she'll do it, Paolo. Can you come over tonight to talk to her?"

"Sure, of course I will. What time?"

"You could come for a meal, if you wanted to."

Paolo heart rate shot skywards and he almost couldn't breathe. Don't fuck this up, he told himself. Trying for nonchalance, he forced his voice to remain level.

"Yeah, sure, a meal would be nice."

"Okay, if you get here at about six then you can talk to Katy while I'm busy in the kitchen. She's less likely to fight if I'm not in the room. See you then."

Paolo remembered Katy's comment from the weekend.

"Lyds, before you go. Katy said something odd to me on Saturday. Are you two getting on okay? No problems?"

He heard a sound between a laugh and sigh before Lydia spoke again.

"Paolo, she's fourteen and I'm her mother, of course we're not getting on okay. She thinks I'm a pain and I think she's deliberately difficult. But as far as I know we don't have any real problems. What sort of odd comment?"

His mouth moved, but the words refused to come out. How could he tell Lydia that Katy felt her own mother would have preferred it if she'd died instead of Sarah? He couldn't do it.

"Oh, she made some remark about believing you hated her sometimes."

There was silence for a moment. "She throws that comment at me at least once a day, usually when I've told her to do something she doesn't want to do. I don't know why she says it, or even if she believes it, but then she's never confided in me the way she does with you. Maybe, while you're convincing her to make the apology to Father Gregory, you could also find out what I'm doing wrong as a mother and put that right, too. After all, you seem to be Mr Fix-it where she's concerned."

Paolo heard the bitterness in Lydia's voice, but before he could say anything the phone went dead.

***

Barbara walked into the pub and swallowed back the bile when she saw Larry behind the bar. Even though she knew he would be there, she'd been hoping that something might have happened to stop him from coming down from the flat upstairs. Preferably something excruciatingly painful, but non-infectious, so that Sharon couldn't catch it. She forced a smile onto her face and walked up to the bar.

"Hi, Leanna's meeting me for lunch. What's today's special?"

Larry's gaze rested just a fraction too long on her breasts before focussing on her face and she felt the usual urge to throw a bucket of cold water over him.

"There's no special today. Sharon's feeling a bit off colour, so I've told her to stay upstairs. The girls in the kitchen can handle all the usual stuff, though, so order whatever you fancy from the menu."

Barbara forced another smile. "Nothing serious, I hope.

Want me to run upstairs and check her over?"

Larry shook his head. "No, best not. I think she's sleeping. I'll tell her you and Leanna were in. You want your usual drinks? Go on over to your table and I'll bring yours now and Leanna's when she gets here."

Barbara walked away from the bar trying to figure out a legitimate excuse to go up to see Sharon. She was no nearer to thinking one up when Leanna arrived five minutes later. By the time her friend had taken off her coat and sat down, Larry was at the table with her drink.

"Here you go. That's my two favourite customers sorted. Give me a shout when you're ready to order your meals."

As he walked away, Leanna turned to Barbara.

"Okay, what's going on? Why was it so important that I changed my lunch date to meet you here?"

Barbara bit her lip. "I was hoping that Sharon would be here. We need to convince her to leave Larry."

"Where is she now? Hiding upstairs? Has he started knocking her about again?" She stopped as Barbara signalled with her hands to keep her voice down. "Am I right about Larry hitting her?" she finished on a whisper.

Barbara nodded and leaned towards Leanna. "Can you think of a way to keep x-ray vision man occupied while I sneak upstairs to talk to Sharon? I can't tell you why, but it's really important that I go up and talk to her."

Leanna sat back against her chair, clearly deep in thought. Then she grinned. "I've just remembered one of the many, many conversations where Larry has bored me senseless. It's payback time. I'm about to play damsel in distress."

Barbara signalled to Larry to come over. When he'd finished writing down their food order and was about to turn away, Leanna laid a hand on his arm.

"Larry, do you know anything about cars?"

"What sort of anything? Makes, engine types, horsepower? I know a bit. Why?"

"Have you any idea why my car would start making funny noises?"

"What sort of noises?" he asked, pulling out a chair and sitting down.

Leanna put on such a soulful look that Barbara had difficulty holding back a giggle.

"It starts okay, but after a while the engine seems to shudder and then there's a sound like metal on metal. It's in the car park if you want to listen to it."

Larry looked around as he stood up. "It's quiet in here for the minute, so Gareth should be all right on his own for a bit. I'll just shout your order through to the kitchen and then I'll be with you," he said.

As he walked away Barbara finally let out her pent up laughter. "You might as well have batted your eyelashes and be done with it. Tell me, though, how did you know he'd fall for it?"

Leanna grinned. "I told you, he's bored me senseless a number of times. One of them was on the subject of being able to be your own car mechanic. Apparently he thinks no one should be allowed behind the wheel of a car unless they can do their own oil change, whip out an engine with one hand and God knows what else. He spent over an hour telling me about the inner workings of his car one lunch time when you were supposed to meet me here but got held up and couldn't make it. I nearly hunted you down and slaughtered you that day."

Barbara smiled. "Lucky I escaped. By that I mean lucky I escaped the car lecture. Hush now, he's on his way over."

Leanna stood up, grabbed her car keys and headed Larry off. "I'm so glad you know about cars, Larry."

"No problem. I can't spend too long though; it'll get busy soon and Gareth won't be able to deal with a rush on his own."

Barbara waited until they'd gone outside and then headed for the door marked private. Once inside, she ran up the stairs and tapped on the door at the top. As she did so it opened slightly.

"Sharon?" she called out. "Sharon, it's me, Barbara. Is it okay if I come in?"

She could hear the faint sound of someone sobbing, so pushed the door fully open. Standing just inside the small hallway, she called out again, but Sharon didn't answer. Barbara could no longer hear the sobbing, so wasn't sure which room to look in first. She decided to try the lounge and walked into the main room of the flat, stopping dead on the threshold. It looked like a scene from a post-apocalyptic movie. The tall standard lamp was lying across the sofa. One of the dining chairs was on its side. Another was pushed back from the table where plates and cutlery had been left in place. From the amount of food on the plates, the meal had clearly been interrupted – and not for any good reason. A red stain spread down the wall behind the overturned chair and glass littered the carpet.

Fearful of the state she might find Sharon in, she called out for her again. No one answered, but the sobbing started up again. Following the sound of weeping, she came to the bedroom. The door was wide open and Barbara found Sharon lying on the bed, fully dressed, but with her face turned away from the doorway. Here too someone had been throwing more than just their weight around. The stool, missing one leg, was across the other side of the room from the dressing table. Laundry littered the floor, as if spilled from the overturned linen basket.

Barbara stepped into the room. "Sharon, what the hell happened? Can I help?"

Sharon continued to cry softly, but didn't turn her head, so Barbara stepped over the debris and walked around the bed. As she saw Sharon's face a gasp caught in her throat. Hardly any of her friend's face was the normal colour, the rest was decorated with deep marks in multiple shades of blue and purple. Both eyes were swollen, one was almost shut. A clump of hair was missing from one side of her head, the bleeding area on her scalp showed it had been torn out.

Barbara dropped to her knees and took Sharon's hand in hers. "Bloody hell, Sharon, what did he do to you?" she asked, even though in her own mind she knew it was a stupid question. It was obvious what Larry had done, the real question was why.

"Barbara," Sharon whispered, taking her hand from Barbara's. It was clearly an effort for her to speak. "I had an accident. It looks worse than it really is," she said. "Please go away."

"Honey, I'm sorry, I don't believe you. I've seen the state of this place – not to mention the state of you. You never got these bruises from any kind of accident. Larry did this to you, didn't he?"

Tears continued to flow, but Sharon made a slight negative movement with her hand. "No. He never touched me. Why are you up here, Barbara? Did Larry say you could come up?"

"No, he's outside with Leanna, looking at her car."

Sharon trembled. "You must go back down. Please, you must go. I'm fine, honestly, just a bit clumsy, falling over stuff. I'll tidy up in a bit. Please go, Larry doesn't like anyone up here, you know that."

"Come with me," Barbara urged. "You can stay at my place. I won't let Larry near you. Please, Sharon, let me help you."

"Barbara, I told you, Larry didn't do this. I did it tripping over the furniture. Please, please, go back down to the bar."

"Did you trash your flat at the same time? I can guess what happened from the way the place looks. Come with me, Sharon. I promise you'll be safe with me. Leanna can get a restraining order so Larry can't harass you."

"Barbara," Sharon said, tears streaming from under her swollen lids, "please go away before Larry realises you're up here. I'm fine. Really I am."

Barbara stood up. "Okay, honey, but always remember you have my phone number. You can call at any time, day or night, and I'll come and pick you up. Okay?"

She waited, but Sharon didn't answer. "The reason I came up was to give you the results of the tests I did for you. At least that's one thing less for you to worry about. You only have a minor infection. A short course of antibiotics will fix you up."

She leaned forward and gently dropped a kiss on one of the few unbruised areas of Sharon's forehead. "Please, call me. I can get you out of this nightmare."

Sharon closed her eyes, but remained mute. Barbara turned and went back through the flat to the main door and closed it to without actually shutting it. She needed to make sure it looked as it had before she went into the apartment. As she ran down the stairs she wondered if she'd be able to stop herself from confronting Larry about the state Sharon was in. But inside she knew that doing so would only make matters worse for her friend. There was nothing to be done until Sharon left him. If Barbara faced up to him now, he'd take it out on Sharon later. All she could do was to pray that one day her friend would decide she'd had enough. When that day came, Barbara vowed she'd move heaven and earth to make sure the bastard paid for what he'd done.

She slipped back into the bar and sat down at the table. She needn't have worried about being away too long. When one of the kitchen girls brought their meals to the table, Leanna and Larry were still outside. Sighing, Barbara stood up and went to find them. With a bit of luck, between them, she and Leanna would be able to persuade Sharon to leave Larry one day.

***

Paolo picked up his phone and slipped it into his pocket as he stood up. He'd be glad to see the back of today even if he didn't have a dinner date with Lydia. Okay, it wasn't a date as such, he reminded himself, but they'd be having a meal together, him and Lydia, in the place he used to call home. That was a better situation than he'd been able to look forward to for a very long time. He thought of his mother's saying of everything happening for a reason. Maybe she was right after all. He'd never have thought Katy almost getting expelled could be a good thing, but it seemed good might come out of it – as long as Katy did what was needed and apologised to Father Gregory.

Paolo had wrestled with what he should do about what Katy had told him. Speaking to Father Gregory to find out the true reason he went to the locker rooms way over the other side of the playing fields seemed to be the best option. If Father Gregory had a legitimate reason for being there, then Katy's take on the situation would be less reliable. If he didn't have a good reason, well, maybe Katy might be on to something. Making up his mind to chat to Father Gregory at school after Katy had made her apology, Paolo reached for his coat hanging on the stand near the door.

He shrugged himself into it and opened the door, almost colliding with Dave.

"Sorry, sir. I've just come from the front desk and ran to catch you before you left."

"I can't stop, Dave. I have a..." He stopped, loath to say the word date when it so clearly wasn't one. "I've got to go," he said.

"Fine, sir. I won't keep you, but I thought you'd want to know that a prostitute went missing Saturday night. Her friend, Sandra Massey, has phoned in to report it. The desk sergeant put her through to me."

"And?"

"It seems her mate went off in a dark car with a trick and the girl hasn't been seen since."

"Albanian?"

"No, sir, and that's another reason I thought you'd want to hear about it. The missing woman and the person reporting it, Sandra Massey, are both part of Azzopardi's stable. She didn't mention him by name, but the patch she and her mate work is definitely run by one of his team."

CHAPTER ELEVEN

Paolo came into work Tuesday morning feeling as though his smile was lit up in neon lights. It was all he could do to stop himself from whistling. As he hung his coat on the stand in his office he realised he hadn't felt this good in a long, long time. Not only had he finally had a relatively untroubled night's sleep, but he might even have a future to look forward to once again. The evening with Lydia and Katy had gone better than he'd dared to hope. Katy, pleased to be, as she saw it, part of an investigation, was prepared to sacrifice her principles on the altar of the greater good. She'd agreed to offer Father Gregory an apology. She hadn't wanted to, but Paolo pointed out she needed to get friendly with the girl from the locker rooms. If she was being abused, maybe Katy could persuade her to tell someone. Paolo hadn't been able to prise the girl's name out of Katy, but he felt certain it was only a matter of time. Once he knew who she was, he'd alert social services to look into the family. If she really was being abused – and he found it hard to believe Father Gregory was the culprit – then the sooner Social took over the better.

Dinner had gone well, Lydia had even laughed at some of his more inane jokes and Katy had been on her best behaviour, not once arguing with her mother. As Lydia had said, once Katy had gone upstairs, it couldn't last, but it was nice not to be on the defensive the whole time.

Paolo hadn't realised how difficult it must be for Lydia,

coping with Katy's rebellions on her own, but maybe she wouldn't be on her own for much longer. He walked across to his desk and his eye fell on a ringed advert for an apartment in the classified section of the previous day's newspaper. He'd intended to go and look at it today, but maybe he should hold off a bit longer before making any permanent moves.

He'd just settled himself into his seat when the phone rang. He saw Barbara's name on the display and instinctively looked at the clock. Not yet eight o'clock. It was a bit early in the day for a call related to work, but she rarely called for any other reason.

He snapped the phone open. "Hi, Barbara, what can I do for you?"

"Morning, you sound in a good mood. Just found out you won the lottery?"

He was about to tell her the reason for being cheerful, but realised in time just how crass that would be. "Yes, I'm now a multi-millionaire, but don't tell anyone because I don't want to give up work. I'd hate to lose out on my police pension."

She laughed. "Understandably so. Tell me, Paolo, do I remember rightly that you and Larry from the Nag and Bag went to the same school? I'm sure you told me that once."

"I did. Why do you want to know? What's he done?"

"What makes you think he's done anything?" she asked and he could hear the surprise in her voice.

"I don't. It was just a joke. Why do you want to know about my schooldays? Or rather, Larry's schooldays?"

Her heard a sound as if she was going to say something and then changed her mind. He waited and finally she spoke again.

"Was he a bully? I have a good reason for asking, but don't want to tell you what it is just yet."

"Larry? A bully? No, quite the opposite, in fact. He was the victim rather than the bully. Poor weedy bloke, he was, even in senior school. His great ambition at one time was to become a priest, but his family weren't too keen on that idea. Larry spent ages perfecting his halo, but went off the rails a bit after his dad beat the holiness out of him. His dad was a bit heavy with his fists. Poor Larry often looked as though he'd gone a few rounds in the boxing ring."

"And the teachers didn't do anything about it?"

"Barbara, no one did anything back then. If parents belted their kids every night, as long as the kid lived, the parents got away with it. Catholic schools were fully behind the 'spare the rod and ruin the child' creed. At least, our school was. I suppose I shouldn't really speak for the others."

Paolo's mind drifted back to his final year in St Swithin's. Frank Azzopardi, Greg Mitchell, Matthew Roberts and Larry Harper were the only members of Matthew's little group. Thinking about it, though, Paolo recalled Larry had never really been a full member of the gang. He'd just been tolerated as someone to fetch and carry for the main three. Paolo, along with the rest of the class, had been desperate to be a member for most of his high school years. Then he reached his final year and started going out with Lydia. Life changed completely and fitting in with Matthew and co wasn't as important as being with her. Nothing was as important as spending every spare moment with her.

Remembering them as they were, he realised Frank had changed the least. He'd been a thug and a crook even back then. If there had been a betting book on anything, from the outcome of exam results to the winner of the Grand National, then Frank Azzopardi was running it. He'd boasted about his uncle's empire and how one day he'd take over from him. No one had taken him seriously, but his boasts had all come true.

The one who'd changed the most was Greg, or Father Gregory as he was now. Who'd have believed that Greg would give up drink, drugs and sex for the priesthood? Especially the sex. He'd been the only one in their class who'd definitely scored. Lots of others claimed they had, but Greg had never said a word about any of his conquests. He hadn't needed to brag, the girls had done that for him; he'd had an aura of confidence about him that the others tried to copy, but none of them had ever managed to carry off, not even Matthew. Greg had been wild for most of their senior school years, even came close to being expelled on more than one occasion. Paolo chuckled. He'd forgotten just how uncontrollable Greg had been. If he turned nasty over Katy's apology, it might be time to remind him of his own less than perfect past.

Matthew had turned out exactly as his parents had planned. Paolo shuddered as he recalled Mrs Roberts' cut glass accent on speech days. She'd been on the board of St Swithin's for years and always gave what she must have thought was an inspirational speech. In truth, she could have won gold medals boring for Britain. Matthew had taken her place on the St Swithin's school board when she'd died ten years or so back. And then, when St Swithin's had merged with the girls' catholic school a couple of years later, he'd been made chair of the joint board. Which was why, if Father Gregory didn't accept today's apology, Matthew would have a say in Katy's future.

"Helloooooooo, are you still there?"

Barbara's voice finally penetrated his reverie and Paolo shook off his memories.

"Sorry, Barbara, I just took a very long walk down memory lane. Was there anything else you wanted to know about Larry as a young man?"

"Do you think his father..." She stopped speaking so suddenly he could almost picture her clamping her lips tightly together.

"Do I think his father what? Come on, Barbara, you wouldn't call at this time of the morning unless there was a good reason for it. Why the sudden interest in Larry's past?"

"I was going to ask if you knew whether Larry's father beat his mother."

"I don't know, I'm afraid, but I'd be surprised if that wasn't the case. I've seen too many cases in my career where the mother and kids were walking punch bags. It seems when the fists fly the bastards don't mind where they land. Now, are you going to tell me why you're asking, or shall I make an educated guess?"

He waited for an answer, but Barbara didn't say anything.

"I think your friend Sharon's getting a taste of what Larry grew up with. Am I right?"

Barbara sighed. "Yes, but that's not the only reason for calling you. I saw Sharon yesterday, Paolo, and it was like looking at a living version of our recent victims. Her face was a mess. She says she fell down the stairs, but even if she'd bounced on every step face first she wouldn't be as battered as she is."

"Barbara, I'd love to step in and do something, but unless Sharon is prepared to—"

"That's not why I'm calling. At least, it isn't the only reason. I could be imagining things, but I'm telling you, Paolo, she looked *exactly* like one of our victims – and Larry has been visiting prostitutes lately. I'm just wondering if there's any connection between the two."

"Bloody hell, Barbara, Larry? I suppose it's possible, but… I wouldn't have thought… But then, we never really know people, do we? You might be right. I'll have someone watch his movements for the next few weeks. If he's our man, we'll get him."

"Thanks, Paolo."

"In the meantime, what about your friend? It sounds like she's in a bad way."

"She is, but until she decides to leave him, there isn't much either of us can do to help her. But if she calls, can you make sure someone responds immediately? If she phones for help it will be because she's in real danger."

Paolo promised to make sure there was a message on the desk telling the force that immediate response was required if Sharon called in. He said goodbye and snapped the phone shut. So Larry was following in his father's footsteps? Was he really surprised? He'd seen domestic violence repeated generation after generation too many times to honestly say he couldn't believe it of Larry. But murder? That he found harder to swallow. Still, he'd have him watched just the same. If Barbara thought the injuries inflicted looked similar to the murdered girls, then she was worth listening to.

He'd no sooner put the phone on his desk than it rang again. This time CC's name came up.

"Storey," he said as he put the receiver to his ear. "What have you got for us, CC?"

"News on Azzopardi's sister and some info on the dead woman. Which do you want first?"

"Tell me about Azzopardi's sister. I know he has three sisters, where does this one fall in the family?"

"She's the youngest and wants nothing to do with her brother. She wasn't at all pleased to get a visit from us. She says the reason she and her husband moved to Liverpool was to get away from her family. Her husband's a butcher, by the way, the type who makes sausages and stuff, not the kind who beats up people – unless he does that in his spare time. The sister's name is Louise; I met up with her at her house. Typical suburban semi, not the rich bitch mansion I'd been expecting. She says she hasn't had any contact with her brother or any other family member for years. I could be wrong, but I'd say she's telling the truth."

Paolo tapped his fingers on the desk. "Pity. It would have been neat to have a connection to Azzopardi we could use. Still, there might be a business association we haven't uncovered yet. What have you found out about the dead woman?"

"Her name was Catherine Andrews. She was well known to the local force. Several arrests for prostitution, small time drug dealing and theft. She'd been on the streets for years, almost an institution up here apparently, but then she disappeared one night and turned up dead about a week later. Beaten and then strangled, but no DNA left behind to match. Either our killer didn't do her, or he wore a condom. No close friends that I could find, but one of her neighbours says she had a young man who visited a few times. Dark haired, tall, good looking. The neighbour, Mrs Bligh, didn't think he was a boyfriend or trick because it was always a Sunday afternoon when he came over. She thought he might be a relative of some kind due to the fact that Catherine used to clean herself up and stay off the drugs until after he'd gone."

"The neighbour didn't catch his name or anything else useful?"

"No, but I'm not really surprised. The noise level in that place is horrific. I don't know how they can bear living there."

"How do you mean?"

"When we arrived it was like listening to half a dozen different radio stations all playing at full volume. Once we'd knocked on a few doors, the sound level gradually went down," CC said. "Anyway, Mrs Bligh didn't hear anything useful. She said she wasn't one to be nosey. I think it's more likely that she is very much a nosey neighbour, but that Catherine wanted to keep the young man's visits private. Apparently she used to wait downstairs and only bring the mystery visitor upstairs when she thought the coast was clear. Which means, of course, that Mrs Bligh must have been peering through a crack in the door or something, or she wouldn't have known any of this."

"I take it she knew Catherine was on the game?"

"She says not, but she must have done. I could be doing her an injustice, but I think she might have been in the same line of business, only she's now retired and can afford to be respectable."

"Good work, CC. Is there any point in you and George staying up there any longer?"

"I don't think so, sir. George and I have made some good contacts with the local force and they've promised to keep us up to date if anything develops. We'll be back in the office bright and early tomorrow morning."

"Fine, I'll bring you up to date with what's going on here then." As he spoke the door opened and Dave peered across at him. Paolo signalled for Dave to come in and sit down. "We'll see you and George tomorrow, CC. Have a safe journey back."

He closed the phone and tossed it onto the desk. "Not much new information from Liverpool, but it seems the sister isn't on good terms with her brother, so there's no reason for Azzopardi to wander on up there. They had a falling out a few years back and she hasn't seen him since."

He went on to fill Dave in on CC's other news and then asked what Dave had found out about the missing prostitute.

"Nothing more than I told you last night, unfortunately. I arranged to meet Sandra Massey last night. Remember she's the woman who's reported her friend missing? Anyway, business must have been good for her because she stood me up. I've tracked down her address, though, so I'll go and disturb her beauty sleep when I've brought my paperwork up to date."

Paolo caught sight of the clock and realised he only had half an hour before Lydia and Katy would be arriving at the school. He'd promised to be there to lend moral support – and also because he wanted to see Lydia again.

"I've got to go out for a couple of hours, Dave, but hang on until I get back and we'll go and question Sandra Massey together. Oh, by the way, before I forget, arrange for some discreet surveillance of Larry Harper, he's the owner of the Nag and Bag. It might be nothing, but I've had a tip that he likes to beat his wife and also spends time in the company of prostitutes."

As he stood up, he toyed with the idea of telling Dave that Larry was an old classmate from his high school days, but decided against it. There was no reason for him to know and explaining the connections would take too long.

Walking across to the coat stand, he issued a few last minute instructions to Dave, grabbed his coat and ran. He had no intention of being late for this meeting. He had a feeling more than Katy's future depended on what happened this morning.

Lydia and Paolo watched from the hallway as Katy walked back to class after she'd made her apology in front of the head and it had been accepted, although not as wholeheartedly as they'd hoped.

"I thought Father Gregory was a bit grudging in his reply, didn't you?" Lydia said.

Paolo caught the note of concern in her voice. "Don't worry, Katy has promised to keep her mouth shut for the rest of the year at least. As long as she doesn't do or say anything else outrageous she shouldn't have any more problems."

"I'm glad you were here," Lydia said, gripping Paolo's arm. "I'm not sure I could have got her to apologise, far less sound as if she meant it."

She looked so lovely, Paolo wanted to gather her in his arms, but this wasn't the place.

"Fancy going somewhere for a coffee?" he asked.

He looked up to see the priest had come out of the head's office and was bearing down on them. He turned, intending to whisk Lydia out but wasn't fast enough.

"Paolo, can we have a chat?"

"Right now?" he said, smiling in what he hoped looked like a friendly manner. "Lydia and I were just off to find a nice coffee shop."

Lydia smiled. "Another time, Paolo. I have an appointment at the hairdressers anyway, so couldn't have stayed long."

She waved goodbye and headed for the double doors of the exit. Paolo watched until the doors closed behind her. He turned back to Father Gregory.

"What's the problem now? Katy has promised to behave."

"I know she has, but I had a call this morning from Matthew and I feel I need to warn you so you can speak to Katy. He wasn't happy about this meeting. He felt Katy's case should have been decided by the school board. You know what he's like,

Paolo, can't stand the idea that anything would damage the school's reputation."

"You mean *his* reputation," Paolo said.

"Yes, maybe, but he does really care about the two schools, Paolo. What I'm trying to say is that Katy needs to be more than careful. Her behaviour needs to be close to perfect. Matthew has lots of supporters on the staff. They'll all be watching Katy. It isn't just my class that she needs to behave in, it's all of them. Matthew only needs one transgression, no matter how minor, and he'll insist on reopening this."

"Well, she needs a friend in that case. You're on the school board, aren't you?"

"I hardly think I'm the right person to plead her cause."

Paolo frowned. "Greg," he said and the frown changed to a smile at the look of shock on the priest's face. "Oh, come on. It's still your name. Just because I give you the courtesy of using your title doesn't mean I don't think of you as Greg."

The priest grimaced. "I'm just used to being called Father. It sounded odd."

"You know, it is odd. I'd forgotten our schooldays. I don't mean completely, but just hadn't given them any thought. Then today someone asked me about one of our old classmates and the memories came flooding back. Now, if anyone should understand about a teenager's rebellion it must surely be you."

"Paolo, that was a long, long time ago."

"I know it was, but that doesn't change the fact that you haven't always been as holy as you now make out." As Father Gregory scowled, Paolo held up a hand of truce. "Okay, sorry, as holy as you are. But Greg, your drinking and smoking were the bane of the teachers, the priests and your parents. As for your other exploits, the parents of the girls you had so much fun with would have strung you up with pleasure if they'd been able to get away with it. Come on, you were the worst behaved boy in our school and the only reason you weren't expelled was because Matthew was your best friend and no one would take a chance on upsetting his family. I didn't realise any of that back then, but I'm older now and know how these things work. The school needed the Roberts' money, so as long as you, Frank and Matthew were as thick as thieves, it didn't matter what any of you did, you knew you would get away with it."

Paolo made himself pause before saying anything else. When he was sure his temper was under control, he continued. "I'm not asking you to let Katy get away with anything, Greg. If she plays up after today's warning then she deserves whatever she gets, but if she's set up by one of your colleagues to suit Matthew's way of thinking, then, yes, I expect you to stand up for her."

There was silence for several seconds. Then Father Gregory laughed. "Talk about a chip off the old block. Your Katy sounds just like you when she gets going."

"I know. She gets worked up and lets fly."

"She almost caught me out a little while ago. I'd sneaked off to the playing field lockers to indulge in one of the vices I haven't given up and there she was with another girl. Luckily I hadn't actually lit my cigarette, but it was a close run call."

Paolo studied Greg's face, but couldn't see anything other than amusement.

"Oh, you still smoking? Me too, but I'm planning to give the patches a try. Katy told me she'd seen you. I don't think she'd realised that you'd gone over there for a quiet fag. She did mention that she'd found a girl in deep distress though. You know anything about that?"

Father Gregory smiled. "Now, Paolo, you know as well as I do, even if I did know anything, I couldn't tell you. Whatever is said under the seal of the confessional is covered by a sacred trust."

Again, Paolo studied the other man's face looking for any sign of discomfort. Either Greg had become a first-class actor, or Katy was way off base.

"Talking of sacred trust, I believe you're spreading the word in our red light district."

Greg's face darkened. "How the hell do you know that? And what's it got to do with you?"

"You preaching the gospel is none of my business, but if you're down there often enough you might notice something that would be of interest to me, or at least to the case I'm working on."

"What sort of something? I'm not there to tell tales on them, Paolo."

"I realise that. I'd just like to hear if they mention who their pimp is, or if there's someone they are particularly scared by."

The priest sighed. "They're scared of everyone. Every single man they meet frightens them, even me. I go there night after night hoping to save just one of them from the life they lead, but it seems as though they can't break free."

Paolo nodded. "I know. It's a vicious trap they're in. Look, Greg, if there's anything you think might be of use in tracking down the killer who's preying on them, you will tell me, won't you?"

Father Gregory's eyes clouded. "If only I could."

"What's that supposed to mean?"

The priest smiled. "Mean? It isn't supposed to mean anything. There isn't anything to tell, that's all. I wish there were."

"Me too," Paolo said and turned towards the exit. He'd almost reached the doors when he heard his name called out. He turned back to see Greg smiling at him.

"By the way, you're right, there's nothing in my past to be proud of, but people change. I'm living proof of that. I changed when God took over my life. I'll protect Katy if I think she's being set up, Paolo, but you should know that if she tries to turn anyone against God's love, I'll do all I can to have her expelled."

Paolo nodded to show he'd heard and understood. He could only hope Katy would keep her head down.

It was heading towards evening before he and Dave were both free to follow up on Sandra Massey. As they pulled up outside a rundown block of flats, Paolo took in the litter strewn road and graffiti covered walls. Two young women seemed to sum up that they weren't possible customers because they immediately walked off as he and Dave got out of the car. A group of young lads, hiding their faces behind hoodies, congregated outside a rundown church hall situated on the corner of the street. Paolo hoped the place was being used as some kind of sports hall, but from the look of the youths hanging around outside, he seriously doubted it. The graffiti on the walls hinted at a different kind of meeting place.

"What's the number of her flat, Dave?"

"According to the voters' register, she's lives in 413, sir."

"She's on the voters' roll? People never cease to surprise me. I wonder who she voted for. None of the main parties seem to be interested in doing anything for this area of town."

Paolo walked towards the communal doorway. The glass panel was shattered, but held in place by the reinforcing running crisscross through it. He pushed the door open, noticing that the security lock was no longer working. The intercom on the side wall had been attacked at some point by someone with a grudge, a hammer and, presumably, a lack of self-restraint.

"We'll have to go up. There's no point in trying to use that thing," Paolo said, pointing to the remains of the intercom. "Fourth floor? What's the betting the lift doesn't work?"

Dave shrugged and walked over to push the button. Amazingly, the lift call light came on. The sound of machinery reached ground level and the doors creaked open. Paolo went to walk in, but staggered backwards as the stench of stale urine hit him.

"Jesus Christ, what is it with people? Come on, Dave, I'd rather climb four flights of stairs than travel in that thing. It's a fucking health hazard."

They went to the stairwell where the smell was slightly less offensive. Paolo tried not to breathe in too deeply as he climbed. He could hear by the strange noises coming from Dave's direction that he was probably doing the same thing. As they stepped out of the stairwell onto the open balcony that provided access to the flats, he and Dave both leant over the edge and dragged air into their lungs.

"This Massey woman had better have something worth telling," Paolo said as he turned to walk along the corridor.

They reached 413 and knocked, but no one seemed to be in. Giving a final rap on the door, Paolo was about ready to accept defeat when the next door along opened.

"What's the fucking noise for? I'm trying to sleep."

Paolo turned to see a woman of about thirty standing on the step. Black mascara smudges under her eyes and leftover lipstick gave the impression of a badly made up doll.

Dave took a step towards her. "We're looking for Sandra Massey. Any idea when she'll be back?"

"How the fuck should I know? I'm not her keeper. Who are you, anyway?"

Dave flicked his badge and introduced the two of them.

"Oh, that's different. I thought you might be the bloke Sandra was avoiding. She got home last night in a right state. Came hammering on my door and said she was fucking off and never coming back."

Paolo walked up to the woman's door. "Friend of yours is she?"

The woman nodded.

"Did she say where she was going?"

"Nope just asked me to take her cat in."

"Did she say why?" Paolo asked.

"Nope. All she said was that she was clearing off because she knew something that meant it wasn't safe for her here anymore."

Chapter Twelve

No matter how many times he used the lash, still he trembled with lust. Was this it? Was he now tainted by those he'd saved? He remembered reading accounts of long-dead missionaries who had gone to save the souls of savages. In trying to bring God's light into the darkest places, many of them had lost sight of their mission and fallen prey to the native way of life and the worship of false gods. Some had even taken native wives and lived in sin with them before remembering God's message. Is that what was happening to him? Was he in danger of losing himself to the way of the flesh?

"Never, Lord, I promise I'll never let this lust into my heart even if I have to destroy my body."

He braced his back and lashed the whip again and again, as hard as he could, first over the right shoulder and then the left, but still his erection stood proud, taunting him with its power to seduce his mind. No matter how many times he used the scourge, it seemed as if his desire was stronger than his pain. It couldn't be. He marked them only to save them, not for his own pleasure, so why couldn't he control his needs?

Falling forward, he let the whip fall from his hand and clutched his arms around his body. He clung tightly, anything to keep his treacherous hands from giving him the release he craved.

Sin. It was sinful to lust in this way.

Please God, give me the strength to resist. How can this be happening? I haven't even looked at the images on screen and yet I can see them in my mind, replaying that glorious moment when she went to meet you, Lord.

His hands moved of their own volition. He had no power to resist as the devil entered his soul and forced his way into his mind. He fell onto his ravaged back in an effort to raise his pain level, but that only heightened the sensations flooding his body. He gave in to temptation and caressed his erection. The devil's hands took over his own and played the sweetest tune. He arched his back, squirming as the evil one brought him to climax.

"Sweet Jesus, it feels so good. So good. So... fucking... good."

He bucked and thrashed as his seed spurted, wave after wave of pleasure flowing from his groin.

Then it was over. The pleasure faded, leaving a void for guilt to fill, taunting him with his weakness. As he lay spent on the floor, tears of despair ran in rivers from under his closed lids. He'd called out the Lord's name. How could he have done such a thing?

What could he do to atone?

He already knew the answer.

***

Paolo looked up from his interminable paperwork as Dave came in. Throwing down his pen, he gestured for Dave to sit down.

"Any joy?"

"No, sir. We have a trace on Sandra Massey's mobile, but it hasn't been used. No one has seen her. No one knows where she might have gone, if she has any family – nothing. She might just as well not exist."

"I'd love to go hammering on Azzopardi's door asking if he's missing a girl, but the chief feels we need something more tangible to go on than a missing person's report phoned in by someone who then deliberately goes missing herself."

Dave laughed. "When you put it like that, it does seem a bit of a stretch."

"Okay, Dave, let's recap where we are so far. Anything to report on Larry Harper?"

"Not a thing, sir. According to the surveillance he hasn't stepped out of his pub all week apart from to go to the market for food supplies. His wife hasn't been seen since Saturday, apparently. He's been telling his customers that she has a nasty case of flu and will be staying in bed for quite some time yet."

There was a knock on his office door and CC opened it. She came in before Paolo had chance to say a word.

"Sorry to intrude, sir, but you need to know. They've found another body. Badly beaten, wrapped in black plastic and dumped in with the garbage."

"Where this time?" Paolo asked, feeling sick at the thought of another woman suffering as the others had.

"She was found at the landfill site, sir. One of the workers spotted her."

Paolo stood up. "Come on, Dave, let's go. CC, I want you to look into the background of Larry Harper. We've got someone watching him, but I want you to see if there's anything in his past that we might be interested in."

"Okay, sir, but what am I looking for?"

"Not sure. He's taken to beating his wife to a pulp and paying for his thrills on the side. It might mean nothing, but we can't ignore any possible lead. God knows, we have little else to go on right now."

The landfill site was just over a mile south of the outer edge of town. When it had first opened no housing had been within three miles of the place, but the housing developers had been given the green light by successive councils to build more and more estates, until now some lucky residents had an uninterrupted view of the steaming piles of garbage from their upstairs windows.

Needless to say, the properties had been sold off plan and on a good day when the wind was in the other direction. From ground level the landfill wouldn't have been seen by anyone visiting to choose the perfect plot. What none of the eventual purchasers had realised was that on a bad day, those living closest to the site would end up complaining of breathing in toxic fumes. Paolo thought they might be right and wouldn't have lived in any of the houses if the developers had paid him.

Dave drove in through the gates guarding the landfill site and pulled up next to the manager's office. Paolo stepped out of the car and tried not to breathe in. They headed towards the office, but stopped as a man came out and walked down the steps to ground level. He strolled over to Paolo and held out his hand.

"Michael McGuire. I run this place."

Paolo shook the man's hand and introduced himself and Dave.

"Your people are already over by where Del found the body. It definitely wasn't there when we packed up and went home yesterday. I ask you, what kind of monster does something like that? Well, I just don't understand the way some people's minds work and that's a fact. I don't suppose Del will ever be the same again. Proper shook up, he was. Well, so was I if I'm honest. But there you go, that's what management is all about. You'd know that, being in charge of folk yourself. You have to put your own upsets to one side and look after your staff, don't you? Of course you do. That's what I did for Del. He's up in my office having a cup of tea. Poor bloke might never be the same again. It's not the kind of thing you expect to happen when you come to work, is it? There he was thinking thank God it's Friday and planning his weekend one minute and throwing up all over the place the next."

"Thank you, Mr McGuire." Paolo said, stopping the flow of the man's verbal assault. "Would you please show my colleague up to your office and stay with him while he questions Del?

Thank you." He turned to Dave. "I'm going to see what the situation is with the body. I'll meet you back here."

He nodded to both men and headed in the direction Michael McGuire had indicated. Funnily enough, he was already getting used to the smell that permeated everywhere. He knew from past experience that the human nose was amazingly adaptable, but maybe he'd been spending too much time in refuse sites because he hadn't expected such a rapid response.

Barbara was already there and busy with her team, so Paolo stood and waited for her to finish up. The body was lying on the edge of the landfill, so anyone dumping it could easily have driven in, thrown the corpse out of the car and rushed off. He pulled out his pad and made a note to ask Mr McGuire if the gates were locked at night, or just closed. If they were locked, then that might finally give them a few definite people to look at. It was also possible that someone saw or heard a car passing by the nearest houses. The most straightforward way into the site was through the Beckett Estate.

He flipped open his phone and tapped CC's speed dial number.

"CC, send some uniforms to question the residents on Beckett Estate where roads runs through to the landfill site. No way could this body have been dumped here unless it had been brought in some sort of vehicle."

As he closed the phone, Barbara rose and spoke quietly to her people, then she came over.

"It's the same killer, Paolo."

"That's not like you, Barbara. I'm used to getting the 'don't ask me questions I can't answer' routine from you." He intended to continue in that vein, but then saw the look on her face. "Sorry, Barbara, that was crass. I can see you're more upset than usual. What is it?"

"Remember our conversation about Larry? I've realised that our killer is going after women who look like Sharon. I hadn't realised it before, but it wasn't that Sharon reminded me of them that upset me so much. It's the fact that *they* all look like *her*. Same hair colour, same build, same bruises. The only difference between the bodies we're dealing with and Sharon is that Sharon was still breathing when I saw her last and the other poor women weren't. Catch him, Paolo. Catch him before he does it again."

"I intend to, Barbara. Any idea on time of death?"

"I'll know more when I get the body back to the lab, but an educated guess would be at least a few days, probably Saturday, but don't..."

"Quote me on that," Paolo finished, smiling at her.

She laughed and returned to her team. Paolo watched them as they worked. Quiet and efficient, just like Barbara. He automatically patted his pockets, reaching for his cigarettes and lighter, then remembered he'd given up. The patches were doing a great job of stopping the cravings, now all he had to do was find a way of stopping his hands from searching for the things when he was thinking. The chemist who'd sold him the patches had told him that the physical habit might be the hardest part to deal with. Right now, he agreed with him.

There were tyre marks crisscrossing the area around the landfill. They virtually covered the place, not much use from the point of view of making a match with the killer's vehicle. Paolo sighed, nothing was ever easy. He headed back to the office, wondering if Dave had managed to stop Mr McGuire talking long enough to ask the employee any questions. He ran up the stairs to the office door and knocked.

As he opened the door, a wall of heat hit him like a physical blow. Dave looked up. He was sitting with his coat and jacket off, but still perspiring. The wooden building was like a sauna. The only difference was that everyone still had their clothes on, although Dave looked as though he wished he could take his off.

"Do you mind if I leave the door open a touch? It's a bit warm in here," Paolo said with a smile.

"Well, I don't know about that. I'd hate anyone to get cold and there's a bitter wind blowing out there. As I said to your young man here, I said, you don't want to take any chances with this weather. Always keep warm, that's what I say."

Paolo jumped in when the man paused for breath. "Yes, I quite agree. Dave, have you got everything? Or do we need to trouble these men any longer?"

Dave looked at Paolo as if he wanted to hug him. He jumped to his feet, grabbed his coat and jacket. "No, sir, I have everything I need. I have their contact details, so can always call with any follow-up questions we might have."

Paolo smiled inside as he watched Dave perform the fastest goodbyes he'd ever seen. He virtually ran from the office and down the steps. By the time Paolo had said his goodbyes and reached the bottom step, Dave was already at the car shrugging himself into his jacket. Without a word, he opened the driver's door and slid in behind the wheel. Paolo walked around to the passenger side.

"Find out anything interesting, Dave?" he asked as he climbed in.

"That man has the worst case of verbal diarrhoea I've ever come across. He didn't shut up from the moment you left me with him until you finally arrived. What took you so long? I thought my fucking eardrums were going to explode."

Paolo laughed at the look on Dave's face. "It was a bit warm in there as well."

Dave almost exploded. "Warm? I've been colder in a heat wave. He's a nut – and interviewing him and the employee who found the body was a complete waste of time because no one saw anything of any use to us."

"Did you find out what time they shut the gates?"

"They don't. Apparently they used to lock them up each night, but then people would dump rubbish outside while the place was closed. Mr McGuire said they often used to have a mountain of refuse to clear before anyone could drive in each morning – only he used about a hundred and fifty more words to say so than I just did."

Dave started the engine. "Where to now, sir?"

"Let's pay another visit to our friend Azzopardi. I have a horrible suspicion that today's find is his missing girl. I'd like to watch his face when I ask him if he's lost one of his assets."

"I thought you said the chief had warned us off Azzopardi?"

"He did, but that was before another body turned up."

They pulled up outside the gates to Azzopardi's mansion. Dave leaned out of the window and pressed the intercom buzzer. After a few minutes of silence, Paolo told him to try again, but the intercom remained non-responsive.

"Strange. There's always someone here. If Azzopardi goes out, he usually leaves someone guarding Maria. Are you sure you pressed it hard enough, Dave?"

"Of course I am, but I'll give it another go."

After another three minutes wait, Paolo gave Dave the signal to give up and told him to head back to the station. Dave put the car in reverse and then slammed on the brakes, sending Paolo shooting forward.

"Damn. The flaming seatbelt nearly cut me in half. What did you stop for?"

In answer, Dave jerked his thumb behind. Paolo turned, his chest aching, and saw a sleek black car had pulled into the entrance drive, blocking their exit. He unsnapped his seat belt and gingerly eased his way out of the car. As he walked towards the black car, the passenger window slid down and Paolo recognised one of the two men who'd greeted them on their last visit.

"I'm looking for your boss. Is he inside?"

"Depends on what you want him for. He wasn't too thrilled to see you before, so I don't suppose he's that anxious to see you again."

The man laughed as if he'd just told the funniest joke the world had ever heard. Paolo leaned on the car.

"Very funny. Now, open the gates like a good boy and we'll drive in together so that I can tell Frank how amusing you are."

The driver of the car leaned over. "There's no point in you coming in. The boss ain't there."

"Really," Paolo asked. "And where is he if he isn't here? Gone on holiday? Hardly likely. He never leaves his little empire."

"He ain't here," the man said again. "And he ain't on holiday neither, Mr Smartmouth. He's sick. He's been sick all week. You wanna speak to him you're gonna have to get past the doctors at the hospital. Now, I'm gonna back up and you can tell your boy to move that heap of shit so that we can go and get Maria the things she's asked for."

Paolo was stunned. Azzopardi must be genuinely ill if he'd been admitted to hospital. From what he remembered of him as a boy, he had a pathological fear of anything medical. He'd never allow himself to be admitted, which must mean he wasn't capable of refusing.

"What's wrong with him?"

"That's none of your business, copper. You want to know, go and ask his doctors. You'll find him in intensive care."

Paolo walked back to Dave's car and got in. "They're going to reverse so that you can back out. Then head to the hospital. Azzopardi's sick. Very sick."

Paolo found Maria and a couple of Azzopardi's men in the waiting area outside ICU. She looked drawn and had clearly been crying for some time. Paolo had never understood why such an attractive woman would stay with someone like Frank, but it seemed as though she really loved him. Or maybe she loved the riches he gave her. Who could tell? Not that it really mattered.

Maria glared at Paolo. "What do you want? Leave him alone."

"We're just here to ask him a few questions, Maria."

"Well, you can't. He's unconscious. The doctor says..." She

stopped to wipe the tears streaming down her face. "The doctor says Frank has... *had* a brain tumour. Says he's had it for years."

Paolo nodded sympathetically, encouraging her to go on.

"He's been suffering with really bad headaches, but wouldn't go to a doctor. Then on Sunday he collapsed."

For some reason that brought on a fresh flood of tears and Paolo had to wait for her to calm down again.

"He was in the middle of his second bottle of wine when he stood up and staggered away from the table. I thought he was drunk." She blew her nose and wiped away more tears. "I only realised he was sick when he collapsed and we couldn't wake him.".

She fell against the wall, sobbing. He went to put a hand on her shoulder, but one of Frank's men stepped between them. Paolo managed to utter a few sympathetic words in parting, feeling like a complete hypocrite, but he could hardly tell someone in such distress that she'd be better off without the man she was breaking her heart over.

He went to find the sister in charge who seemed to think it was touch and go whether Azzopardi would leave upright or in a box. Deciding there was nothing to be gained until the man regained consciousness, Paolo arranged for the nursing staff to call him when, or if, that happened.

"Who'd have believed Azzopardi even had a brain," Dave joked as they pulled into the car park at the back of the station.

"Don't underestimate him, Dave," Paolo said. "I've known him for a long time. He may not be a contender for the world's most intelligent man, but he's a cunning bastard. He didn't just take over as a matter of right when his uncle died. He fought off takeover bids by various uncles, cousins and siblings who each felt they should run the streets."

"You still think he's behind these latest murders?"

"I don't know. Yes. Maybe. I'm convinced there is a connection between him and the dead girls. I've just no idea at the moment how to prove it, or even what the link is."

They walked into the station together, passing a group of WPCs on their way out. Paolo expected Dave to follow his usual pattern of stopping to chat to them, but he acted as if they didn't exist. Paolo hoped it was because his words to Dave about cleaning up his act had hit home, but for some reason he didn't think that was the reason.

Snatches of conversation reached his ears as he opened the door. The words seemed to be spoken slightly louder than they needed to be, which convinced him they were meant to be heard.

"Fancy that. You reckon it's true? What a poor excuse for a man..."

He held the door open for Dave to go in ahead of him. The younger man's face was rigid with anger and he looked as though he was about to explode.

Chapter Thirteen

Paolo headed for his office, calling for CC and George to follow him as he passed. Should he speak to Dave about his reaction to the words they'd overheard? He'd stormed into the station ahead of Paolo and disappeared in the direction of the canteen, muttering something about being thirsty. Paolo realised Dave was just using that as an excuse to get away on his own. If he'd really been thirsty he'd have used the drinks dispenser outside the main office. If whatever was going on between Dave and the WPCs was affecting Dave's ability to do his job, then Paolo knew he had to step in and do something about it. What had Dave done to make him so disliked in such a short space of time? He'd acted like an idiot when it came to boasting about his so-called conquests, but the acid in the women's voices had made it sound as though he'd done something far worse than that.

CC and George followed him in, closing the door and settling themselves in the chairs opposite Paolo.

He filled them in on what they'd learned from the landfill site and also the news about Azzopardi being in hospital.

"That isn't good news for us, sir, is it?" George asked.

Paolo sighed. "No, it's the worst possible news. With Azzopardi out of action, too many people are going to decide they'd like a piece of his business. Quite apart from all the family members he upset when he took over from his uncle, we also know there's the Albanian gang just waiting for the chance to expand – and we've found squat on who's running that set up."

He drummed his fingers on the desk. Too many thoughts crowded his head and he needed to get some clarity.

"I want you two to go down to the district and chat to the girls from both sides of the street, Azzopardi's as well as the Albanians. See if anyone is missing apart from the girl that Sandra Massey was going to tell us about. In fact, if she's the only one who is AWOL, find out what you can about her. We didn't even get the poor kid's name before Ms Massey did a bunk."

Paolo waited until they'd gone and then phoned Lydia.

"Hi, just checking it's still okay for me to come over tomorrow. I thought I'd take Katy to the movies if there's something she fancies watching."

"Hi, Paolo, of course it's still okay. I don't know what you've done to our daughter, but I haven't seen her in such a good mood for... well, for a long time."

Paolo heard the hesitation in her voice and knew why she struggled to continue. Katy hadn't been the same since Sarah's death. None of them had, but maybe they were finally moving on.

"You still there, Paolo?"

"Yes, sorry, my mind wandered a bit. I'll be over at midday. Katy and I can go and have one of those horrible meals she seems to think contain real food before we go in to watch the film. There's a whole range of fast food places at the cinema complex. Is that okay with you?"

"Of course, I'll tell Katy. Paolo, I've, er, I've got something to discuss with you, but I don't want to talk about it on the phone. It's something I think we should talk over face to face. When you drop Katy off tomorrow evening, would you have time to come in for a drink?"

Hope surged and his heart almost burst. Surely the only thing she would want to discuss with him was suggesting they try again. Although, it could be something to do with Katy, a dark voice in his brain reminded him. But she could do that at any time, he thought, forcing the negative tone to disappear. He'd always believed deep inside that they would get back together again one day. Divorce didn't have to be final, did it? Not for two people who were meant to be together. But he mustn't rush things, especially if she'd only just started thinking of him in that way again. Softly does it. Sound like it's no big deal, he thought, even though your mind is running berserk.

"Yeah, sure, no problem. I can drop in for a chat and a drink. See you tomorrow."

He closed his phone and felt a smile spreading across his face. Should he take flowers? No, don't push it. Let the first move come from Lydia. Trying to control his grin, he stood up and headed towards the door. Then he remembered where he had to go next and all desire to smile disappeared. Looking at dead bodies was nothing to smile about.

Paolo followed Barbara into her office. She'd indicated that she had something more to say than just outlining her findings. From the look on her face, it was something fairly serious.

She settled herself behind the desk and sighed.

"Would you like some coffee?"

Paolo sat down opposite her. "No thanks. You have something to add to what we know so far?"

She sighed again. "No, not really, but... yes, maybe. I don't know to be honest. I've given approximate time of death as Saturday evening. I know for a fact that Larry was out last Saturday until late. Sharon was with me and she only left the pub once Larry was safely out of the way. I can't tell you why," she said as Paolo sat forward. "Sorry, what passed between me and Sharon is private, but, well, Larry could be... might be. Oh fuck it, I don't know."

Paolo laughed. "Barbara! I didn't think you even knew that word. I think that's the first time I've heard you say anything worse than damn."

"It isn't funny."

"No, I know it isn't. It just sounded funny coming from you. Look, I don't think Larry is our killer, but I'd had him under surveillance since you raised concerns about him earlier this week. If he puts a foot wrong, we'll be there to see him doing it. I've already spoken to uniform this morning. Larry didn't leave the pub last night, so it doesn't look like he dumped the body. Besides, you said this one had been kept somewhere for nearly a week. As far as we've been able to check, Larry doesn't own or rent anywhere that doesn't have neighbours or workers nearby. The bodies are being kept where no one raises the alarm when the smell of rotting flesh starts to leak out."

"I know you've got someone watching Larry whenever he *leaves* the pub, but no one is watching what he does to Sharon inside the place."

"Barbara, you know as well as I do that there is nothing we can do for Sharon until she asks for help."

"No, I know. God, that man gives me the creeps. It wouldn't surprise me at all to find out the pub has a secret underground cellar where he can keep the bodies to screw until they no longer turn him on. It's possible, isn't it? I mean no one realised what Fred and Rose West got up to under their house for years."

When Paolo returned to the main office Dave was sitting at his desk, but his mind was clearly anywhere but on his work. He hardly registered Paolo's entrance until Paolo was right next to him. Then he looked up, shook his head as if to get rid of some unwelcome thoughts, and smiled, but Paolo could see it was an effort.

"You okay, Dave?"

"Sure am. CC called, sir. She's had a bit of a breakthrough. The missing girl's name is Mandy Ward. One of the other girls claims she saw Mandy getting into a dark and expensive looking car. Apparently the girl's English isn't all that good, but she says

Mandy went off with a star from television."

He looked down at the notes on his desk. "CC said the girl's exact words were, 'He famous. Like star.' So that makes our job nice and easy. All we have to do is find a television star with a fetish for screwing the dead, who drives a dark car and may or may not have connections to Liverpool. Simple, let's nab the first actor who covers all of those aspects and the case is solved."

"Very funny, Dave. Have uniform come back yet with anything from the estate near the landfill site?"

Dave consulted his notes again. "Nothing at all useful. A couple of residents woke in the early hours; both reported hearing a car heading in that direction and returning about twenty minutes later, but curiosity didn't make either of them leap out of bed and rush to the window, unfortunately. So they didn't see the car or the presumably famous driver. Wouldn't it be great if it was someone off one of those old shows like *The Bill*?"

Now Paolo was really concerned. Dave was going out of his way to come across as chirpy and without a care in the world.

"Come through to my office for a moment, please, Dave."

As Dave closed the door behind him, Paolo gestured for him to sit down, all the time wondering how to phrase his questions. He decided to jump straight in and hope for the best.

"Dave, we didn't get off to the best of starts, but I think we can put that behind us. You're a good copper. If there's anything troubling you, anything at all that I can help with, please, just tell me."

Dave looked uncomfortable. "Like what? I didn't mean what I said out there. I just thought you'd appreciate the joke – you know, on television they get a couple of clues that mean fuck all and by the end of the episode they know who did it and why, where they live and everything else needed to draw a line under the case before the credits come up on screen."

"I wasn't referring to what you said out there. It's... I don't know, it's just that you seem to have the weight of the world on your shoulders recently. As I said just now, if I can help in any way..."

Dave's face, which had been alight with laughter, darkened as Paolo's words registered. "There's nothing," he snapped. "Nothing that you and everyone else in this place staying out of my personal life wouldn't cure."

He stood up so fast the chair nearly toppled backwards.

"Is that all you wanted, sir? Only I've got a job to do and I seem to recall you telling me to keep my private life private. So that's what I'd like to do, if you don't mind, *sir*."

The emphasis on the word made Paolo wince. Dave walked to the door, yanked it open and made a dignified exit, back ramrod stiff, his entire body radiating anger.

I really handled that well, Paolo thought. Just call me Mr Sensitive.

Paolo recognised the ringtone on Dave's phone as he disappeared towards his own desk. Within a couple of minutes Dave was back in Paolo's office with a look of complete incredulity on his face.

"I've just had a call from Sandra Massey, sir. I couldn't get her to stay on the line long enough for a trace, but I think she's most probably using a pay as you go phone anyway. She said she won't come back, so not to bother trying to track her down."

Paolo waited. There had to be more to come. No way would Dave have come rushing back just to tell him Sandra Massey had relocated.

"You'll never believe who she said picked up her friend Mandy Ward that night."

"By the look on your face it has to be someone I'd never suspect, so go on, confound me."

Dave grinned and sat down, looking relaxed, which was completely at odds with the way he'd looked as he'd stormed out only seconds earlier.

"Oh, I think I'm going to confound you all right, sir.

Whether or not we take her seriously... well, that's up to you. She swore to me that she definitely recognised him," he said with a laugh in his voice.

"Are you going to share the secret with me, or take it with you to your grave?" Paolo asked.

Dave's grin grew even wider. "Oh, I'll share my knowledge, sir. Ms Massey says she saw her friend getting into the car of no less a personage than... Matthew Roberts."

Paolo heard the name and felt like joining in with Dave's laughter, but the desire to laugh didn't last long. Whether Sandra Massey was telling the truth or just yanking their chain, he would have to follow up on it. The thought of interviewing Matthew Roberts and asking the solicitor a load of questions that was bound to get him yelled at by the chief was no laughing matter.

"Bugger it, Dave. What on earth made her pick on him? I mean, can you imagine him cruising the district looking for a good time?"

"She says she's almost sure it was him."

"Almost?"

"Yeah, sorry, sir. I messed with her wording a bit. What she actually said was it was someone who looked like him. I just couldn't resist seeing what your face would look like if I told you she had definitely identified Matthew Roberts."

Relief flooded Paolo's body. "Very funny. Well, you got your moment of laughter, but in fact your Ms Massey has given us some help."

"How do you work that out, sir? You can't arrest Matthew Roberts just for looking like the bloke who picked up Mandy Ward."

Paolo stood up. "No, but we can use a picture of him in with a load of others to see if the girl on the street also says Mandy Ward was picked up by someone who looked Roberts. It would at least give us an idea of what our maniac looks like."

Paolo reached the door and yelled for CC to come in. As he

walked back to his desk he couldn't help but smile. This could be the breakthrough they needed. If they used Matthew's face as a starting point, the girl might be able to help them to build a decent identikit mock up of the killer.

Chapter Fourteen

He closed the curtains against the feeble early morning March sunlight. Incense filled the air and he inhaled its sweet perfume, drawing the holy scent deep into his body. Candles burned at his makeshift altar. He knelt and begged for the honour of continuing the Lord's great work. He was getting stronger each day, pushing back the other one – taking over the weakling's mind and body. But it wasn't enough. He needed God's blessing. He needed a sign that God was pleased with his progress.

As he prayed he felt the Lord's presence drawing closer. The candlelight grew brighter and the sweet sound of angels singing lifted his soul. Fearful of looking on the Lord's beauty, he kept his eyes on the patterned rug in front of the altar.

"I am not worthy, Lord," he whispered.

A voice clearer, brighter and almost more beautiful than he could bear touched his soul.

"You are more than worthy," the Lord said. "You are my special one. My saver of souls."

He prostrated himself before the altar as the singing reached a crescendo and the Lord's love washed over him in perfect waves.

"What do you want of me, Lord?"

"You must save them all, my child. Save every one of them, as I saved the Magdalene."

As the Lord finished speaking, the glory of His presence

faded until only the flickering candlelight remained and the singing became no more than a whisper on the edge of hearing. He remained face down, naked and trembling with awe. The Lord had blessed him. The Lord had touched his soul. He was above mankind, at one with God's son. Sobs wracked his body. He had not been worthy before today. But this morning he had been sanctified by the Holy Spirit. He was ready. The other within him could no longer fight. He'd been granted a decree from the heavenly powers and none could stand against it. Tomorrow was the Sabbath, the day on which God rested and so must he, but after that blessed day, he would collect another soul. He'd been confirmed as the Lord's instrument and would prove himself worthy of His sacred trust.

***

Paolo woke up smiling on Saturday morning. For the first time in what felt like eternity, he had an entire weekend to look forward to. He would be spending today with Katy, but later, after he and Lydia had spoken, who knew what might happen? He half sat up and put his hands behind his head. Settling back against the pillows, he allowed his mind to wander down a *what if* path.

What if Lydia asked him to move back into the house? Hmm, possible, but not probable. She was more likely to say they should take things slowly and rebuild their relationship. Okay, so what if she suggested he spent weekends there? That was a definite possibility. He'd settle for that. He grinned. Right now he'd settle simply for Lydia telling him she wanted him to be part of her life again.

He climbed out of bed, still smiling. Today was going to be a good day. Whatever Lydia suggested would be fine by him. It was going to be better than good; it was going to be a great day.

After his shower, Paolo dressed with greater care than usual. It felt like going on a date. Or, at least, he assumed that was the feeling. He'd not been on a date since his high school days and those youthful dates had all been with Lydia. He smiled again – talk about a one-woman man. Then he laughed out loud at himself. Thank God no one could hear his thoughts. He sounded like an idiot even to his own mind.

Still chuckling, he left his dingy bedsit and headed across town.

Lydia opened the door, looking as gorgeous as ever. Paolo had to stop himself from asking her to tell him now what was on her mind. The last thing he wanted was to mess up whatever she had planned for later.

"Come in, Paolo. Katy isn't quite ready, but she'll be down in a few minutes. Would you like some coffee?"

"Sure thing, why not if you have some ready?"

They walked through to the kitchen and Paolo sat at the table, angling his chair so that he was facing Lydia as she busied herself with the cafetière. She poured the water into the pot and then turned to look at him. Her smile made him feel seventeen again. He wanted to chuck up all responsibilities and take Lydia on a picnic by the river. Okay, maybe not that at this time of year, but something equally romantic.

"What?" she asked. "Why are you looking at me like that?"

Paolo shrugged. "No particular reason. I was just thinking how nice it was that we weren't arguing any longer. It's pleasant just sitting here."

Lydia smiled and sat down opposite him. "Yes, I know, that's what I wanted to talk to you about later, but we can chat now if you like."

Paolo was about to reach across the table and take Lydia's hand when he heard Katy's footsteps coming down the stairs. Before he could say anything, Katy was in the room.

"Hi Dad, I'm ready whenever you are," she said, dropping a kiss on his cheek as she went past to open the biscuit barrel.

"Katy, I think your mum wants to speak to me. Can you give us a few minutes?"

She turned, custard cream midway to her mouth. "Is it about me? What now, Mum? What have I done wrong this time?"

Lydia stood up and went over to the cafetière. "No, it isn't about you, Katy, and you haven't done anything wrong. It's something completely different. You know what I want to discuss with your dad." She turned to Paolo. "We can talk now if you want. You haven't even had your coffee. Would you still like some?"

He looked across at Katy who was shaking her head and mouthing the word no.

"Thanks, Lydia, but I think Katy and I are going to get going." He looked over at Katy who was swallowing the last of her biscuit. "Have you decided what you want to see yet?"

Katy picked up her bag and slung it over her shoulder. "I decided to let you choose. That way, if it's rubbish I can blame you for a change. You never like any films I pick."

Paolo laughed and turned to Lydia. "I can see that whatever I decide is going to be a disaster. This should be fun. We'll see you in a few hours. Still okay to chat later?"

"Yep. Don't hurry back, you two. Have a great time."

Paolo nodded towards the door. "Right, come on, kiddo. I don't know about you but I'm starving. So hungry in fact that I could even eat some of that lovely non-nutritious stuff they serve in all your favourite eating houses. What shall we have today? Something with the texture of cardboard, loaded with sugar and fat, or shall we treat ourselves and have cardboard, sugar and fat with fries on the side?"

Katy punched his arm as she went past. "You can be such a jerk, Dad."

"I know, kiddo, it's why you love spending time with me," he called after her.

Giving Lydia a final wave, he followed Katy to the door.

The noise of the burger house made it impossible to speak

quietly. Crowds of young kids screeched to get the attention of waiters and waitresses dressed as clowns. Paolo looked over at the party closest to where he and Katy were sitting and remembered Sarah's birthday party held in the same spot a few years before she died. His heart still ached every time he thought of her, but somehow he'd learned to cope with the pain. If only he hadn't shut Lydia out, she most probably wouldn't have had the affair. He'd blamed her for deserting him, but in truth, he'd deserted her, emotionally at least.

"I take it you know what your mum wants to talk to me about?" Paolo said, raising his voice to be heard over the noise of a child screaming because her neighbour had poured juice over her head.

Katy just smiled in response and shrugged as if to say there was no point in saying anything.

"Shall we go and sit outside the cinema? I can't bear this noise any longer," Paolo said, feeling like a grouchy old man and hoping that wasn't who he'd turned into.

Katy nodded and they gathered up their belongings. As soon as he was outside the restaurant, Paolo let out a sigh of relief. Even the noises echoing around the complex, which appeared to be entirely made up of kids screaming and parents yelling, seemed quiet compared to where they'd just been. They walked over to the area outside the cinema entrance and sat down on a wooden slatted bench opposite the posters displaying the films on show.

"So, which one?" Paolo asked. "Are you going for too young for both of us, but cute? Too old for you, but the film you're determined to see? Or the family adventure that promises to entertain all age groups from five to a hundred and five?"

Katy laughed. "None of the above. We're going to watch the all-action spy film."

Paolo was so surprised he nearly fell off the bench as he spun towards Katy. "You're having me on, right?"

"Nope," Katy said, grinning at him.

"Okay, I know I'm going to regret asking, but why the spy film? Or are you picking that because you know it's the one I'd like to see?"

"I love you, Dad, but not that much. I picked it because of the drop dead gorgeous Matt Damon who's playing the secret agent."

For the first time ever in his dealings with Katy, Paolo was speechless. He hadn't even realised she was interested in boys, far less ready to drool over a man at least twenty years older than her and probably even older than that. Fortunately for him, Katy had moved on to a new topic, so he didn't need to comment.

"I've been keeping close tabs on the girl I told you about. So far, Father Creepy hasn't been near her. Have you got someone watching him?"

Paolo wondered if Katy would accept him speaking to Father Gregory as having done enough. From the way Greg had spoken, it seemed fairly clear that the girl had told him something in the confessional that he couldn't repeat. But would Katy believe that?

"I bet I know who it is."

"Know who what is?"

Katy laughed. "The person watching Father Creepy of course. Don't worry, I won't let on to anyone."

"Look, Katy, I wanted to explain to you, but haven't had chance yet. I can't put anyone in to watch Father Gregory. I don't have any evidence to tie him in to a crime."

To his surprise Katy squeezed his arm and winked. "It's okay, Dad. I know you can't tell me who it is, but I've already worked it out. It's the new caretaker, Mr Shaw, isn't it?"

Bewildered, Paolo shook his head. "I didn't even know the school had taken on a new caretaker."

Katy grinned and stood up. "Nice try, Dad. Don't worry, I won't let on to Mr Shaw that I've twigged. Shall we go and watch the film?"

In the car on the way home Paolo remembered that Katy hadn't answered his question about whether or not she knew what Lydia intended to discuss with him. He was tempted to raise it again, but then decided it wasn't fair to Lydia.

As they stopped outside the house, she opened the car door and pulled out her phone.

"You're coming in, right, Dad? Okay, I'll see you before you go. I have to let Jenny know which film I've just seen. She is going to be sooooo jealous."

She towards the house, already deep in conversation before she'd even reached the front door. Paolo pressed the locking button on his car keys and followed her in. He was just in time to see her disappear into her room at the top of the stairs as he closed the door behind him.

"Lydia," he called out. "We're back."

She came out of the lounge, smiled and nodded towards the room she'd just left. "I've got a fresh pot of coffee in the kitchen. Take a seat through there and I'll go and fetch it."

Paolo went in and sat on the sofa. Looking around he realised the place had never stopped feeling like home to him. All the photographs, ornaments, even the furniture, had stories behind each piece. Memories of good times and bad. It suddenly hit him how much he wanted that life back again. Not just being with Lydia, but turning back the clock to how things were before Sarah's accident.

Lydia coming in with the coffee on a tray broke his reverie. He wasn't sorry to put those thoughts behind him. It was time to move on, not look back. He smiled at Lydia as she handed him a mug.

"So, what is it you want to talk about?" he asked, settling back against the cushions.

"I'm not sure where to start really," she said, looking more nervous than he'd ever seen her.

"Relax, Lydia. We've known each other too long for you to be nervous of telling me anything. Whatever you have to say will be fine by me."

She smiled. "I hope so. Paolo, Katy needs stability in her life. She's in danger of going off the rails. This business at school and the way she acts with me are sure signs she's not happy with the way things are. No, don't say anything yet," she said as Paolo moved forward on the couch. "Seeing you here on Saturdays, or going out for a few hours with her every second week isn't enough. She loves you, Paolo, you know that, and she needs to spend more time with you."

Paolo felt like singing, except that he had a dreadful voice. "Lydia, you don't have to—"

"No, Paolo, let me finish. I'm also not happy with the way things are. I need love in my life. I'm not someone who wants the single life. You know me well enough to understand that. And I can't believe for one minute that you actually enjoy living in that horrible bedsit."

"Lydia, just say it. Whatever changes you want to make to the way things are, just tell me."

As he said the words Paolo thought about packing his belongings and moving home. It wouldn't take him more than a couple of hours to get his stuff together. He smiled at Lydia, but she seemed to be having difficulty getting her words out. He leaned over towards the armchair where she was sitting and took her hand.

"It's okay. I agree with you. I can't wait to move from the bedsit."

She smiled and squeezed his hand. "Great, but how soon do you think you'll be able to find somewhere better?"

He sat back, shock freezing his brain as Lydia continued speaking.

"You'll need to have at least two bedrooms so that Katy can stay with you for a full weekend. She says she'd like to come over on Friday evenings and stay until Sunday. I told her I didn't think you'd have a problem with that."

"Lydia, sorry, I'm confused. You said you needed love in your life and I thought..."

Lydia's face turned ashen. "Oh God, Paolo, I'm so sorry. You thought I meant we, that is, you, me. Oh God, I'm sorry."

Paolo's heart drummed faster, so fast that he felt sick. "I thought you meant for me to move back in. So why.. who...? Sorry, I can't seem to think straight."

She looked down at her jeans and pulled at a loose thread until it came out. When she looked up Paolo thought she'd never looked more distressed – or more desirable.

"I want us to start divorce proceedings. Jack has asked me to marry him and I've said yes. I want to sell this house, Paolo, and move in with him."

"But, I hadn't even realised he was still on the scene. You never mention him, neither does Katy. How's she going to feel about this?"

Lydia shrugged. "Katy is fine with the idea as long as she still gets to spend time with you. She said she's okay about Jack, but that you'll always come first with her. As for not mentioning him to you, I think Katy and I must have avoided talking about him for the same reason. We didn't want to hurt you." She sighed. "Obviously, once we move, it would be a bit awkward for you to come to his home, our new home, to visit Katy as often you do here. But it will be better all round once you have a new place and Katy can stay with you for weekends and such like. Katy will see more of you, not less."

Paolo put up his hand to stop the flow of Lydia's words. She was babbling. She always did that when she was nervous. He couldn't bear the thought of her being married to anyone else, but he had to say something. He had to pull himself together and get out. He stood up on legs that felt too shaky to hold him, but was determined to leave with whatever dignity remained.

"I'm, er, I'm going now. I'm fine with whatever you want to do. Tell Katy I said goodbye, will you?"

He walked to the front door. Held himself together until

he'd climbed in the car and driven around the corner. Then he pulled over, switched off the engine, laid his head on the steering wheel and wept.

Chapter Fifteen

Paolo walked through the main room, barely nodding at colleagues as he passed, and headed towards the safety of his office. Mondays were bad enough at the best of times – and this was hardly the best of times. He'd spent the rest of the weekend in his bedsit, squirming after his humiliating conversation with Lydia. Eventually he'd come to the realisation that she was right – they all had to move on, but right now that felt more of a challenge than he could cope with. Work was the answer. If he submerged himself in his cases then he could push his messed up personal life into the background for a while.

He reached the door of his office, but stopped as he heard footsteps behind him. He turned to find CC grinning at him.

"Morning, sir," she said. "We've got Denada in the interview room looking through some photographs of tall, dark, handsome men."

"Sorry, who?"

"She's the young prostitute who saw Mandy Ward get into the car, sir. Her English isn't very good, but we've got across what we need from her. We've put a recent picture of Matthew Roberts in a book of mug shots, so it'll be interesting to see what happens."

Paolo had difficulty concentrating on CC's words. Not enough sleep and too much thinking had left him with a headache to beat anything he'd ever experienced, but he managed to force a smile.

"Great. Thanks, CC. Let me know when she's done with the photofit profiler. I can't wait to get a glimpse of who we're looking for."

When CC left, Paolo sat staring into space, as he had for all of Saturday night and most of Sunday. His mind kept asking the same stupid question – *how could he have made such a complete bollocks of his life?*

When CC came back an hour later, he hadn't moved an inch. The cup of coffee on his desk had gone cold long before, but he picked it up and pretended to take a sip. Anything to appear normal.

"We've got a problem, sir. Our girl is fixated on Matthew Roberts' photo and we can't seem to get through to her that we need to make changes to it to make a mock up of the person she actually saw."

Paolo stood up. "I'll come down to the interview room. We might need to bring in an interpreter. See who we have available, please, CC."

He followed CC from his office into the main room and looked around, suddenly realising Dave was nowhere to be seen.

"Anyone know where Dave is this morning?" he asked the room at large, but the answers were all in the negative.

Making a mental note to call Dave later, Paolo carried on to the interview room. The young prostitute didn't look any older than sixteen, but she seemed completely at ease, which surprised him, but maybe she was being treated better in the nick than on the streets.

"Good morning, Denada," he said. "I believe you've found a photo of someone who looks like the man you saw in the car when Mandy Ward disappeared. We need you to tell us how to change the photo so that it looks exactly like the man. Can you do that for us?"

"Sorry? How change? Is man on TV."

Paolo pulled out the chair from the table and sat opposite

her. "Yes, I know that's the man from television, but..."

"No, is man. Is not like man. Is man."

Paolo smiled to show he understood. "I understand that's the man you've seen on tv, but we need to change his image so that he looks like..."

Denada grinned, showing teeth in desperate need of a good dentist, and pointed at Matthew's photo.

"Is not like. Is him."

"You think the man who picked up your friend was this man?"

"*Po!*" she said, nodding vigorously. "*Po!* Is not like. Have seed man. On TV."

Paolo sighed and stood up. He turned to CC who'd just come into the interview room. "Any joy with locating an interpreter?"

"Yes, sir. That's what I came to tell you. He'll be here in about half an hour."

"Fine, thanks, CC. Let me know when he arrives. I'll be in my office. In the meantime, can you organise another cup of coffee for this young lady?"

As he walked back along the corridor he pulled out his phone and speed dialled Dave's number. After several rings it went to voicemail, so he left a message for Dave to call him back. It was strange, Dave was annoying in many ways, but he'd always shown up for work and was never late.

Paolo stopped by the coffee machine on his way to his office. The first cup had gone cold and he now really needed a caffeine fix. Just as he was about to pick up the cup his phone rang.

"Storey."

"Morning, sir. Sorry I'm late. I had a bit of an accident over the weekend, nothing serious. I'm on my way in."

"An accident? What happened?"

The silence from the other end of the line told Paolo that Dave was thinking about how to answer. He decided to save him the trouble of thinking up a lie.

"No need to tell me, as long as you're okay."

"I'm fine, sir. Just injured my back a bit, that's all. I'll be there in about twenty minutes."

Dave arrived just before the Albanian interpreter, Gazmend Dushku, so Paolo didn't have chance to check that Dave wasn't seriously injured by whatever had happened to him. The three men went to the interview room, picking up the photofit profiler en route.

After everyone had been introduced, Paolo asked the interpreter to explain to Denada what they needed from her. Warren, the profiler, sat next to Denada and set out the various pieces he would need to create an image according to her instructions.

Denada barely looked up as Gazmend Dushku spoke to her. She seemed almost more ill at ease with a fellow Albanian than she had with the police. Paolo wondered if she felt embarrassed by her way of life and wished he could speak her language enough to show he sympathised with her. None of these kids wanted to be out on the streets.

Gazmend spoke rapidly, pointing first to the photo of Matthew and then to Warren. As he did so, Denada looked at him briefly and then pointed once more to Matthew's photograph. The Albanian spoke again, this time his voice was sterner and he jabbed his finger towards Warren. Denada shook her head, leaned away from the table and crossed her arms.

"Is there a problem?" Paolo asked.

"Yes, is problem," said Denada, looking scared. She then let rip with a stream of Albanian.

The interpreter shook his head. "She thinks you're trying to trick her."

Paolo looked at Denada. "Why do you think that? We simply want you to help us make a likeness of the man you saw. Can you help us do that?"

He looked over at the interpreter who translated Paolo's words. As Gazmend spoke, Denada stood up, snatched

Matthew's photo from the table and threw it at Paolo, all the time yelling in Albanian. Bewildered, he looked to the interpreter to explain.

"It seems that Denada believes that this man *is* the man she saw. Not someone like him. Not even someone very close in looks to him, but that man himself. She says she recognised him because she'd seen him on television the night before he picked up her friend. She won't budge from that." Gazmend smiled. "I can understand your confusion, Mr Storey. I recognised Matthew Roberts' photo when I first came in. He does a lot to help minorities in this town, so I have had some contact with him through various committees. He is one of the most decent men I've ever met. I don't envy you having to follow up on this because it is almost certainly a waste of your time. However, Denada insists that Matthew Roberts is the man she saw driving off with her friend."

Paolo thanked Gazmend for his help and asked Dave to show him and Denada out. They had her details. If necessary they could always bring her back in again. He'd have to pay a visit to Matthew, find out where he was on the night Mandy Ward disappeared, but it wouldn't be more than a formality surely. One thing was certain though, whoever drove away with Ms Ward must look amazingly like Matthew Roberts.

Paolo was sitting at his desk by the time Dave came back from his escort duty. As he came in, Paolo noticed that Dave's face was covered in a film of sweat and he was holding himself stiffly, as if his back was painful when he moved. When he sat down gingerly, Paolo was sure the other man was suffering from chronic pain.

"Should you be here, Dave? You're clearly suffering."

Dave winced. "I'm fine, sir. What do you make of our witness? She seems pretty convinced."

Paolo sighed. "I know. I've just been trying out a few sentences in my mind, wondering if I can get to the end of even one of them before Matthew Roberts sues me individually and the force as an institution."

"We have to follow up on it, though, don't we?" Dave asked, moving as if trying to find a more comfortable position.

Paolo looked through the phone book, then picked up his phone and pressed the numbers. "We sure do," he said as he listened to the ringing tone. Then he held up a hand to Dave to signal not to speak. "Good morning, could you put me through to Mr Roberts, please. Ah, okay, thank you. I wonder if you would be kind enough to ask him to call me as soon as possible. My name is Storey, Paolo Storey."

He gave his phone number, said goodbye and snapped the phone shut as he looked over at Dave. "He's with a client. His secretary will get him to call me back."

"Okay, I've got some paperwork to catch up on. Give me a shout when you need me," Dave said, getting up with some difficulty and turning to leave.

As Dave moved to the door he shrugged off his suit jacket. Paolo called out for him to wait.

"Dave, what the hell happened to you?" he asked as he hurried round his desk.

Dave stopped in the act of reaching for the door handle. "What do you mean? I told you, I had an accident and I've hurt my back. What more do you want to know?"

"It must have been quite some accident," Paolo said. "Your back is bleeding. The blood has stained your shirt."

***

Barbara finished the last of her reports and moved the file to one side. She still couldn't understand why the prostitute killer was deliberately leaving DNA behind. Unless it wasn't his? Could all of the dead women have been with the same client and the killer stepped in after that? Was there a connection between the killer and whoever was having sex with them before they died? The sexual partner and the killer might not be the same person.

She picked up the phone, but then put it down again. Convincing herself that it would be better to talk to Paolo about this possibility face to face, she left her office.

Barbara tapped on Paolo's open door and went in. He'd been staring into space, but smiled as she sat down.

"Hi, Barbara, what brings you to our building?"

She was taken aback at the sadness in his voice. Studying his eyes as she answered, she was convinced he'd been crying. Whatever he'd been going through over the weekend, it couldn't have been good. He looked like he was on the brink of a breakdown.

"I came to discuss our latest case with you, but that can wait. Are you okay, Paolo? You look a bit stressed."

He smiled, stretching the crescent scar on his cheek. "I'm fine, Barbara. Just finding it harder to stop smoking than I'd thought it would be. The patches are working, by the way. Good idea of yours. But I'm struggling over what to do with my hands."

"Don't give me that, Paolo. I can see you're on edge, but if you would rather not talk to me about it, fine. I'll keep my distance."

"Sorry, it's been a bit of a weird day. Dave's gone off to see his doctor. He had some kind of accident over the weekend and injured his back. It was bleeding, but he refused to go to our doctor on call. Our one and only witness who's prepared to stand up in court has picked Matthew Roberts as suspect of the month. And we have no other leads, so it's not been a great start to the week. Anyway, how can I help you?"

Barbara shifted in her seat and leaned forward, resting her forearms on Paolo's desk. "I've been thinking about the DNA left on these girls. It makes no sense, Paolo. Why not wash it off when he's cleaning up the rest of the body?"

Paolo shook his head. "I agree with you, but we've been over this so many times. We're only going to solve that riddle when we find our killer."

"But what if the person who ejaculates on the girls isn't the one who kills them?"

"You think we have some sort of double act? Two people working together? I suppose it's possible. If that was the case then we might not be limited to looking just at men. In your opinion, could it be a woman who strangles them?"

Barbara mentally reviewed her findings, then shook her head. "No, I'd have to come down on the side of a man as suspect. But what if the two men weren't working together? What if the killer is tracking the man who gets his kicks from ejaculating on prostitutes?"

Paolo nodded. "Could be. If he's out to frame someone else, that would at least explain him leaving the evidence on the bodies, nice and easy for us to find."

Barbara studied Paolo as she got up to leave. Talking about the case had banished the haunted look from his eyes. She wondered whether or not to say anything more. Before she had made her decision, his phone rang.

"Storey. Oh, hello, Matthew. Thanks for calling me back."

She went to the door and made a farewell gesture with her hand. Paolo nodded and signed that he would call her, but it was clear that his mind had already moved on. She walked away, wondering if he'd even remember she had been there.

Chapter Sixteen

Paolo slowed the car outside the luxury block of flats that housed Matthew Roberts' apartment and followed Dave's directions to the parking area. They'd gone in Paolo's car as Dave was clearly still in some discomfort; even though he'd insisted he had nothing more than a few grazes on his back. As Paolo drove into the private yard and located the visitor's bay that Roberts had told him to look out for, he glanced over at his passenger. Something wasn't right. It went deeper than his injuries and Paolo found himself feeling more sympathy than he would have believed possible just a few weeks earlier.

He switched off the engine and looked at his watch. They were early. The rush hour traffic had been kind to them for a change and they still had twenty minutes to waste before they met Roberts in his apartment at six.

"So, are you going to tell me how you injured your back?"

The look Dave gave Paolo almost took away the sympathy he'd felt earlier, but he decided to ignore it.

"Come on, Dave. You can't come in my office with blood seeping through your jacket and not expect me to ask questions."

"You can ask, but I don't have to answer," Dave said, shrugging and then clearly regretting the gesture as a spasm of pain shot across his face.

"Look at you. You can't even move without it hurting. What the hell happened? You know I'm going to keep asking until you tell me, so you might just as well get it over with."

"Paolo, it's none of your damn business, okay?"

"If you're bleeding over my car seat it's my business. Look, Dave, I'd like to help if I can. You aren't happy…"

Dave laughed. "Oh, and you are? You aren't exactly the picture of ecstasy about the place. So what gives you the right to pry?"

Paolo sighed. "You're right, Dave. I'm sorry. I should mind my own business. I think trying to fix other people's problems is easier than dealing with my own. I won't ask again."

"I fell down a flight of concrete stairs," Dave said so quietly that Paolo almost didn't catch the words.

"What? How? When?"

Dave turned in his seat to face Paolo, grimacing in pain. "It happened last night. I was on my own and got to thinking about things. One thing led to another and I got depressed. Opened a bottle of vodka. Then I decided to go and see Rebecca. Remember you asked about her? Well, I've sort of fucked up in that area and I need to try to sort things out. Anyway, I was so totally and absolutely plastered I didn't even reach my car, thank God. I must have tripped or something because I woke up in the early hours at the bottom of the stairs leading up to my flat. I was shivering with cold but my back felt on fire. I knew I'd grazed it, but I hadn't realised how badly scraped it was until you pointed out the blood. So that's my sorry tale. What's your problem? Or is that private?"

It was Paolo's turn to shrug. "I know what it's like to feel depressed enough to want to drink a bottle or two, but I stopped drinking some years back." Paolo smiled at the knowing look on Dave's face. "No, I wasn't an alcoholic. No AA meetings or pledges for me. I just stopped enjoying booze, so gave up drinking it. You asked what my problem is. You were honest with me, so I'll return the courtesy. My ex-wife is going to marry the man who broke up our marriage. Life's shit, hey?"

Dave nodded agreement.

"The reason I didn't go to our doctor on call was because I don't want this leaking out, Paolo. You will keep it to yourself, won't you?"

"You didn't need to ask."

Paolo felt as though they'd reached some sort of understanding, but wasn't sure it was strong enough to last. He looked at his watch. "It's five to six. Let's go and get yelled at by Matthew Roberts. He is going to love this."

They climbed from the car, Dave with some difficulty, and headed towards the entrance of the recently redeveloped building. Amazing what they could do with the old factories, Paolo thought. The thought reminded him that he needed to do some flat hunting. Pity his salary didn't run to this level. They entered into a lobby where a uniformed porter greeted them from behind a security desk.

"We're here to see Mr Roberts," Paolo said. "Storey and Johnson."

The man looked down at his clipboard. "Ah, right, sir, Mr Roberts told me to expect you, but not your colleague. I'll just need to check with Mr Roberts before I let you both go up."

He picked up the phone, looked away and spoke briefly, and then turned back to Paolo and Dave. "That seems to be in order. If you could both just sign here, please." He waited while they complied. "Take the elevator to the penthouse suite. Mr Roberts is waiting for you."

As they rode up in the elevator Paolo wondered how rich you'd have to be to afford the best apartment in the most upmarket development in town. Very rich indeed, he decided, and then couldn't make up his mind if he disliked Matthew more because he was clearly so incredibly successful, or just the same amount as he had when they'd been in the same class at school.

The elevator stopped and the door opened. Potted palms and ferns filled the lobby they stepped into. At the end of a short corridor was a single door. It opened and Matthew stood in the frame looking relaxed in casual clothes.

"You must excuse me," he said, standing to one side to let them in, "but I am going out this evening, so don't have much time to spare. Could we get to the point nice and quickly, Paolo? You were very mysterious on the phone. I'd supposed it was to do with Katy, but as you've brought your sidekick with you, I can only assume it's police work instead. So, gentlemen, what can I do to help with your enquiries?"

Paolo looked around the spacious lounge and tried not to feel envy. His pokey bedsit would easily fit three times at least in this one room. What Paolo could only assume was expensive modern art adorned the walls, but he felt he could have come up with something similar if he'd attacked a canvass while blindfolded, using only his left hand to daub several brushes simultaneously, each one dipped in a different colour. Oriental rugs covered areas of polished oak floors and side tables held fragile looking porcelain. Matthew waved towards a white leather couch and Paolo took him up on the invitation, sinking into the soft upholstery. Dave settled into one of the two matching armchairs. Matthew positioned himself opposite Paolo in the other armchair.

"Why so serious looking, Paolo? Don't tell me you're continuing with your vendetta against Frank? You do know he's seriously ill in hospital, I assume?"

Paolo nodded. "I saw Maria there. It looks bad for Frank."

"And you are, no doubt, heartbroken," Matthew said with a smile that made Paolo want to thump him. Supercilious bastard.

"Not heartbroken at all, just concerned at what sort of war is likely to break out if he dies, but that isn't why I'm here." He took a breath and decided to jump right in. "The fact is that someone has put you in the frame for what started out as a missing person's inquiry."

Matthew looked amused. "Started out as? What did it finish up as, or is that not yet decided?"

"It's now a murder inquiry and we have a witness who claims she saw you entice the victim into your car and drive away with her."

Matthew laughed. "Me? Is this your idea of a joke, Paolo? If it is, I have to tell you I'm not really amused, even though I laughed."

"Sorry, no, it isn't a joke. We actually have two independent witnesses who say they saw you pick up a prostitute, Mandy Ward. She has subsequently been murdered." Paolo took his notebook from his inside pocket and flipped it open. "So, I have to ask you. Where were you on evening of Saturday 23rd March at about..."

Matthew jumped to his feet. "Are you mad? Have you completely lost your mind? Or is this some petty game to get back at me because Katy nearly lost her place at school? And, let me tell you, from what I've heard from Greg she may still be out on her ear. Is that what this is about? Some sort of bargaining chip to protect Katy's place?"

Paolo struggled to keep his temper. In Matthew's place he'd have been as mad as hell, so wasn't surprised at his reaction, but he had to do his job.

"Matthew, you know me better than that. This has nothing to do with anything other than two witnesses who both named you as the last person seen with the victim. You're a solicitor, for God's sake; you know I have to ask you these questions. You're not above the law just because you practice it."

Matthew sat down again, but he looked as though the slightest word or action could make him explode. Glaring at Paolo, he nodded for him to continue with his questions.

"Where were you on..."

"I was here, all evening, on my own. I hadn't been feeling well, so went to bed early and read. I can tell you the name of the book if that helps."

Paolo smiled, but refused to rise to Matthew's goading. "Any phone calls during the evening? Anyone who can vouch for you being here? What about your man downstairs?"

"You can ask him on the way out, but all he'll be able to tell you is that he *didn't* see me go out."

"I know," Paolo agreed, "but that's better for you than him saying he did see you go out, isn't it?"

Matthew seemed to calm down. "Look, Paolo, let's make this easy for both of us. How reliable would you say your witnesses are?"

"That's a strange question, Matthew. What do you want me to say to that? I'm hardly likely to be here if I felt I could disprove what they'd said."

Matthew looked at his watch. "I need to leave in about five minutes. Let's wrap this up, shall we? What have you got in the way of fingerprints and DNA?"

Paolo smiled. "Now you know I can't answer that. Why do you want to know?"

"If you have any physical evidence then it's the easiest thing in the world for me to prove I had nothing to do with your victim. If you have the killer's DNA then I'll give you a sample. If you have fingerprints then you can compare them to mine. So, I'll ask again, do you have any physical evidence?"

Paolo nodded. "No fingerprints, but we have DNA."

Matthew stood up. "Look, I'm sorry I went off at you. As a solicitor, I know you have to follow up when someone points at a suspect, but it felt very different to be on the end of that pointing finger than it does when I'm advising a client. I'll come by tomorrow and let your people take a mouth swab." He held out a hand. "Let's shake on a truce. We can't have old St Swithins' boys at loggerheads, now can we?"

Paolo hesitated, but took Matthew's hand. For some reason he was convinced he'd been played for a fool, but couldn't quite figure out how. As Matthew gripped his hand, Paolo looked into the other man's eyes and saw such hatred that he almost fell backwards. Matthew tightened his grip as Paolo attempted to pull away.

"And while I'm there giving my swab and being a good citizen I'll drop in to see Chief Constable Willows. I shall have a lot to say to him about your exemplary zeal in following up on leads – especially when it gives you the opportunity to get back at those you have it in for."

Paolo pulled his hand free. "Matthew, do what the hell you like. You know as well as I do that I had no choice about coming here." He turned to Dave. "Come on, let's go. We're keeping Mr Roberts from his social engagement."

They walked to the lift in silence and didn't speak until they'd reached the ground floor. As the lift doors opened and they stepped out Paolo pointed over to the security alcove.

"We'd better check with him about Matthew Roberts' movements on the Saturday before last, but I bet he confirms what Roberts had to say."

He was right. The man checked his register. Matthew hadn't left the building that night.

They thanked him and left. As they walked towards the car, Dave turned to Paolo.

"St Swithins' old boys?"

"Yeah, I went to school with Matthew and Frank Azzopardi."

"You've never mentioned it before."

"Dave, there's lots of stuff in my life I haven't mentioned. If it isn't important to the case, then it isn't worth bringing up."

"Is that why you hate Azzopardi? Something left over from your schooldays?"

Paolo stopped walking and turned to Dave. "I hate Azzopardi because he's the worst kind of garbage. He uses other people as if he owns them, as if they have no value as human beings, only as his chattels. And before you ask, I hate Matthew Roberts because he knows what Frank is, has always known since we were boys, but he defends him and makes him out to be the victim of injustice. Now, if you want to make something of that, fine. No doubt the chief will feel the same way tomorrow after Matthew visits him."

Paolo's anger, which had been bubbling under the surface all day, suddenly erupted and he turned on his heels and strode off. He only realised Dave wasn't keeping up when he'd almost reached the parking bay. He stopped and looked back. Dave swayed as though a strong wind would blow him over. Paolo strode back towards him.

"Jesus, Dave, I'm sorry. I shouldn't have taken my temper out on you. How's the back? You don't look good at all. Come on, let's get you home."

He helped Dave into the passenger side and closed the door. As he got in and settled himself behind the wheel his mind went back to Dave's words. Were they true? Was there something in his subconscious that made him want to take Azzopardi down that had nothing to do with the man's crimes? He certainly hoped not, but how could he be certain?

He put the key in the ignition and started the car. As he backed out of the space, Dave interrupted his musings.

"Didn't you think that was pretty weird?"

"Think what was weird?"

Dave fidgeted, obviously trying to find a more comfortable position. "Offering to give a DNA sample. Most members of the public freak if you ask for one, yet Matthew Roberts offers without even being asked. I just found it a bit weird."

Paolo nodded. "It's odd, I agree, but what's the betting that by the time he's spoken to the chief that he'll be saying I demanded one? I felt that he'd played me somehow and I couldn't put my finger on what he'd done, but as soon as he said he was going to call in on your uncle, I realised he'd stitched me up. Still, once we've eliminated him, we'll be able to concentrate on the Matthew Roberts look-alike who really did drive off with that poor girl."

CHAPTER SEVENTEEN

Paolo stood in front of Chief Constable Willows and stared at the carpet. The words washed over him in angry waves, but he knew the chief would run out of steam soon and then he'd get his chance to put his side of things. It seemed that Matthew hadn't let this opportunity go to waste. Paolo heard the slant Matthew had put on the interview and wasn't surprised the chief was almost apoplectic. From the way the chief was raging, Matthew must have put across the worst possible interpretation of the interview and then added in a bit of spin just to make sure Paolo would get hammered. If he'd wanted Paolo to be chewed over and spat out in tiny bits then he'd achieved his desire.

"And then to ask for a DNA sample on the flimsiest of evidence. What were you thinking, Paolo? Or weren't you thinking? Matthew Roberts seems to feel you have moved your vendetta to him personally, now that Frank Azzopardi is out of the picture."

Paolo fixed on the final sentence. "Out of the picture, sir? Last I heard he was recovering."

"Apparently he had a serious setback over the weekend and has slipped into a coma. It's touch and go whether or not he's going to make it. No doubt we'll be seeing some takeover fallout over the next few weeks, but that is neither here nor there at the moment. What on earth made you demand a DNA sample from someone you know hates the force?"

"Sir, I didn't demand it. I didn't even ask for it. We went to see him as a result of a witness saying she'd seen him driving off with a victim. And she wouldn't be budged from that, sir. She swears that's who she saw. What would you have had me do, sir? Ignore the evidence because it led to someone we don't want to upset?"

Willows sighed. "No, of course not, but you've given Roberts plenty of ammunition for his next round of television appearances. Unless you have good reason, and by that I mean a reason *I* would find good, stay away from him, Paolo."

"Yes, sir," Paolo said. "Was there anything else?"

The chief smiled. "Not this morning, Paolo, but who knows, by this afternoon you might have managed to upset the mayor if you work hard enough."

Paolo laughed. "He isn't on my list of people to annoy, sir, but I can add him if you want."

"Not today, Paolo, but I'll let you know if I change my mind," he said and picked up a file.

Realising he'd been dismissed, Paolo turned and left. He kept his anger under control until he'd reached the safety of his office and then, shutting the door behind him, he leaned against it. He could almost understand why some cops fabricated evidence against people they knew were guilty. Right at that moment, if he could have found a way for Matthew to spend a few weeks behind bars he'd have been very tempted. Not because Paolo felt Matthew was guilty of any crime, but he sure as hell was guilty of being a first-class prick.

Eventually his temper calmed and he moved away from the door. As he walked around his desk he spotted the photofit picture that Warren had made up of Matthew. Even though it was just a drawing, the likeness was unmistakeable. Paolo started to laugh. Matthew Roberts was going to have a fit when he saw his face on wanted posters, but what other course of action was there? Somewhere out there was a nut job who was killing prostitutes and apparently he looked very much like the media's darling. They'd be mad not to make use of that fact, but how to do it without being sued was another issue. Paolo had been relieved to hear that the chief was going to take that up with Matthew Roberts himself – and good luck with that, sir, he thought.

On Saturday morning the first thing Paolo saw as he pulled up outside his former home was the for sale sign in the front garden. He knocked on the door and prayed that Katy would answer it, but his prayer wasn't granted. The door swung open and Lydia stood on the step.

"Come in, Paolo. Katy is just tidying her room. Or, at least she says that's what she's doing. I think it's more likely that she's shoving stuff in the wardrobe or under the bed."

She led the way into the kitchen and picked up the coffee pot. "Would you like some?"

"No, thank you. I won't be staying long. I've got some viewings lined up. I thought Katy might like to come flat hunting with me."

She stopped pouring and looked over at him. "I'm sorry, Paolo, really sorry about last week. I hadn't intended to—"

Paolo held up his hand to stop her from saying anything else. He couldn't bear to hear her say the words again. She'd made her choice, fine, but he didn't have to listen to her professing love for another man.

"Forget it, Lydia. You were right about one thing and that was that I needed to find a decent place to live. I've made appointments to look at four flats today. They all sound about right, so I thought I'd get Katy to help me make a decision."

"Make a decision about what?" Katy asked, coming in and sitting down.

"Don't get comfortable, kiddo. We're going to find me a new home."

"Oh wow, great. Do I get my own room?"

Paolo nodded and then grinned. "And you get to clean it, too."

"That sucks," she said. "You should get a cleaner in." She stood up again and moved towards the door. "Come on, then, Dad."

Paolo smiled at Lydia. "Have fun. I'll drop Katy back this evening."

After trailing around the four apartments, Katy and Paolo headed for her favourite restaurant. The waitress greeted them like long lost friends and led the way to a table near the salad bar.

"Would you like your usual, or are you going for something different this time?" she said to Katy, offering both of them menus.

"The usual, please," Katy said, ignoring what else might be on offer.

"Right, that's one Hawaiian deep pan, a salad and coke with no ice," the waitress said, then turned with a smile to Paolo. "Do you need a bit more time?"

He grinned. "Nope, I'm having the same as my daughter, but lemonade in place of the coke – also no ice."

The waitress went off to pass through their orders. Paolo leaned back against his chair and looked across at Katy.

"I thought all four flats were okay, but for me it's between the first one and the last one. I didn't like the middle two as much."

"Me neither," she said. "I liked the last one best. It had the biggest second bedroom."

Paolo nodded. "Right, last one it is then. I'll sign for it on Monday and hopefully I should be able to move in on the first of next month."

Katy nodded, but looked a bit troubled. She toyed with her napkin and then threw it to one side.

"Mum told you about her and Jack. You okay with that, Dad?"

Paolo wanted to change the subject, but Katy deserved an honest answer.

"Not really, but there's nothing I can do about it. Your mum and I are, well, your mum and me... it's... it's complicated."

Katy smiled. "I know, Dad. You still love Mum, don't you?"

Paolo nodded. "I always will, kiddo, but she's moved on. I have to accept that. How do you feel about your mum getting married again?"

She shrugged. "Okay, I suppose. He's nice, but it'll be pretty weird living in his house. I'm glad you're getting that flat, can I come every weekend?"

"You can stay over any weekend I don't have to work. How does that sound?"

She laughed. "You want the truth? It sounds rubbish. You work most weekends. But you will take some off, won't you?" She suddenly looked serious. "I'm okay with Mum getting married again. I'm even okay with moving, but if it means I won't see you as much, then that stinks. At the moment I get to see you most Saturdays, but if you have to work, say on Sunday, does that mean I can't come over to stay with you? That wouldn't be fair, would it?"

"Katy, I promise that you can come to stay with me most weekends. If I have to go into work, say to the station or something like that, then you can come with me. But if I have to go out to a crime scene then I'll drop you at home first."

"Aw, come on, Dad. Why couldn't I stay in the flat and wait for you?"

"Because your mum would have a fit if I left you on your own, that's why. So, if I go to a crime scene, I take you home first. Deal?"

She nodded. "Deal. By the way, I see your man at the school is still keeping an eye on Father Gregory. Has he found out anything yet?"

"Katy, I've told you, he's nothing to do with me. He's not an undercover cop; he really is working for the school."

"Okay, Dad. I get that you can't tell me about it. I've been following the girl during school breaks and she's definitely avoiding Father Gregory. When she sees him coming towards her, she ducks out of sight until he's gone past. It's really funny. Or, at least it would be funny if I wasn't convinced she's scared of him. Can't you do something, Dad?"

Paolo had visions of adding Father Gregory to the list of people Chief Constable Willows had told him to stay away from.

"Katy, unless I know a crime has been committed, or your school friend accuses Father Gregory of a crime, there's nothing I can do. Have you thought that there might be an innocent explanation? Maybe she told Father Gregory something in confession and now wishes she hadn't, so is avoiding him. That's a possibility, isn't it?"

Katy looked shocked. "Dad, you don't believe that, do you? I told you what I saw and what I heard. He's a creep and she's scared of him. You'll see I'm right one day. I'll prove to you that Father Gregory has something to hide."

Matthew Roberts' words about Katy's position at the school came into Paolo's mind. Whatever happened, he couldn't allow her to jeopardise her place there.

"Katy, you just keep your friend under surveillance and don't antagonise Father Gregory."

She looked away, avoiding eye contact. "Sure thing, Dad. Whatever you say."

Paolo reached across and grabbed her hand. "Katy, I'm not joking about this. Stay away from Father Gregory. Your apology was accepted by the school, but not all the board members felt you should have been allowed to stay. I know for a fact that your place there isn't as secure as it could be, so don't do anything stupid." He squeezed her hand. "Promise me, Katy. Promise you'll behave."

She smiled and nodded. "Of course, Dad. I'm not going to do anything stupid."

"Promise?"

She nodded again. "Promise."

On Monday Paolo went to work via a trip to the estate agent's. By the time he reached the station he was the proud new tenant of a two bedroom apartment that he wouldn't be embarrassed to call home. He walked into the main office feeling better about life than he had for some time, so didn't at first notice his team's air of excitement.

Giving a general good morning as he headed for his own office, he was surprised when Dave and CC both jumped to their feet and followed him.

"What's going on?" he asked as he hung his coat.

CC pointed to his desk. "It's Matthew Roberts' DNA report, sir. You should read it."

Paolo stopped moving, hand still holding his coat above the hook. Various thoughts chased themselves through his head. He finished hanging his coat and turned to Dave and CC.

"Don't tell me it's a match?"

"Not exactly, sir," Dave said.

"What does that mean, not exactly? You two are like kids at a Christmas party where Santa's arrived but not yet given out the gifts."

CC laughed. "That's what it feels like, sir, except that we know what the gift is. Roberts' DNA isn't a match, but it shares enough strands with the killer's to prove that it's most probably a sibling."

Paolo snatched up the report as he sat down at his desk. "But that isn't possible."

"Why not, sir?" Dave asked, sitting down opposite Paolo. "It would make sense if Roberts' brother was the guilty one. We know it's someone who closely resembles Roberts' and presumably a sibling would look very like him."

Paolo shook his head. He signalled for CC to take the other chair and then went back to reading the report. At the end of it he started again from the beginning. He heard Dave and CC fidgeting, but ignored them. This simply didn't make sense.

Eventually, he looked up.

"I've known Matthew Roberts for more than twenty-five years and one thing I can say for certain is that he doesn't have any siblings – male or female. Matthew is an only child."

There was silence for a few minutes as the news was absorbed and then both Dave and CC came up with possible explanations.

"Maybe the father played around," Dave offered. "There might be a love child out there who you don't know about."

"Or it could be the mother had a child and gave him away at birth. If it happened before she met and married Mr Roberts senior then she could have kept it quiet," CC said.

Paolo grinned at her. "If you had met Mrs Roberts you'd never have suggested that. She was the most terrifying woman I'd ever known. I was always convinced as a boy that she knew all my darkest thoughts and by that I mean what every young boy thinks about nearly every minute of every day. Straight-laced doesn't even come into it, the woman was an iceberg. I'd have said she was the last person in the world who might have had a child out of wedlock, but maybe that's why she was the way she was. Maybe she was hiding a guilty secret. It's a pity we can't question her. She died a few years back." He sighed. "You know what this means, don't you? It's back to questioning Matthew Roberts, only this time it's to ask him which of his parents might have given him a half-brother I'd take bets he doesn't know anything about."

CC whistled. "He's not going to like that, sir."

Paolo nodded. "I know, which is why I'm going upstairs to discuss this with the chief. I am not going to put my head in line for the guillotine without first letting Willows know so that he can arrange for a basket to catch it."

Paolo and Dave spoke in whispers while waiting for Roberts to finish with a client. Once Paolo had explained the DNA possibilities, Willows himself had picked up the phone to organise the meeting and had conveyed the need for it far more tactfully than Paolo would have been able to manage.

It was the first time Paolo had been to Matthew's place of work and he was surprised by its lack of ostentation. He'd been expecting something plush and expensively decorated, rather along the lines of the penthouse they'd visited, but it seemed as though the workplace persona and the private one were completely separate identities. The waiting area was basic to say the least. All that was offered in the way of decor was a line of padded upright chairs against one wall, a couple of side tables holding an assortment of tired looking magazines, and two tall plants, both in need of some TLC.

Matthew's secretary was also very different to what Paolo had expected from her voice over the phone. The female he'd spoken to had sounded young, maybe in her early twenties. The woman sitting opposite them, typing so fast her fingers were a blur, couldn't be a day younger than sixty. Her iron grey curls didn't have a hair out of place and her face was devoid of any make up. From a distance she looked formidable – capable and without charm – but when they had arrived for the appointment she'd apologised on Matthew's behalf for being delayed with a smile so sweet that she'd instantly been transformed into everyone's favourite granny. And, without doubt, hers was the youthful voice Paolo had heard on the phone.

His mobile rang and the sudden noise breaking the silence of the office made him jump. He checked the display and saw Katy's name. It wasn't like her to call during school hours. He flipped the phone open, hoping she wasn't calling to tell him she'd done something dreadful.

"Hi, kiddo, I'm about to go into a meeting, so can't stay on long, what's up?"

"I don't know, Dad. I need you to find out for me."

"Well, that really makes sense," he said, relief that she wasn't in trouble making him feel lightheaded. "You want to give me a few more details?"

"It's Valerie. Something's happened to her, but I don't know what."

"Firstly, who is Valerie? Oh, hang on, is that-?"

"Yes, she's the one I told you about. She hasn't been in school since the middle of last week and whenever anyone asks a teacher where she is they go all funny and won't answer."

"Maybe she's sick, Katy. It's not really any of our business, now is it?"

"No, but, Dad, you don't understand. I haven't told you the rest. Father Gregory has been sent away. What do you think of that?"

"What do you mean? Sent away where? Katy, I'm going to get called in to see someone any minute now, so tell me quickly what you think is going on."

"That's just it, Dad. I don't know where Father Gregory has gone or why, but I'm worried about Valerie. It might be something to do with her, mightn't it? Can you find out if she's okay? Her full name is Valerie Simmons. Please, Dad."

Paolo couldn't resist the pleading note in her voice. "Okay, I'll see what I can do."

The phone rang on the secretary's desk.

"Katy, I've got to go. I'll call you if I find out anything. Okay? Love you," he said and closed his mobile.

The secretary picked up her phone and murmured a few words Paolo couldn't catch. She stood up and smiled at them.

"Mr Roberts will see you now," she announced and went across to the only other door in the room apart from the one they'd entered by. She opened the door and announced Paolo and Dave, holding it open until they'd gone inside and then she closed it quietly behind them.

Paolo wondered what had happened to Matthew's client, but then saw his office had another door. Presumably that one also led to the corridor and enable Roberts to show clients out without them having to pass whoever might be in the waiting room.

"Please, sit down. I hope Jennifer looked after you."

"Yes, she did, thank you."

"She's amazing. Did you know she was my dad's secretary? Oh, no, of course, you wouldn't have any reason to know that. I inherited her with the practice and thank God I did. I dread to think how I'll ever replace her when she finally decides to retire. But you didn't come here to discuss my secretary. Chief Constable Willows says it's to do with my DNA sample throwing up an anomaly. Something to do with a possible family connection?"

He raised his voice on the final sentence and Paolo realised the moment he'd been dreading had arrived.

"Hmm, yes," he said. "But it's not just any family connection. Your DNA matches partially with our killer's. It's almost certain that the DNA we recovered from a series of murdered prostitutes belongs to a sibling of yours."

"But I don't have any," Matthew said. "There must be some mistake in the test procedure."

Paolo leaned forward. "That's what we thought, but the test results have been checked. Is it possible that either of your parents might have..."

He left the unspoken words dangling in midair. Maybe if Matthew himself joined the dots he might not be so ready to explode. Paolo watched his face, waiting for him to start chucking threats of lawsuits around, but instead, incredibly, Matthew laughed. A genuine laugh of pure enjoyment.

"Which one did you have in mind, Paolo? You met both my parents. Can you really see either of them providing me with a sibling and keeping quiet about it?"

Paolo was stunned. Whatever reaction he'd been fearing, this wasn't it.

Matthew still looked amused. "Sorry, I'm not laughing at you, or at my parents, I'm not sure why I found it funny. I suppose it must be a reaction to shock. You see, you've just told me something I didn't know, which is that I have a sibling. Now I'll tell you something that you didn't know – my parents are not my biological parents. I was adopted as a child. So, whoever this mysterious sibling might be, he isn't a product of my parents' mucky past."

"God, Matthew, I had no idea. In fact, I've always thought you looked like your father, which just goes to show that we see what we think should be there."

Matthew smiled. "Knowing how efficient my mother was, she most probably picked me because I had the right colouring and would fit the family."

Dave had been sitting silently, but now took out his notebook. "Do you know anything about your natural mother, Mr Roberts? We need to trace the person whose DNA has been left on the bodies and the only lead we have is through you."

Matthew shook his head. "I've known I was adopted since I was about ten or eleven, but funnily enough have never wanted to find out who my mother was or why she gave me up. I suppose it's because I had a very fortunate upbringing. I didn't need to find out where I came from because I've always been happy with who I am."

Paolo stood up. "We're going to have to look into your adoption records to find out if your birth mother had other children. If she didn't, then we'll have to try to track down your biological father. You do understand that I have no choice about this, don't you? It isn't part of any plan to cause you problems in any way whatsoever."

Matthew sighed. "Yes, I realise that."

"I suppose the next question is, do you want to know what we find out? I mean, if we discover anything about your birth family, would you like the information?"

"I don't know, Paolo, and that's the truth. You're saying a sibling I didn't even know I had might turn out to be a serial killer. That's not easy to take. Give me a few days to process what you've told me and I'll let you know if I want to hear all the grisly details of how he ended up as he did."

Paolo nodded. "One last thing before we go. Do you know where the adoption took place? Do you have any paperwork, any records that might help us?"

Matthew smiled and picked up the phone. "Jennifer, would you come in here, please?"

Within moments the door opened and Matthew's secretary came in. "Jennifer, please find whatever paperwork is available to do with my adoption and make copies for these gentlemen."

"Certainly, Matthew, I'll get on to it at once. Your next appointment is waiting for you."

As she left the room, Matthew stood up. "If you wouldn't mind going out through that door, I'd appreciate it. It gives my clients a degree of privacy if they don't have to pass each other coming in and out. Jennifer will send the copies of whatever she has on record over to you later today."

Matthew held out his hand. Paolo shook it, feeling as if he'd trespassed on private ground, which in a way he had. It couldn't have been easy for someone like Matthew to give access to his personal life and allow others to claw through it.

"We'll be as discreet as we can, Matthew, but unfortunately this relationship is bound to come out at some stage. You might want to think about how you'll deal with the press when the time comes."

Matthew nodded. "I hadn't thought of that," he said and gave a wry smile. "I imagine it's going to be very different being questioned about this on television compared to the normal stuff I do. That's always supposing anyone would be interested in my connection to the case."

Paolo didn't say anything, but knew deep inside that the press would be all over it as soon as they got wind of Matthew's family involvement. The flip side of being a media darling came when something happened that you didn't want splashed on the front page and you discovered that you were big news for all the wrong reasons.

Chapter Eighteen

Paolo looked back over the last few days, reflecting how weird things had been since discovering Matthew's adopted past. Matthew's secretary had been as efficient as he'd promised she would be and copies of the files had arrived within a couple of hours of Paolo and Dave leaving Matthew's office. Dave had been set the task of following up on the information contained in the photocopied pages. He'd been hard at work chasing every lead and had phoned nearly an hour ago to say that he was on his way in.

Paolo looked at his watch for the tenth time and seethed with frustration. Surely to God Dave should have been here by now? He was about dial Dave's number to chase him up when the door opened and he came in clutching a file. From the grin on his face, it looked as though he'd won the lottery.

"Morning, sir. Sorry I kept you waiting but I got waylaid on the way here. I received a call with a bit more information to add to the rest," he said holding the file aloft like a trophy.

"Judging by the Cheshire Cat grin I think you must have some good news for me. What have you found out? Please tell me that Matthew Roberts has a brother who looks just like him, you've tracked him down and he's in the cells waiting to be put away for a long stretch."

Dave sat down and grinned across at Paolo. "Not quite as good as that, sir, but you're going to like what I've found out so far. That's for sure."

"Great. I like good news on a Wednesday. It makes the week go faster." He waited, drumming his fingers on the desk while Dave sat silently reading from the file. "Come on, Dave, don't keep me in suspense. What have you got for me?"

Dave looked up from the file. "Hang on, sir. I want to make sure I give you the pieces in the right order. It will make more sense if I tell it to you chronologically." He read for a few seconds longer and then closed the file. "Right, here goes. Let's start with Matthew Roberts. He was adopted just before he was three years old. I have no idea whether or not the Roberts' lived up in the Liverpool area at the time, but I couldn't find any records of them doing so. It's possible there might have been something suspect about the adoption, because the records are, to put it bluntly, a bit strange. Not all the information about the mother and her background had been filled in, but the adoption took place in... you're going to love this, sir... Liverpool."

Paolo smiled. "And so we come back to the city where we believe the murders started."

"Wait, sir, it gets better. The natural mother was..."

Paolo sat up straighter in his chair. He knew what was coming. It had to be... "Catherine Andrews, the Liverpool victim."

Dave looked deflated and Paolo regretted saying the name out loud.

"Sorry, Dave. It just seemed to fit. It brings us full circle in a way. Tell me the rest. I promise to keep quiet and listen. Unless, of course, you tell me something truly astounding."

"Okay, I'll hold you to that. You're right in your guess about the birth mother, of course. The woman was a prostitute called Catherine Andrews, but she wasn't on the game when her boys were born. At least, there's no record of it. She was married to a local thug who used to knock her around according to the court records."

"Court records?" Paolo asked. "For what?"

"For the case against her when she was on trial for murder. She stabbed her husband in a drunken rage, although to be fair, her defence was that she killed him to protect herself from yet another beating. The jury wasn't convinced, but that might have been because she didn't stop even after the husband was dead. There were twenty-one stab wounds on the body; most of them inflicted long after the husband was in no fit state to fight back. Anyway, they found her guilty and she was sent to prison. She ended up serving fifteen years. She had no family that anyone could discover so her children were taken into care. There was less than a year between them. The youngest, Sean, was just a baby at the time and Matthew wasn't even two."

Paolo sighed. "Poor kids, but at least we know that Matthew landed in a good home within a year. What happened to Sean?"

"He went into various foster homes until he was ten, but no formal adoption. It seems that he was a disruptive kid as he grew up. He was passed from pillar to post, no one keeping him for more than a few months at a time. He was blamed for burning down the last foster home he was in, but there was never any proof he was guilty. Although he did boast about it afterwards, but that might just have been trying to gain extra street cred with the gang he ran around with."

Paolo nodded. "Sounds like the type of thing a boy in that position would do."

"Burn a house down, sir, or claim he'd done it even if he hadn't?"

"Either, both, it doesn't really matter which. What does matter is that he was clearly a troubled youth. What happened to him after the arson, if it was arson?"

Dave looked back at the file. "No one was prepared to take him in after that. He spent the next six years in the Catholic orphanage and then—"

"Catholic orphanage?"

"Yes, sir. Apparently the mother was Catholic and begged the social services to respect her religion when they placed her boys. Why do you ask?"

"I was surprised, that's all. Carry on with your tale."

"Okay, he left the orphanage at sixteen and completely dropped off the radar of social services and anyone else who might have taken an interest in him. Liverpool has been able to pick up his scent again by checking the unemployment records. He's been out of work for years, signing on as regular as clockwork until ten months ago when he disappeared and hasn't drawn any money since. He never returned to the flat he shared with his girlfriend, but as they'd had a flaming row the night before she simply assumed he'd left her for good. Apparently they'd broken up quite a few times before and she was glad to see the back of him. She bundled all his stuff into a black bag and shoved it under the stairs."

Paolo grinned. "That sounds encouraging. Let's hope there's lots of lovely DNA on a comb or toothbrush to match with our killer's."

"The bag was collected yesterday, sir. If there's anything to test, it will be treated as urgent. Liverpool have promised us the results as soon as they get them."

"So, he disappeared around the time his natural mother was killed. Do you know if there was any contact between them?"

Dave shook his head. "Liverpool weren't able to establish whether or not Sean had tracked her down, but the ex-girlfriend says that he was trying to find her." Dave grinned. "You'll love this next bit. She told the inspector up there that Sean had decided to trace his family after he saw Matthew Roberts on television. She says he was astounded by how alike they were and was convinced they must be related. Apparently he went mad over the idea. Wanted to know everything about his past."

The phone rang and Paolo looked at the caller display. Holding up his hand to ask Dave to wait a moment before continuing, he flipped the phone open.

"Barbara, hi, I'm in the middle of something really

important. Can I call you back in about half an hour or so?"

"Sure thing, Paolo, there's no urgency. Well, there is, but not for me."

"Sounds intriguing. I'll call you as soon as I can."

He shut the phone and nodded for Dave to go on.

"The girlfriend says that up to that point he'd never been interested in knowing anything about his background, but once he'd seen Matthew he started going on about what a great life the two of them could have, that's Sean and her, not Sean and Matthew, if he was really related to someone rich and famous. She doesn't know exactly what he meant by that because he went AWOL soon after. Maybe he was planning to blackmail Matthew, you know the type of thing, pay me x amount and I won't tell the redtops that your mother was a whore and your brother an out of work loser."

"Good theory, Dave, but we don't know if he found out who his mother was. If he hadn't, then he might not have known for sure that Matthew was his brother. All he'd have been certain of was that he looked like Matthew."

"Yes, sir, but the mother was killed within a couple of weeks of Sean spotting Matthew on the television. It certainly looks like he traced her."

Paolo nodded. "Okay, fair enough, but then why kill her? What would have made him strangle her when they'd only just met again?"

Dave shrugged. "Maybe he was pissed off that Matthew had lived the life of luxury and been adopted while he'd been abused by the system. Maybe he blamed his mother for his shitty life. Who knows what's going on in his mind? If he's our man, he certainly seems to have it in for prostitutes, so that's a clue right there to the way he's thinking."

Paolo sat forward and leaned on the desk. "How come Liverpool didn't connect Sean to Catherine when she was killed?"

"There wouldn't have been any reason for them to know

about Sean, would there? I mean, if he'd only just found out who she was, there might not have been a trail to follow leading back to him. To be honest, sir, I'm not sure they investigated that deeply. The inspector I spoke to up there seemed to think that she wasn't worth too much police time."

Paolo sat up in surprise. "Dave, you sound like you disapprove of that attitude. Are you feeling okay?"

Dave grinned sheepishly. "I'm turning over a new leaf, sir. I'm trying to treat everyone the same. My boss told me he'd kick my arse if I didn't."

Paolo smiled back. "Your boss sounds like a good bloke. You should listen to him more often. Go on, what else is in that file?"

"Sadly, sir, that's about it. We know he was tracing his mother and can only assume he found her. We know he believed he was related to Matthew Roberts, but presume he hasn't made any contact with him. At least, Roberts hasn't mentioned it and surely he would have done if Sean had been in touch."

Paolo tapped his fingers on the desk. "Okay, so why hasn't he made contact? If he felt there was a relationship what would be a good enough reason to avoid getting in touch with Matthew?"

"The only thing I can think of is that he's waiting for the right moment."

Paolo nodded. "Yes, it could be that, but I think there might be a more sinister reason. Our killer has made no effort to hide his face when picking up the girls he later kills. He's operating in the town where Matthew lives and is easily identified. He's driving a dark car, similar to the one Matthew drives. What if Sean is setting Matthew up? Leading us deliberately to think Matthew is involved. What better revenge could he have on the sibling who has it all than to destroy his life and leave him with nothing?"

Dave closed the file and stood up. "I'll get copies of this to CC and George, sir."

"Good work, Dave. Is there a recent photo of Sean available that we can use in a public appeal?"

Dave nodded. "Yes, sir. The ex-girlfriend is sorting some out for us. At this stage she hasn't been told what Sean is wanted in connection with. I believe she jumped to the conclusion the police were looking for him to do with some kind of benefits fraud. Apparently Sean moonlighted in a few places while claiming unemployment."

"She's going to get quite a shock when she sees his picture on the news in connection with this case. I'll tell the chief to go ahead and set up a press conference as soon as we have a good photograph to use."

When Dave had gone Paolo picked up the phone and called Barbara.

"Hi, you wanted to ask me something?"

"Thanks for calling me back, Paolo. I want to ask you for a favour. It's not for me as such. Well, it is for me, I suppose. Oh crap. I'm making a right mess of this. Can I explain over lunch?"

Paolo thought of all the paperwork he needed to clear up. If he spent the next three days doing nothing but filing and writing up reports he still wouldn't have made a dent in the pile. His delay in answering was misunderstood.

"What's wrong, Paolo? I'm not coming on to you. I just don't want to talk over the phone or while we're both on duty," she said.

"Sorry, Barbara, I was just trying to reconcile spending my time going out to lunch instead of getting on with the admin tasks. Lunch just won. Where would you like to meet?"

"Great. How does the Nag and Bag sound?"

"Suspicious, that's how it sounds. I haven't been in there for ages, but I know you go quite often. I get the feeling there's an ulterior motive for suggesting it. Am I right?"

Barbara laughed. "Of course you're right, but gloating doesn't suit you. What time will you be free?"

Paolo checked his watch. "Now's as good a time as any. See you there in about fifteen minutes?"

Paolo walked into the pub trying to remember when he'd last been in there. It must have been shortly after Larry and Sharon took it over, so quite some time ago. It didn't look as if any changes had taken place in the intervening years. Larry was behind the bar and looked surprised to see Paolo.

"Good God, what brings you in here? I didn't think pubs were your scene."

He held his hand out and Paolo shook it.

"I'm meeting a friend for lunch. She tells me Sharon makes the best pub food for miles around."

Larry nodded and grinned. "Sharon's a good cook, but I hadn't realised her fame had spread far and wide."

The door opened. Barbara came in and walked to the bar.

"Hi, Paolo. Thanks for coming. Shall we sit over there," she said, pointing to a corner table.

"What am I, invisible?" Larry said as Barbara went to walk away.

She turned back. "Hello, Larry."

Paolo could hear the anger in her tone and wished he'd said no to the lunch invite. Barbara's greeting couldn't have been colder if she'd been standing on an iceberg.

Larry must have picked up on it as well because there was a decidedly acid note in his voice as he addressed Paolo.

"Ah, now I know who you're meeting. The raving about Sharon's cooking makes more sense. Barbara is Sharon's number one fan. Isn't that right, Barbara? Although I don't think everything Barbara believes about Sharon is necessarily true."

Barbara slowly looked Larry up and down. Her nose twitched as if the scent of the sewers had wafted through the room. Then she smiled and shook her head. Paolo was pleased she'd never smiled at him in that way. If Larry had been in any doubt before about Barbara's view of him, she couldn't have made it any clearer.

"There are some things I know which I wish weren't true, but there isn't much I can do about it. Speaking of Sharon, how is she? I haven't seen her around for ages. Last I heard she'd had yet another accident. Can I go through to the kitchen and say hi?"

Larry glared at Barbara. "Not just now, Barbara. It's our busiest time of the day, but I'll be sure to tell her you were asking after her."

Barbara nodded. "You do that." She turned to Paolo. "Shall we go and sit down? I'm famished."

Paolo followed her rapidly, retreating back to the table she'd pointed out earlier. It was as far from the bar as it was possible to be. He stood for a moment, watching her as she removed her coat and slung it on one of the chairs. She dragged out another chair and sat down, glaring in Larry's direction. Paolo waited until she finally looked away before saying anything.

"Well, this is going to be an interesting lunch. Is it safe for me to sit next to you?"

Barbara forced a laugh. "Yes, of course it is. I might want to stab *him* with the cutlery, but you're relatively safe."

Paolo dropped into the seat opposite. "Only relatively? What do I have to do to ensure complete safety? I take it that's why I'm here? It's not for the joy of my company, but because you want me to speak to Larry about his violence?"

Barbara nodded. "Paolo, you didn't see what he did to her last time. If you had—"

"If I had I'd have arrested him for it, but I didn't see it, Barbara. Legally, I can't do anything. You know that as well as I do."

She kicked his shin hard, letting fly with her booted foot under the table. Before he could ask her what the hell she was playing at, he heard Larry's voice and understood.

"Have you two decided what you'd like to eat?"

"Paolo," Barbara said, "I know the food here. Have the

bobotie, you'll love it."

"Sounds weird, what is it?"

"It's a South African Cape Malay dish. Trust me, it's wonderful."

Paolo agreed to try it out. As soon as Larry was out of earshot, Paolo turned to Barbara.

"As I was saying..."

"Paolo, I know you can't do anything legally. I'm not stupid. But you could speak to Larry as an old acquaintance though, couldn't you? Isn't there something you could say that would make him think twice before he hits her again?"

"Like what? You're being naive, Barbara. Do you think just because I went to school with Larry that he'll listen to anything I have to say? He didn't listen to me then, so it's not likely he will now."

"Paolo, please, won't you at least try? I haven't seen Sharon recently because Larry won't let me anywhere near her. She'd not answering her phone and she's never seen in here. I'm scared for her. You know how domestic violence escalates. I'm sure you've seen enough of it. Please, drop a threat or something."

Paolo sighed. "If all it took was a threat there wouldn't be anyone still lashing out at their spouses. Don't you think that —" He stopped. "Don't look at me like that, Barbara. It's not... I can't... oh, all right. When we've eaten, you push off and I'll have a chat with Larry. But don't expect miracles," he warned as a wide grin spread over her face.

"I don't," she said. "But I'm hoping a small change now might lead to bigger changes later."

Half an hour later Paolo put his knife and fork together on the plate and patted his stomach.

"She was right," he said to Larry who came over a little while later to clear away the plates. "That was absolutely delicious. I'd love to give my compliments to the chef. Is she still in the kitchen?"

Larry scowled. "No, she's already gone upstairs. We were busy today and she's tired out, so needs a lie down. Maybe next time. Would either of you like coffee?"

Barbara shook her head and stood up, gathering her things together. "Not for me, thanks. I have a meeting in fifteen minutes. If I don't run I'm going to be late. See you soon, Paolo. I'm sure you two have lots to talk about as you haven't seen each other for so long," she said with such a meaningful look that Paolo almost laughed out loud.

He looked around the bar. "It's quiet in here now, Larry. Why don't you come and join me for a coffee and we can catch up on what's been happening in our lives."

Back at the station Paolo reflected on his conversation with Larry. He could only hope he hadn't done any harm. Larry hadn't seemed to be listening most of the time, but maybe enough of Paolo's words hit home to make a difference.

He'd already let Barbara know about his chat with Larry, so now all that was left was to fill Matthew Roberts in on the news regarding his parentage and sibling. Finding out about his natural mother was going to be hard for someone like Matthew to swallow. Paolo smiled wryly. This could mean yet another trip to Willows.

Picking up the phone again, he dialled Matthew's office number. The ever-efficient Jennifer answered and put Paolo through to her boss.

"Matthew, good afternoon. I have some news about your natural parents which I feel you should know. I—"

"Paolo, this isn't something I want to hear about by phone. Why don't you come over and tell me what you've found out. I'm sure you can understand that all this has been a shock for me. I would like to think that you would treat me with the same degree of respect that you'd give to anyone else in my position."

"Matthew, are you implying that I'm not treating you with

respect?"

"That is the way it appears to me, yes. I'm quite sure if you were going to be given news about your natural parentage that you would like to be given the information face to face and not impersonally over the phone."

"You're right. When can you fit me in?"

Paolo heard the sound of pages being turned.

"I appear to be free for the next hour. Can you come over straight away?"

"I'll be there in twenty minutes," Paolo said, cursing himself for not realising that this could be traumatic for Matthew. "I'll see you then."

He put the phone down, grabbed his coat and called out to Dave.

"We're going to pay a courtesy visit to Matthew Roberts. He will most probably have a million and one questions, so bring your file."

As they walked out to the car Paolo realised Dave was no longer walking stiffly.

"You found some magic medicine to ease the pain in your back, Dave?"

"No, sir. I found a magic way of getting the ointment rubbed in. I'm well and truly on the mend now."

Paolo waited for the wisecrack about some girl being lucky enough to massage Dave's body, but it didn't come. He smiled to himself. It seemed Dave was learning when to keep quiet. Miracles did happen after all.

Chapter Nineteen

Paolo and Dave went directly to the door leading into Matthew's office rather than going via the reception and waiting area. He had made it quite clear that he wanted to see them immediately they arrived. Paolo tapped on the door and heard a curt command to enter. He opened the door to find Matthew pacing up and down in front of his desk. He looked distraught, entirely at odds with his usual 'I'm in control of every situation' persona.

He stopped his aimless wandering as they came in and gave a weak smile.

"I'm sorry I snapped at you on the phone, Paolo. I am completely on edge and I have no idea why I should be. I'm actually nervous about what you've got to tell me. How weird is that? I'm never anxious about anything as a rule, but this is a situation I simply don't know how to deal with."

Paolo felt a measure of sympathy for Matthew he wouldn't have believed possible and wondered how to put the man's mind at ease. Considering what they had to tell him, it didn't seem likely that anything he said would help for long.

Matthew moved to the side of his office where a small couch and two armchairs were arranged around a coffee table. He sat in one of the armchairs and signalled to the other seats.

"Won't you please sit down? Jennifer will be bringing in coffee shortly. We might as well be comfortable while you tell me all about my serial killer brother."

Paolo sat on the other armchair and left the couch to Dave. "We don't know for certain that he is the one we're looking for, Matthew."

"I thought you said the killer's DNA proved it was a sibling of mine? Or are you telling me I might have more than one brother? Dear God, is that what you've got to tell me?"

Paolo crossed his legs and made himself more comfortable. "No, it's almost certain that the brother we've discovered is the man we want, but we haven't yet been able to match his DNA, so we can't prove it at this stage."

"You're talking about the legal aspect. I'm looking at it from a more personal point of view."

The door from the secretary's domain opened and Jennifer appeared carrying a tray which she placed on the low table.

"Thank you, Jennifer," Matthew said, reaching for the coffee pot. "Please hold all calls until further notice." He waited until she'd left the room and then passed a cup to Dave and smiled. "I see you're clutching a file. Does it have any information I might actually want to know about, or is it full of details I'd rather you didn't tell me?"

Dave accepted the cup, but looked to Paolo instead of answering the question.

"Oh hell, that look tells me I'm not going to like what you've got hidden away in there." He handed Paolo a cup. "So which one of you is going to hold the floor?"

As gently as he could, Paolo told Matthew what they knew about Sean and his life in Liverpool, hoping against hope that he could gloss over their birth mother's background, but Matthew asked the question he'd been dreading.

"So poor Sean had a terrible life while I lived a life of privilege. He must hate me for it. I think I would have loathed him if our lives had been reversed. But what happened to our natural mother?"

Paolo sighed. "I'm sorry, Matthew, but she's dead," he said, determined not to go into detail unless he absolutely had to.

"I can't pretend to feel sad about it. I didn't know her, had no idea whether she was even alive. Whenever I've thought about her, which wasn't very often, I'd always assumed she'd died. It had never occurred to me that she might still be living or why would she have given me up?" Matthew laughed. "I've just realised how narcissistic that sounds. I don't mean it like that. I just meant... I don't know what I meant, to be honest."

Matthew stared at the wall for a few seconds. Paolo stayed silent, happy to give him time to digest what he'd heard so far.

"When did she die? She couldn't have been very old."

Paolo hesitated. The words prostitute and murdered formed in his head, but refused to come out of his mouth. Matthew had handled the news very well so far. It seemed almost cruel to tell him the rest.

"Oh God, Paolo, you really need to work on your people skills. I can see the wheels turning in your brain trying to work out the best way to break something unpleasant to me. Now I'm really concerned. Did she die from something that might affect me? Is there a hereditary disease I should be worrying about?"

Paolo shook his head. "No, it's nothing like that. She was murdered."

"Christ! Where? How?"

Paolo told Matthew how Catherine Andrews met her end.

"So she might have been killed by her own son?"

Paolo nodded. "We don't know for sure yet, but it seems likely."

Matthew stared at the wall again, but then, almost as if a further unpleasant thought had forced its way to the surface, he turned his head slowly in Paolo's direction.

"But all of the victims featured on the news have been prostitutes. Why would... was she... oh Christ, Paolo, come on, spit it out. Was my natural mother a prostitute?"

Paolo thought back to his school days when he would have given anything to be able to humiliate Matthew, to dish out the kind of spite that Matthew gave to others. Now, all these years later, here was his chance and all he wanted to do was protect the man as much as he could. He nodded in answer to Matthew's question.

"Paolo, I can see by your face that there's more. It's something worse, isn't it? What the bloody hell could be worse than what I've already heard?" He swallowed. "What else have you found out?" Matthew asked, his voice barely above a whisper.

Paolo told him about his mother's prison term and why she'd been sent down. Matthew looked shattered. He dropped his head in his hands and stayed that way for several minutes before looking up again.

"I'd like you to leave now, Paolo. Please, just go."

"There is one more thing, Matthew. It's also possible that Sean is watching you. Has been watching you for some time. We don't know where he is, but the fact that he came to our town to kill women suggests that it was to be closer to you for some reason. You could be in danger. What I'd like to do is arrange for someone to watch over you. Are you okay with that?"

Matthew shook his head. "No, I'm not okay with that. You think I want someone following me around? Checking out my every movement?"

"It's for your safety. We don't know why Sean is here. He might have been setting you up so that it appears you committed the murders. He might be waiting for a chance to hurt you in some way. We simply don't know."

Matthew stood up. "I'll take my chances. Many of my clients have been badly treated by the police, Paolo. I don't intend to lose their trust by having a policeman logging their visits to me." Paolo went to interrupt, but Matthew held up a hand to stop him. "I said no and I meant it. If I find that you've had anyone following me without my permission I swear to God I'll have you fired from the force. My clients deserve their privacy and I won't have you invading it."

The previous atmosphere of friendly cooperation was gone in an instant. Matthew had reverted to type and there was nothing more Paolo could do. He signalled to Dave that they were leaving.

"Matthew, I'm sorry you feel that way," Paolo said holding out his hand. "We wouldn't have been watching you to see which clients were coming in and out, but simply to keep you safe should Sean have you down as a target."

Matthew managed a weak smile and took Paolo's hand. "Do I look like a prostitute? I appreciate the concern, Paolo, but my clients must come first."

Paolo nodded. "I don't suppose Sean will make contact, but if he does, don't arrange to meet him. Or at least, do arrange to meet him but don't go unless you've told us about it so that we can pick him up."

Matthew nodded. "The sooner you find him the sooner my life can go back to normal. Don't worry; I want him found and locked away as much as you do."

Matthew walked with them to the door leading into the corridor, but stopped with his hand on the handle.

"Thanks, Paolo."

"For what? I haven't exactly made your day with my news."

Matthew smiled at him. "No, you haven't, but you haven't rubbed my nose in it either. I appreciate the fact that you tried to spare me most of the unsavoury details. I'm just glad that my mother, the woman you and everyone else knew as my mother, isn't alive to hear about that woman's background. I doubt my parents would have chosen me if they'd known what she was. My mother loathed prostitutes, you know." He opened the door. "If she'd had her way, they would all have been rounded up and left to rot somewhere."

Paolo didn't speak until they were back in the car.

"That went better than I'd expected," he said. "I didn't think Matthew would take the news like that."

"What did you think he'd do?"

Paolo laughed. "I wouldn't have been surprised if he'd picked up the phone and made a complaint about us to the Police Complaints Commission right there and then."

"He's a strange bloke, isn't he?" Dave said. "Won't have us watching over him in case it violates the trust of the criminals he acts for. I've heard him on television loads of times and he always comes across as someone who just wants to protect human rights, but he's a criminal lawyer, so what about the rights of their victims?"

Paolo grinned at Dave. "You know, you need to be careful. I think you've caught some sort of disease."

Dave looked horrified. "What are you talking about? What disease?"

Paolo turned the key in the ignition, gave Dave one last grin, and pulled out of the car park.

"It's called being human and the symptoms are terrible. You start to care about people. I think you've definitely caught it because you're beginning to sound remarkably like a human being and less like a pillock."

"Bollocks," Dave said, but Paolo could see the smile on his passenger's face in his peripheral vision.

Chapter Twenty

The police think they're so clever, but they cannot stop the Lord's work. They don't even know where to begin looking for me. He frowned as he prepared for the night's exertions. How he hated Matthew. The golden child, the special one.

He forced his mind away from thoughts of anger and retribution. *He* had been anointed by God. *Him.* Not Matthew. He dressed with care, choosing the clothes that made him look like a successful man. The whores seemed to think that going with someone wealthy would mean they were safe. All it meant was that they were stupid.

He looked around the cottage bedroom. Everything was in place. He loved Friday nights. The Lord had died for mankind on a Friday, so it was only fitting that he did the Lord's work on His special day. He felt the Lord's presence in the room and fell to his knees.

"I am not worthy of your love," he cried with head bowed.

As the light of God's blessing filled the room, he prayed for strength. The strength to choose wisely. The strength to save her soul. The strength to abstain until only the shell of the body was left. It was getting harder to wait, but the Lord had explained that he had to. If he entered a living whore he was damned for all eternity.

"I will not fail," he cried, raising his voice above the angels singing the Lord's praises. "I am ready to do my duty."

He cruised the streets until he found one who matched the woman in the photograph. His mother. His mother before she took to whoring and murder. He'd been too late to save her soul, but the Lord had forgiven him. He'd sent him out to find others. Others who could still be saved.

He slowed the car to a stop and pressed the button to lower the window on the passenger side. The girl was alone in the deserted street. It couldn't be better. She looked around, as if she wanted to run. Word must have got out. He waited. If the Lord had chosen her, she would come to the car. If He didn't think her worthy of saving, He would make her turn away.

The girl hesitated – looked over at him. He smiled and waited. She took a step towards the car. Still he said nothing. She took another step, still looking around as if someone would call out to stop her, but there was no one else around. The streetlight made her bleached hair look yellow, which angered him. Maybe this wasn't the one. But then she took another hesitant step towards the car and then another and another, away from the glare of the yellow light. Out of the circle of yellow lamplight, he saw that she looked very like his mother. When she was young and that picture had been taken.

He could barely breathe waiting for the Lord to show him if this was one of His chosen lambs. She stopped just a couple of feet from the car.

Still he waited. She had to come to him. It was the only way he could be sure that the Lord was giving his consent. She took another two steps and spoke through the car window.

"You wan' good time?"

He exhaled the pent up breath he hadn't even been aware he'd been holding and nodded. She smiled and opened the car door. As she slid into the passenger seat he slipped the photograph of his mother and brother into his pocket. The Lord had spoken. It was time to do his bidding.

He drove out of town in silence, not looking at the whore. Nervousness must have loosened her tongue because her prattle began to get on his nerves.

"Shut up," he said. "I don't want to hear you speak."

"Okay. Where we do fuck? Is long way."

He slammed on the brakes and swerved to the side of the road.

Grabbing her hair, he pulled her head towards him. "One more word and I'll break your neck. Now shut up."

He let her go and accelerated away, smiling as she tried to open the car door. The child lock stopped her from escaping, but even if she'd been able to jump out, he'd simply have dragged her back into the car. She was his to save. There was no other option for one who the Lord had chosen.

The car pulled smoothly into the driveway. As he stopped the car, he turned to her.

"Don't be afraid. Come inside and we'll dance for a while. You like to dance?"

She nodded, her eyes wide with fear. He could smell the anxiety and it excited him, but he forced his mind and body to think only of the Lord's work. He would find his release later, but for now he had to drive the devil from her.

He opened his car door and closed it, locking her inside. Walking the short distance to the cottage, he slipped the key in the lock and pushed the door open. Reaching in, he flicked the light switch, illuminating the entrance hall. Then he returned to the car and opened the passenger door. As he did so she pushed herself past him. They all tried to run, but none of them ever escaped. He grabbed her arm, digging his nails into the soft flesh.

"Stay by my side or I'll break your arm," he whispered into her ear, inhaling her cheap perfume. "We're going inside to dance. You said you like to dance."

She opened her mouth and screamed as he dragged her towards the open doorway. The countryside was in darkness, the only light coming from the cottage itself.

"There's no one to hear you," he said. "No one to care about you. But don't worry; the Lord and I are here to save you."

As they reached the cottage he shoved her hard. She fell over the threshold and he kicked her away from the opening before locking the door. He slipped the keys into his pocket and took a good look at her. She scrambled away from him, her face disfigured by black mascara-stained tears mingled with snot, but she still looked enough like the girl in the photograph to excite him.

This was the test. Making him want her while she still lived was the devil's way of tempting him, but he had the Lord in his heart, so could never be corrupted. He kicked the whore in the stomach and she doubled over.

"Get up," he said.

She didn't move, simply screeched in her foreign tongue as the devil took deeper root inside her. He reached down and grabbed her hair, dragging her to her feet.

"I said, get up. I want to dance. My fucking whoring mother liked to dance. She said so when I found her. It was too late for her, but I'm going to save you. You should say thank you."

The girl's eyes darted from side to side.

"You're looking for a way out. There isn't one." Still holding her hair he shook her head backwards and forwards. When he stopped, he pulled her face close to his. "I said, say thank you."

"F... fank you."

He let her go and she slumped to the ground.

"That's better. I'm going to put on some music and you can dance for me. We're going to have such a nice time."

He left her in the hallway and went into the lounge. As he switched on the light, the figure of the Lord on the giant crucifix against the far wall smiled in encouragement.

"You have done well, my child," Jesus said.

He dropped to his knees before his Lord and prayed. This was always the hardest part. He had to keep himself clean and not enter her too soon, but already he could feel his excitement ready to betray him. To make him defile his body.

"Give me strength, Lord. Don't let me fail you."

The Lord's light filled him and he rose to his feet. He was ready.

He woke early on Saturday morning sprawled on the bedroom floor. Unbidden, an image of her disfigured face swam into focus. As his erection rose, he was filled with disgust. Even in death the whore continued to entice him. His lust had been sated during the night over and over, yet still his body craved release. This was surely the devil at work. He crawled away from the bed where the whore's body lay spread-eagled and opened the cupboard against the far wall. Even as he reached in for the whip and promised the Lord not to touch the whore again, he knew he'd fail. He'd continue to anoint her until the stench became too much to bear.

He knelt and put out his left hand to steady himself against the wall. Raising his right hand he flicked the lash over his shoulder. As the barbs bit into his skin his erection subsided and he found a measure of peace. He'd keep her for the next few days and then dump the body at a different illegal refuse tip. Fortunately for him, the inhabitants of the town found new places to tip their rubbish faster than the council could clean them up.

His glance fell on the camcorder he'd set up. When the whore was gone he'd still have the memories to see him through.

***

Paolo pulled up outside Lydia's house and felt a sense of relief that he wouldn't be coming here for much longer, just a few more weeks. He couldn't wait for the day he would be able to move into his new flat. It would mean seeing less of Lydia, but with her forthcoming wedding that was just as well.

He walked up to the front door and was about to ring the

bell when the door flew open and Katy came hurtling into his arms.

"Dad, you're late!"

"I am not. We said ten and it's only twenty past, so how can that be late?"

She punched his arm and yelled back into the house. "Dad's here. We're going now. Bye, Mum."

Although Paolo hadn't wanted to see Lydia, he felt cheesed off that she hadn't even come to the door. Katy must have picked up on how he felt because she dragged him towards the car.

"Believe me, Dad, you don't want to get in her way today. Bad mood doesn't come into it. She's been planning... stuff."

Paolo stopped halfway to the car and felt the familiar gaping hole in his stomach. "You mean her wedding?"

Katy nodded. "Sorry, I didn't mean to upset you."

"It's fine, kiddo," he said pointing the keys and pressing the button to unlock the car. "I'll have to get used to the idea. So she's planning the wedding and getting into a state? Your mum has always been a manic planner."

"Tell me about it! Actually, no, don't. Let's just go."

Paolo smiled. "Suits me. Where to?"

Katy leaned on the passenger door and grinned at him over the top of the car. "Bowling. Let's see if you can get anywhere near my score this time."

"You're on. I have a feeling I might have a few strikes," Paolo said and climbed into the driver's side.

As she slid into the passenger's seat, Katy laughed. "Why not? There's a first time for everything."

Afterwards, as they settled themselves at a table overlooking the bowling lanes, Katy was still smirking over her incredible score and Paolo's dismal attempts to match it.

"You really are pretty bad at this, Dad."

"Don't rub it in, kiddo, or we won't come back here again.

What do you want to eat?"

"I'll have a burger and chips, please."

Paolo went to the counter and ordered their food. He was dreading having to tell Katy what he'd found out about her friend, but couldn't put it off any longer. As he sat down he decided to attack the subject head on, but would have given anything to avoid having the discussion with his daughter.

"Katy, you know you asked me to find out why the girl from your school has been missing for a while? I'm afraid the news isn't good."

Katy stopped sucking on the straw and put her can of lemonade on the table.

"What's happened to her, Dad? Is it Father Gregory? He's been missing for ages as well."

Paolo shook his head. "I don't know where he is, but he has nothing to do with your friend's problem." As Katy opened her mouth to speak Paolo put up a hand to stop her. "No, let me finish. I've had to call in a few favours to find out, so don't you dare tell anyone what I'm going to tell you. I'm trusting you on this, Katy. Give me your word."

She nodded. "Dad, you know I wouldn't blab to anyone about anything you tell me. I can't believe you asked."

"I know, but this isn't my story to tell – and it isn't yours either, but it's bound to come out when the court case starts."

"Court case? Why? What's happened to her?"

"You know her mother has a drink problem?"

Katy nodded. "Everyone knows that. Sometimes her mother could hardly walk when she came to the school. We just pretended not to notice."

"Well, it seems that while her mother has been passed out drunk her new boyfriend has been over friendly with Valerie. That's why she was hiding out in the lockers after school. She didn't want to go home."

"So where is she now?"

"She's been taken into care. The boyfriend has been arrested and so has her mother, but it's not likely the CPS will be able to bring a case against the mother."

"Why not? If she let it happen then—"

"Because the boyfriend used to ply her with drink until she passed out. Valerie says her mother didn't know. Maybe she did, maybe she didn't, but unless the CPS can prove she knew, there isn't a case to answer. They may not be able to convict her of encouraging or allowing child abuse, but social services are going to make sure she gets sober before they allow Valerie back into her care."

"So when will Valerie be coming back to school?"

"I don't know, Katy. I don't even know if she'll be returning to your school. It's possible that she'll be placed in care outside the school catchment area. If that's the case then she'll go to the nearest school."

"And it's nothing to do with Father Gregory?"

Paolo shook his head. "Nope, nothing. No need to look so disappointed."

"I'm not. Well, I am a bit disappointed. I still think he's a creep. I wonder where he is."

Chapter Twenty-One

Paolo ripped Tuesday's page off his calendar with more force than was necessary. Wednesday had come round faster than he'd have liked. If there was one thing he hated about his job it was taking part in television broadcasts. Fortunately they didn't come up too frequently, but once Liverpool had supplied them with a useable picture of Sean Andrews, the request to the public had been organised.

He looked down at the photograph on his desk and was amazed once again at how alike the two brothers were. The only difference he could see was that Sean had the slightest sign of a harelip on the right-hand side of his mouth. It was a pity it hadn't been on the left, as then one of the witnesses might have spotted it, but being on the driver's right, there was no way it could have been seen from the street. But would that have made any difference? He would still have known the witnesses had described someone who looked very like Matthew Roberts, with the exception of a harelip. Would he still have looked into Matthew's family history? Possibly not without the DNA Matthew had supplied.

Dave tapped on the door and came in.

"The chief sent a message to say they need you upstairs in ten minutes, sir."

"Thanks, Dave. I've just been looking at this picture and wishing they'd found some DNA to go with it. That would have made it much neater, but I suppose we can't have everything."

"I know, sir. It seems the girlfriend kept the valuable stuff in case he came back for it, but ditched all the personal goods. I can't say I blame her. I wouldn't have held on to someone else's toothbrush or comb, would you?"

"No, I wouldn't. Apparently all she kept was the playstation, games and blu-rays. She donated his clothes to charity shops after a few months and binned everything else." Paolo looked at his watch. "Okay, Dave, let's go and get this over with."

As they left the office Dave grinned. "Are you taking the lead, or is the chief doing the talking?"

Paolo sighed. "He wants me to do it. God knows why. I suck in front of a camera."

They headed for the stairs leading to the conference room where the press had set up their equipment. Paolo still held a copy of Sean's photograph. The harelip was barely noticeable, but he wondered if it had been more so when Sean was younger.

"Do you think his harelip might have been why he was passed over so many times and yet Matthew was adopted?" he asked Dave. "I've been trying to work out why a toddler was placed, but the baby wasn't. It usually works the other way round, but maybe it was enough of a disfigurement to put off prospective parents."

By this time they'd reached the next floor. Dave held open the door to the conference room to allow Paolo to go in first.

"Could be, sir. I believe people want perfection when they adopt." He grinned. "A bit like me in my search for the perfect girlfriend."

Paolo decided to let the comment pass. He was almost certain that Dave said it just to see what sort of reaction he got. Maybe he was developing a sense of humour at last.

They approached the long table set up with mikes and a few of the leaflets that were going to be passed out into the community. Paolo's nerves got the better of him and his hands started shaking. He'd have to remember to keep them out of sight when he spoke into the cameras. He hoped the sudden onset of nausea didn't show on his face. Dave moved to the side of the room. Paolo walked up to the table and sat on one of the two chairs that had been put out for them. Putting down his notes, he looked over to where Chief Constable Willows was chatting to one of the camera men. Paolo nodded to show he was ready to begin the ordeal and Willows came to sit next to him.

The cameraman signalled the countdown and then called for filming to begin. Paolo took a deep breath, trying to control his rapid heartbeat. His mouth was so dry the water in his glass looked like ambrosia, but he didn't dare reach for a drink because his hands were shaking so much he'd be sure to spill water all over the leaflets. He coughed and began, praying that his voice wouldn't give out on him.

"We are appealing for the public's assistance in locating this man," he said, raising the photograph. "His name is Sean Andrews and we believe he can help us with our enquiries into the murder of several prostitutes in the town..."

Twenty minutes later he answered the last of the questions from the journalists, feeling as though he'd run a marathon. The cameras stopped rolling and Willows rose. Paolo remained seated. He wasn't sure if his legs would hold him.

"Well done, Paolo. You handled that very well. The leaflets and posters are already being circulated. I believe this will go out on the local news immediately. It will be on the national stations this evening. I've also arranged for you to brief the people at *Crimewatch*. With a bit of luck we can get this included in the next show."

Paolo smiled. "Great, sir," he said. "I can't wait."

And if you believe that you'll believe anything, he thought. He watched as Willows did the rounds of thanking the television crew and the journalists, thinking how well the man handled these situations. Hoping that the wobble would now have left his legs, he stood up, gave a general thanks to everyone in the room and headed for the door. This type of thing had to be done, but he'd rather get on with hunting for Sean Andrews than talking about him on television.

Paolo put the phone down and slammed his fist against the desk. Was Sean Andrews laughing at him? It certainly felt that way. The news footage had no sooner been shown than a member of the public had found another body.

He got up and walked to the door of his office.

"Dave, CC, George, I need you in here. Now"

He went back to his desk and waited for them to arrive.

"I've just had a call from uniform. Another body's been found at a fly-tipping site on the east side of town. This bastard really likes making a point about how he sees these women, doesn't he? From what I can make out so far, he dumped the body during the night. Forensics are already on the way. Dave, you and I are heading over to where the body was found. CC, you and George go over to the district and find out who is missing. We haven't had a missing person's report, but someone must know who this latest victim is." He picked up a pile of leaflets. "Take these and dish them out to the girls on the streets. They need to know to be reminded not to get into a car with this bastard."

Barbara was finishing up as Paolo and Dave arrived at the scene. She looked tired and far from her usual immaculate self. Paolo wondered if she was getting enough sleep or maybe someone was keeping her up late at night. Then he wondered why he'd had that thought. It wasn't as if he had any reason to pry into her private life. Shaking his head, he walked towards where she was waiting for him.

"Our killer strikes again, Paolo. He's keeping the bodies for a few days after he strangles them. He's certainly a sick bastard, that's for sure. These girls are beaten almost to death before he finishes them off. The last one had semen on her breasts that couldn't have been more than a few hours old when the body was found. I think this one might be the same."

She sighed and pushed a stray hair from her face.

"You'll call me when you know more?" Paolo asked.

Barbara smiled. "Don't I always? Don't hold your breath while waiting though. Yours is not the only case I'm working on."

Paolo nodded. "I know that, but we need to put this one away."

"Ah, but that's your department, Paolo, not mine. I don't think we're going to learn anything new about him from this body. He seems to be a creature of habit."

"What's the estimated time of death?" Paolo asked, not really expecting an answer, but Barbara surprised him.

"Friday night some time, I would imagine. I'll know definitely later."

Paolo turned to Dave. "I think we need to find out where Matthew was on Friday night. The appeal to the public only went out today. On Friday he would still have felt that Matthew was in the frame – assuming he really is trying to set Matthew up. Come on, let's go and pay another visit to Matthew Roberts."

Paolo watched Matthew pacing around his office, feeling sorry for the man. From the moment they'd arrived to tell him another murder had been committed he'd been pacing up and down, unable to keep still even for a moment.

"I'm sorry, I just can't take this is. Are you telling me that Sean Andrews is watching me?"

Paolo nodded. "It certainly seems that way, Matthew. We've checked back on all the dates and every murder coincides with a night when you have been home alone, and so wouldn't have an alibi if you needed one. It looks very much as if Sean Andrews is setting you up. He looks so much like you it's uncanny and he's made no attempt to hide his face when picking up the girls he later kills."

"But why? Why would he want to destroy my life? What have I ever done to him? I didn't even know he existed until you told me about him," he said, finally coming to rest and throwing himself down in an armchair opposite Paolo and Dave on the sofa.

"Our theory, and we could be way off base, is that he hates you because you were chosen for adoption and he wasn't. You were given a wonderful life in comparison with his. He had a crap time growing up. From what we have found out so far, he was in and out of foster homes, in and out of care. Possibly when he realised you were his brother he resented the fact that you'd had such an easy and somewhat luxurious life. That could be why he killed your natural mother. At this stage it's all supposition, but it seems feasible that he's out to ruin your life to even the score."

"And you have no idea where he is?" Matthew asked.

"Not at the moment, but he has to be close by to know when to strike. If he's setting you up then he would need to be certain you were at home for the evening. There wouldn't be any point if you were out at a function with loads of witnesses, which means he has to be near enough to know where you are. I think the time has come to have you under surveillance, Matthew. The most likely way for us to pick up Sean is to catch him when he's tracking your movements."

Matthew shook his head. "No! How many times do I have to explain to you that my clients' privacy is paramount?"

Paolo's sympathy evaporated. "You can tell me as many times as you like, but are you saying that the poor girls Sean beats up and then kills don't deserve some of your concern? If we don't catch him he'll kill again and again, you do realise that, don't you? We have no intention of upsetting your clients in any way. We'll put a discreet tail on you – hell, you wouldn't even know anyone was following you, so your clients definitely wouldn't know."

Matthew jumped up and towered over Paolo. "You're missing the point. I don't care about that. I care about your men gathering information on who comes to visit me and who they bring with them. I'm telling you now, Paolo, if you set someone to watch my movements after I've specifically said no, I'll make sure you end up in front of the Police Complaints Commission. I'm sure the PCC would agree that I'm an innocent party in all this. My clients even more so. Go and do your job. Find Sean Andrews and take him in, but stay away from me and the people I represent."

Paolo got to his feet and signalled to Dave to do the same.

"Don't threaten me, Matthew. You know as well as I do that we aren't trying to catch out any of your clients. We don't need to do that. Sooner or later they do something stupid, or try one job too many and end up getting caught anyway. I can't put a tail on you without your consent and I certainly wouldn't give you the satisfaction of turning round and catching some poor officer who's just doing his or her duty, so you can relax."

Paolo took a breath to calm down. What the hell was it about Matthew that made him want to knock him flat?

"If Sean gets in touch, or you see someone who looks even remotely like you, contact me directly," he said, passing Matthew a card. "All my phone numbers are on there. Call me any time, day or night. And do me a favour, please. Get your secretary to make up a list of any public engagements you have lined up over the next few weeks. If Sean *is* watching you then we can be fairly sure that those nights are not going to be when he goes on a killing spree."

Paolo nodded goodbye and left without another word. He was vaguely aware of Dave following behind him. He was still furious when they reached the car. He unlocked the doors and got in; wrenching his seatbelt into place as if the thing had done him a personal injury and it was payback time, he forced it into the slot to snap it in place. As he waited for Dave to buckle up, he drummed his fingers furiously on the steering wheel.

He became aware of Dave's stillness and stopped his rapid finger movements. Turning, he had to force himself not to yell at Dave for staring at him. Jesus, he had to calm down.

"He really gets under your skin, doesn't he?" Dave said.

Paolo didn't trust himself to speak, so he nodded.

"Why?" Dave asked. "You deal with people like Azzopardi and don't react the way you do with Matthew Roberts. Why does he rile you so much?"

Forcing himself to think logically, Paolo rejected the first response that popped into his head, which was that the guy was a prick.

"Do you know, Dave, I have no idea. I don't know what it is about him that gets under my skin. Maybe it's that he's too perfect. You know, too well dressed, too well spoken, too... I don't know, too everything. All I know is that there's something about him that makes me want to aggravate him as much as he does me." He laughed, feeling the tension leaving his body. "Maybe it's my inner teenager rearing its ugly head. I hated him back then, so it might just be unresolved issues. Who knows. You hungry? Let's go and eat."

Chapter Twenty-Two

Chief Constable Willows didn't look as if anything Paolo might say was what he wanted to hear. If Paolo was honest, he didn't blame the man. He had nothing to give him that would be worth listening to.

"Paolo, this is ridiculous. It's been a full week since the first appeal to the public. We've featured on *Crimewatch*, the news channels have been brilliant, the press have run the story for days and yet you're telling me that not one person has called in?"

"No, sir, I didn't say that. In fact we've had more calls than we can cope with. I've told you about those."

"Don't get funny with me, Paolo. I'm not talking about the cranks who believe Hitler is camping at the bottom of their gardens, or those who confess to every crime they hear about, I'm talking about genuine leads. You're seriously telling me that not one call has been genuine?"

Paolo sighed. What could he say apart from the truth?

"Sir, we've had a few calls from people who saw Matthew Roberts and believed they'd spotted Sean Andrews, but other than that, we've had zilch. The man is keeping himself well hidden. If you'd give me permission to—"

"Paolo, we've been over this again and again. You cannot put a tail on Matthew Roberts. If he could prove you'd done so we'd end up being massacred by him – and by the press who are being so helpful at the moment. You know how hot Roberts is on human rights." Willows broke off and glared at him. "What did you say? Come on, if you've got something worth hearing, don't mutter it under your breath."

"I said, he worries about human rights when it suits him and his clients."

Willows pulled a face that Paolo couldn't quite decipher. He decided not to put his boss on the spot by asking what he meant by it.

"Any news from Liverpool, Paolo? I suppose it's possible that Sean Andrews might have gone back up there."

"We're in constant contact with them, sir, but they haven't had any new information. The ex-girlfriend has been out of the country for the past week. She went with a group of workmates to Spain, but was due back yesterday, so they'll be getting in touch with her. Still, if she's been away it's not likely she'll be able to add anything into the mix."

Paolo's phone rang. He looked over at Willows, who nodded permission to answer it. He didn't recognise the number on the caller display, so flipped it open and gave his name by way of greeting.

He listened for a few moments and then scribbled down a time. Closing the phone, he smiled at Willows.

"I do believe we might have had our first breakthrough, sir. That was the ex-girlfriend, Lizzie Cooper. How's that for coincidence? It's almost as if she heard us talking about her. Anyway, she switched on her computer when she woke up this morning and saw Sean's face plastered all over the Internet. It came as quite a shock to her, as you can imagine. Anyway, the good news is that she's on her way down from Liverpool. She was calling from the train, which is due to pull into the station in," he broke off to look at his watch, "twenty-three minutes from now. She says she has information that will help us."

For the first time that morning, Willows smiled. "I take it you're off to meet the train?"

Paolo nodded. "I am, sir. Let's hope her journey was

worthwhile, for all our sakes."

Paolo stopped at the doorway to the main office and called across to Dave who was busy typing up his reports.

"Leave that for now, Dave. We've got a train to meet."

Dave jumped up and grabbed his jacket from the back of his chair.

"Really, sir? Who's on it?"

Paolo filled him in on the way to the parking area.

"You can drive this time, Dave. Your back seems to be okay again now."

He waited to see if Dave was going to tell him anything, but the younger man stayed silent. Paolo smiled to himself. He'd seen Dave and Rebecca talking as he'd left the station the night before and it looked as though Dave might have finally met his match. He'd certainly been nodding in agreement with Rebecca, which was a breakthrough in itself.

Dave drove to the railway station entrance and stopped the car. Paolo jumped out.

"Wait here, Dave. I'll see if Ms Cooper's train is on time."

He walked into the station concourse and studied the arrivals board. The Liverpool train was due in one minute from platform three, so he sprinted down the stairs and along the underground passageway to the sign pointing to another set of stairs leading up to platform three. He took a deep breath and forced himself to sprint up them. He got to the top just as the train was pulling in. He'd told Lizzie Cooper that he'd wait for her under the exit sign. He positioned himself out of the way of anyone wanting to go past and scanned the passengers as they disembarked. The only youngish looking woman to get off had a suntan that owed nothing to the weak April sunshine in the UK. Even if she hadn't described what she was wearing, Paolo would have had a good guess that the woman was Lizzie Cooper.

He stepped forward to meet her. "Ms Cooper? I'm Detective

Inspector Paolo Storey. Thank you for coming all this way."

She glared at him, which was the last thing he'd expected.

"I bloody well had to come, didn't I? You lot have made a right balls up."

If he'd been surprised by her look of loathing, that was nothing compared to the shock he felt at her words. Feeling off balance, he tried to make sense of the situation.

"Ms Cooper, I'm sorry, I think we've got off on the wrong foot somehow. I thought you'd come to give us information that would help us to track down Sean Andrews, your former boyfriend."

She hitched her shoulder bag higher, but Paolo got the distinct impression she'd have preferred to hit him with it.

"He is my former boyfriend, as you put it, but that doesn't mean I'm going to help you lot to stitch him up. I haven't come to help you catch him; I've come to tell you what a load of arseholes you are. Sean wouldn't hurt a frigging fly."

Paolo almost rocked backwards from the venom in her voice.

"Look, this isn't getting us anywhere. Why don't you come back with me to station? We can discuss everything there. We can tell you why we think Sean is the man we're looking for and you can tell us why we're wrong. How does that sound?"

She sniffed. "It sounds okay, I suppose, but I'm not having a hand in stitching Sean up for summat he didn't do. He might be a right prick most of the time, but he isn't a bloody nutter."

Paolo nodded and turned to go back down the stairs. After a moment's hesitation Lizzie Cooper followed him. He led the way through the passage and back up the stairway leading to the main part of the station. He was desperate to ask a few questions, but the woman beside him was angry enough to start screaming abuse in the middle of the concourse if he asked something she didn't like, so he took the safer option of heading to the car in silence.

He opened the nearside rear door and held it while Lizzie Cooper got in and settled herself on the back seat. Not feeling that sitting next to her would be a good idea, he moved around to the front of the car and climbed into the passenger's seat. Dave glanced at him with a look of enquiry and Paolo shook his head slightly.

"Dave, this is Ms Cooper. Ms Cooper, this is my Detective Sergeant, Dave Johnson."

He smiled at Dave. "Let's head back, Dave. Ms Cooper wants to put us right on a few things."

Dave nodded and manoeuvred the car away without saying anything, although Paolo could see by the look on Dave's face that he had a million questions buzzing through his head. The car wove smoothly through the traffic and reached the police station in less time than the outward journey had taken, although it felt much longer. The short journey back had been enlivened by non-stop muttering from the back seat – all of it along the lines of the police taking the easy route to crime solving.

As Dave pulled into the parking bay, Paolo jumped out and opened the door for Lizzie Cooper.

"Thanks very much," she said. "It's nice to see someone with some manners. Most blokes don't bother with opening doors and such like anymore. But don't think that means I'm going to let you carry on with this pack of lies about Sean, because I'm not. You're all the same, you coppers. You think you can stitch some poor bugger up instead of doing your job. Well you're not going to do it to Sean."

Paolo glanced across the roof of the car. Dave was about to lock the doors when he looked up. Raising his eyebrows, he looked heavenwards. If it hadn't been so serious, Paolo would have laughed, but Lizzie Cooper's accusation was no laughing matter.

If nothing else, she was at least consistent in what she had to say. By the time they reached Paolo's office he felt as though he'd been listening to a recording stuck on repeat. His head ached and his temper was simmering just under boiling point.

He gestured to one of the chairs facing his desk.

"Please take a seat, Ms Cooper. I'll organise something for you to drink, which would you prefer, tea or coffee?"

"Coffee, please, white and no sugar. This is a nice office. Do all right for yourselves, you lot, don't you?"

Paolo swallowed the retort he wanted to make and decided to sort out the drinks. Maybe by the time he got back he'd have found a way to deal with his visitor. As he turned to leave the office he collided with Dave who'd hung back when they left the car on the pretext of needing to find something in the boot.

He grinned at Paolo and whispered: "Do I have to come in? I think I might strangle her."

Paolo laughed and whispered back: "Go and fetch us some coffee. Make hers white with no sugar – and don't even think of hiding in the kitchen until she's gone."

He watched Dave walk away and then squared his shoulders before going back to face the next barrage of insults. By the time Dave reappeared with the drinks Paolo felt verbally battered.

Dave placed the coffee on the desk and sat in the chair next to Lizzie Cooper.

"Ta very much, but you needn't think being nice to me is going to stop me from sorting you lot out."

"Ms Cooper," Paolo began.

"Lizzie," she said.

Paolo nodded. "Lizzie it is. Lizzie, we appreciate you coming all this way down to see us, but for the benefit of my colleague, could you repeat your reasons for making this trip."

"I've already told you, it's to stop you and dopey there from fitting Sean up for summat he didn't do. I've known the daft bugger for nearly fifteen years on and off. He's a complete wanker, but he's no killer. Bleeding hell, he couldn't even swat a spider when I asked him to."

Paolo put a hand up to interrupt the flow. "I believe you and Sean broke up? Do you know where he went after that?"

"He most probably went to meet that brother of his, the one from the telly. That's where he said he was going. Said he was onto a winner there. Told me he'd be set for life and would take me with him. I told him I didn't want any part of a scam."

Paolo scribbled that down on the pad in front of him. "Did he say where he was going to meet Matthew Roberts?"

Lizzie shook her head. "No, but I wish he'd come home that night. We had a blazing row, but I never meant it when I told him to sod off and not come back. I expect he got money from that Roberts bloke and is off chatting up birds on the Costas. Bastard that he is."

Paolo heard the affection in her voice as she said the last words and realised she'd take Sean Andrews back if he turned up even now. That surprised him. From the picture they'd formed of Sean Andrews he didn't seem to be the type to engender that much affection.

"You seem fairly certain that Sean had made contact with Matthew Roberts. Why is that?"

Lizzie laughed. "Because I heard them, didn't I? Sean called the Roberts bloke using my phone. He was always running out of credit and I knew he'd been using mine up, even though he said he hadn't. I came into the kitchen that last night and Sean was bloody using my phone. I went off on one, didn't I. Told him his bloody fortune. I'd had at least a fiver's worth of credit in the morning and there was sod all left when I looked after he'd gone."

Paolo tried to make sense of what Lizzie was saying, his mind numb. "Are you telling me that you heard Sean talking to Matthew?"

Lizzie nodded.

"And he used your phone to make the call?"

She nodded again.

"Can you please tell us exactly what you heard? Word for word if you can."

"That's easy," Lizzie said. "I came in, and Sean was looking a bit shifty. That's when I realised he was using my phone. Anyway, he said, 'okay I'll meet you at the station.' Then he laughed and said, 'I won't have any trouble recognising you.' Then, when I yelled at him about stealing my credit, he tried to turn me up sweet by saying that he'd be able to buy me a dozen pay as you go phones if I wanted them because he was off to meet his rich brother to shake him down."

"Did he say what he intended to shake him down over?" Paolo asked.

"Not exactly," Lizzie said. "It was something to do with their mother being a prostitute, but Sean always had these grand schemes to get rich. You know, a bit like Delboy on *Only Fools and Horses*. Sean was always going to be rich next year. He'd do anything to earn money apart from actually go to work."

"Do you still have the same mobile number as you did when Sean left?"

She nodded. "Yeah, I've changed the phone a couple of times, but kept the number. Why?"

"We'd like to check the phone records to see which numbers were called on the night you last saw Sean. If you still have his number, we'd also like to check Sean's phone records. Are you okay with that?" Paolo said.

"Will it help Sean?"

Paolo nodded. "It might. I can't make any promises, but it might."

"Okay," she said and gave Paolo both numbers. "But I've rung him loads of times and the daft sod's either been ignoring me or he's changed his number since he left. Look, let's get on to the real reason I've come down here. It's not to play silly buggers with you lot; it's to prove it wasn't Sean what murdered them women."

Paolo smiled. Whatever Sean might have done to Lizzie, she still seemed to have faith in his innocence.

"And you think you can prove it?" he asked.

"I know I can," Lizzie said with a triumphant note in her

voice. "I watch all the crime shows, *CSI* and suchlike. I know how DNA works."

Paolo sighed. "Lizzie, those shows are far from the way things are really done. To test for Sean's DNA we would need a sample that we could prove came from him and there wasn't anything in the bag of his possessions you gave to the Liverpool police."

"Maybe not," she said, "but that don't mean I don't have summat you could test. You seem like a decent bloke. If I give you stuff I know Sean licked, will you promise you'll use it to clear the silly bastard's name?"

Paolo leaned forward. "Lizzie, I can't promise you that. All I can promise is that if Sean's DNA doesn't match the killer's then I'll make sure Sean is cleared. Will that do?"

She put her head on one side, clearly trying to decide if Paolo could be trusted. Suddenly she nodded and picked up the massive handbag she'd been carrying on her shoulder when they'd met at the station. She rummaged inside and extracted a number of envelopes, of the type that usually held greeting cards, which she put on the desk.

"There you go," she said. "You're bound to get summat from at least one of those. He was a romantic bugger when he remembered to be. There's cards there for me birthdays and a couple of years he actually remembered Valentine's Day, so I chucked them in as well. The writing's really crap. He always said that was because he was left-handed and made to use his right hand when he was a kid. I've brought all the ones he'd licked to seal the envelope. I told you, I've watched *CSI*, and I bet you can get DNA from at least half a dozen of those."

Paolo glanced over to Dave. "Log these in and get them over to forensics, smartish. When you've done that, get the phone companies to give us their records on these two numbers."

Lizzie stood up. "Yeah, and don't let them screw up the tests when they do the envelopes. I've seen it done on shows where they mess up the case because someone does summat stupid.

You look daft enough to make the odd mistake." She turned back to Paolo. "I'm off back to Liverpool. If you find Sean tell him... tell him... I dunno, tell him I said hello would you?"

Paolo smiled and got up. "He's a lucky man, Lizzie. Not many would go the extra mile to help someone as you have. Would you like a lift back to the station?"

"Nah, it's no bother to walk. The next train's not due for hours yet and I want to see a bit of the place before I go home."

Paolo walked with her to the door. He stopped and held out his hand. "It's been a pleasure to meet you, Lizzie."

She shook his hand. "Yeah, likewise. You're not a bad sort for a copper."

He watched her walk through the main office and then went back into his own. Dave was gathering the cards into an evidence bag, but looked up as Paolo went past.

"Bloody hell, sir, she could talk."

"She sure could, Dave, and she's opened up a whole new avenue for us. What if Sean really had made contact with Matthew Roberts? That would mean Roberts already knew about his sibling when we spoke to him, but lied about it. Now why would he do that?"

"I suppose he might be covering up for his brother. You know, just found out about his family and wants to help, although being a solicitor hiding someone from the police doesn't really fit. Maybe we should just ask him, sir."

Paolo nodded. "We could, but I want proof before I approach him again. If his number appears on Sean Andrews' phone records, or the call that Andrews claimed was to Matthew Roberts is on Lizzie's, then we'll have good reason to question Roberts again. Until then, you can get to work with what Ms Cooper brought to us." He smiled. "I'm going to see Willows. I'm hoping I can convince him that we have good cause to check Matthew Roberts' phone records, but I'm not counting on it."

Chapter Twenty-Three

Paolo glared at the calendar. Another bloody week gone past and they were still no nearer to finding Sean Andrews. He grabbed the phone to call Barbara. The DNA results from the envelope samples were taking forever to come through, even though they'd been fast-tracked. He pressed the speed dial number for her and waited.

"You have reached the number for…"

Paolo snapped the phone shut. Where the bloody hell was she?

He wished he could go outside and have a cigarette. Even though the cravings were kept in check by the patches, he still found times like this, when he was hanging around waiting for news, really difficult. It was more a case of keeping his hands busy than actually wanting to smoke. His phone rang and he jumped. Snatching it up, he was intrigued by the display. The number wasn't one that was instantly familiar.

"Storey."

"Paolo?" asked a man's voice he vaguely recognised.

"Yes, who is this?"

"Paolo, it's Greg."

"Greg? Katy tells me you haven't been in school for weeks. Where are you?"

There was a brief silence before Father Gregory replied. "I've been sent away on a rehab retreat, Paolo. Drugs and drink, just like the old days. No, sorry, that's a lie. They say to get better I have to tell the truth, especially to someone I'm asking for help. The truth is I never stopped with the alcohol, Paolo, but I did lay off the drugs for years. But then a while back... well, I found out something that I couldn't handle without something to take the edge off."

"In confession?"

Greg's silence told Paolo all he needed to know. He'd never thought about it before, but priests heard the worst of humanity in confession and had to keep it to themselves.

"Greg, why are you telling me about your rehab?"

"Because I need a friend, someone I can trust. Please would you come to visit me?"

Paolo continued the conversation feeling as though he'd stepped into a twilight world. No wonder Katy had found Greg's actions suspicious when he'd surprised her with her friend; it seemed he'd been using the old changing rooms to stash his drugs and wanted to get rid of the girls so that he could get his fix. Paolo put the phone down and stared at the piece of paper where he'd written the name and address of the rehab centre. He shook his head. He and Greg had never been friends, even back during their schooldays, but it seemed Greg needed a completely new start. Paolo wondered if he'd be allowed to stay in the priesthood once he was out of rehab. Funnily enough, he hoped that would be the case. Whatever Paolo might think of religion, he thought Greg most probably needed the prop.

The phone rang again and this time Barbara's name showed on the LCD. He snatched it up.

"Hi, what have you got for me?"

"Paolo, you're not going to like this. They've lost the DNA results."

"What?" he thundered. "Who has? Please tell me this is a joke, Barbara."

"Sorry, Paolo. No joke. I've just been on the phone chasing for answers. I've been promised the results haven't been lost completely, but no one knows where they are. It's a mess."

Paolo swore under his breath, but realised shouting at Barbara was both unfair and counter-productive. She wanted the results as much as he did.

"I take it you've told them to drop everything until they've found the missing file?"

"I have," she answered. "They will be sending a copy directly to your office as soon as they're available again."

He sighed. This was turning into a weird day.

"Paolo, you still there?"

"Yep."

"I'm going to the Nag today. Want to join me for lunch? My treat."

"Is this a way of getting me to put more pressure on Larry?"

Her silence told him he'd hit the spot.

"Barbara, I've done all I can there. Short of standing over your friend and forcing her to make a complaint, there is nothing more I can do."

"That's easy for you to say, she isn't your friend."

"That's bloody unfair and you know it."

"Is it?" she shot back. "I've never asked you for a favour, Paolo, other than to lean on Larry a bit. If that's too much to ask of a friend, then maybe we aren't friends."

"No, Barbara, that's not the case. What you want me to do is storm in there like some caped crusader and save *your* friend from her husband. The only person who can do that is Sharon herself. I've leaned on Larry, as you put it. Now it's up to Sharon to do her bit and either leave or find a way of dealing with him. I can't do any more. I wish I could, but it's a domestic situation."

Paolo stopped speaking as he realised the line had gone dead. Damn Barbara to hell and back. She'd left him feeling as guilty as sin for not saving Sharon. He'd done all he could with Larry. Barbara had worked with enough marital abuse victims to know that unless Sharon chose to leave no one could really help her.

The police couldn't go storming into someone's home unless they were called in or the neighbours complained.

***

Barbara sat opposite Leanna in the pub. At least she'd been able to rely on one of her friends to turn up when needed. After she'd slammed the phone down on Paolo, she'd called Leanna. Maybe, if Larry saw that Sharon had friends who cared he'd be less likely to let fly with his fists whenever he felt like it.

On the other hand, from the whispered words she'd had with Sharon when she'd arrived, it was possible that Paolo's talk with Larry might have done some good after all.

Larry cleared their plates from the table. He seemed to be unusually subdued and hadn't passed any comments about their looks or their love lives. Something Barbara hadn't thought he was capable of keeping out of his normal conversation. She watched as he headed towards the kitchen with the dirty tableware and then leaned across the table and lowered her voice.

"From what Sharon said while Larry was off changing the barrels, he's been as good as gold recently."

"Let's hope he's more scared of what Paolo might have threatened him with than you'd thought, but you know as well as I do, Barbara, it's not likely to last."

Barbara nodded. "That's why I wanted Paolo to come here. To give Larry a little reminder that he's being watched."

She stopped speaking and pointed at the television. Leanna glanced up at the screen. The newscasters were reading out yet another appeal for anyone knowing the whereabouts of Sean Andrews to please come forward. Pictures of him laughing with friends, just days before he went on the run, showed a good-looking dark-haired man with an uncanny resemblance to Matthew Roberts.

"They look so alike. I suppose they must take after their

natural mother. Strange, isn't it? Neither of them knew her, but they both carry her genes."

Leanna gave a bitter laugh. "If he's anything like his brother, I wouldn't be at all surprised to find out he's yet another woman hater. We seem to be surrounded by them in this bloody town."

"Another woman hater? You mean Matthew Roberts? Or are we still talking about Larry? I wouldn't have said Matthew Roberts was the type; he's always got an adoring woman hanging on his arm at all the big functions."

"Yes, but it's rarely the same one. He's a pig."

Barbara turned away from looking at the screen to study her friend's face. Leanna had turned a deep crimson.

"You're flushed. Is that from anger or embarrassment?"

"Both. Matthew Roberts was responsible for the most humiliating thing that's ever happened to me. I still cringe when I think about it, but it makes me bloody furious as well."

Leanna sighed and Barbara noticed her hands were shaking as she took a sip of her drink.

"I've never spoken of it. Never trusted anyone enough to tell them without thinking they might, I don't know, think I deserved it, I suppose."

Barbara touched Leanna's arm. "Want to talk about it now?"

Leanna nodded and took a deep breath. "I met Matthew when I was a freshman at uni. He was in his final year of law. We met, hit it off, or at least I thought we did. He was helping me with my studying. I ended up back at his room one night and we almost slept together. Funnily enough, if we had, I think it might have been his first time."

"What? You're kidding? If he was in his final year I'm amazed he hadn't had loads of partners."

Leanna nodded. "I know, I thought the same, but he definitely wasn't experienced. You know what I mean? He was so gentle and shy, wouldn't even get fully undressed. I thought he was the answer to a girl's dreams." She pulled a face. "Well, who wouldn't? He was gorgeous looking, well spoken, intelligent, funny – but he turned out to be a complete jerk."

"What happened?"

"We were sitting on the edge of his bed, kissing. He was shaking. Mind you, so was I. Then the phone rang. Jed had the genetic test results and was so excited I could hear him from my side of the bed, even though Matthew had the receiver pressed to his ear."

Barbara put up her hand. "Whoa, slow down a bit. I'm confused. Who is Jed and what's he got to do with your story?"

Leanna smiled. "Sorry, I need to back up a bit to explain it all properly. I most probably would never have met Matthew, or at least, not socially, if it hadn't been for Jed. He was a geneticist doing his masters and had put up a poster calling for volunteers for his programme. I've always been interested in genetics, so thought I'd go along. Matthew was there, as well as about ten others. He and Jed were in the same hall of residence, so they knew each other fairly well."

Barbara smiled. "Okay, at least I know who called, but what happened after that?"

"Hmm, I think I'm going to have to tell you what happened during the tests, Barbara, for it to make any sense. Jed took samples of everyone's blood, hair, saliva and other, you know, *bodily* fluids. The men provided samples of their semen. Jed said he'd use the results anonymously in his research. Anyway, that was the last I'd heard of the tests until that night when I was with Matthew and the phone rang with Jed yelling with excitement about something fantastic and for Matthew to come over to the lab immediately."

Leanna fell silent as tears filled her eyes. Barbara took her hand. "Don't go on if you'd rather not, Leanna. You don't have to tell me."

"No, it's okay. I want to tell someone, Barbara. I've kept this to myself for too long. Matthew couldn't calm Jed down over the phone, so said he'd go to look at whatever the amazing results were. He slipped the rest of his clothes on and said he'd be right back. The bastard even kissed the top of my head, but he also seemed a bit relieved that we'd been interrupted. It was all so weird. I couldn't figure him out at all."

Barbara was wondering how to respond when she saw that Leanna was shaking and tears had flooded her cheeks. Eyes clouded with pain, she took another gulp of her gin before continuing.

"I waited for ages, but Matthew didn't come back. I didn't know what to do – wait for him or go back to my own hall. In the end I must have dozed off because the phone woke me. It was Jed asking if Matthew was there. I looked at the clock and saw it was eight in the morning. Jed was concerned about Matthew. Apparently he'd reacted oddly when he'd seen the lab results. I asked Jed what he'd told Matthew, but he said he couldn't tell me. If Matthew wanted me to know, he'd tell me himself. But he was clearly worried about whatever it was he'd told Matthew because he made me promise to get Matthew to call him as soon as he came in. I was now really worried as well, but didn't know where to go looking for him. I decided to wait in his room until he came back. About an hour later, he came in."

She stopped speaking, her body wracked with silent sobs. Barbara got up and moved round to sit next to Leanna on the other side of the table. Reaching out, she put her arms around her.

"Leanna, honey, whatever it is, whatever happened, it's in the past."

"I know, Barbara, but you don't know what he did."

Barbara looked around. The pub was still virtually empty and the people sitting at the bar were too far away to hear anything Leanna said.

"If you want to tell me, it's okay. I'm a safe place to unload. Whatever you say will stay with me, Leanna. I promise."

Leanna pulled back from Barbara's embrace and blew her nose. That seemed to give her the strength to continue because she managed a weak and slightly watery smile.

"Okay, I'm ready to finish this," she said. "I was sitting on the edge of the bed. Matthew walked over and dragged me off it by my hair."

"What? Why?"

"Barbara, to this day I have no idea. When he left to see Jed he was normal, when he came back he was a maniac. He was ranting that I was a whore who'd invaded his room. He... he... I'm sorry, Barbara, this bit is really hard. He dragged me to the door and threw me out into the corridor, yelling at me all time. Doors opened and people cheered like it was some kind of entertainment laid on to brighten up their Sunday morning."

"Oh bloody hell, but surely he didn't leave you out there? What about your notes and stuff?"

Leanna laughed, but there was no humour in it. "When the door opened again I thought Matthew was going to take me back inside, say it was some sort of bizarre joke. But no. He opened the door and chucked my notes and books at me. The edge of one of the books hit here, under my eye; you can still see the tiny scar where it cut. The papers scattered everywhere. Then he shouted to everyone in the corridor that I was a whore and not to touch me because they might catch something."

Barbara would cheerfully have disembowelled Matthew at that moment if it had been possible. "What happened? Surely someone must have helped you."

Leanna nodded. "The girlfriend of the guy who lived opposite Matthew helped me pick everything up and took me to the hospital to get my cut stitched. It was only a tiny cut, but there was blood everywhere." She laughed a little hysterically. "So, that was my big romance with the wonderful Matthew and now it seems like his younger brother is even more of a bastard."

Barbara thought about the part genetics played in shaping people. Something Leanna had said pushed its way to the forefront of her mind.

"Leanna, can you remember the last name of the guy who did the tests? It wasn't Lawrence by any chance, was it?"

"Yes! But how did you know?"

"Because I think I've missed something and it might be really important. I know what field Jed Lawrence specialised in. He is, or rather was, famous for his research."

"What do you mean, was?"

"I don't know if you remember, but a few months back the newspapers were full of stories about a world-renowned geneticist who was killed by a hit and run driver in London. That was Jed Lawrence."

Leanna turned pale. "I didn't see that. It must have been while I was in the US. Are you sure it's the same person?"

Barbara reached across the table and grabbed her handbag. "I'm pretty sure it was, but I can easily check. If your Jed and the geneticist are one and the same, then I've got some urgent research to do – and I have to let Paolo know what I suspect."

Leanna's confusion showed on her face. "I don't understand. Is it something to do with Jed's tests?"

Barbara nodded. "Yes, but I have to check my facts before I call Paolo."

Barbara pulled some notes from her purse and headed for the bar to pay for their lunches.

Leanna followed her over. "I've got some time to spare this afternoon, so just tell me what you need and I'll help you with it."

Barbara took her arm and propelled her to the door. "I don't think we should waste any time. What you've told me changes everything."

***

Dave burst into Paolo's office waving a computer print-out. Before Paolo could say a word, Dave chucked the page on to the desk.

"Look at the highlighted numbers, sir. Bloody Matthew Roberts has been helping his brother from the outset."

Paolo picked up the printed pages and scanned through the entries highlighted in bright yellow. There were at least ten items – all to the same mobile phone number. Every one of them had been made several months earlier at a time when Matthew had claimed he didn't even know he had a brother, far less that he'd been in contact with him.

"Willows really didn't want to authorise us to get Roberts' phone records. I wonder what he'll have to say now. Well done, Dave. I take it there's been no contact recently?"

"Not to the number Lizzie Cooper gave us."

Paolo's phone rang and Katy's name flashed on the screen. She should be in school at this hour. Worried that she might be in trouble yet again, he flipped the phone open.

"You okay? Why aren't you in class?"

"I've slipped out. Told my teacher I needed the bathroom. Listen, Dad, I've had a thought about how I can find out what Father Gregory's up to."

"Is that all? Jesus, Katy, I thought something bad had happened to you."

"Why do you and Mum always think I'm in trouble? No, don't answer that," she said. "I've come up with a plan to find Father Gregory."

"I haven't got time to explain right now, but forget about him. Where he is and what he's doing is nothing to do with you."

"But, I..."

"Look, Katy, I really can't talk. I know all about Father Gregory. I'll call you this evening, okay?"

He waited a moment, but Katy remained silent.

"Did you hear me?"

He heard her sigh. "Yeah, I heard you. But, Dad, I really think..."

"Katy, we'll talk tonight. I have to go."

The phone went dead. He was tempted to call her back, but decided to make his peace with her later. He'd no sooner put the phone on his desk than it rang again. He picked it up, saw Barbara's name and switched his calls to voicemail. As guilty as he felt about not going to the pub with Barbara, he had to stick with his priorities. Larry and Sharon's problems would have to wait until after they'd found Sean Andrews.

"What about the night Sean went missing, was Lizzie telling the truth about Sean calling Matthew that night?"

Dave nodded. "They spoke for several minutes, sir. There's no way now that Roberts could claim not to have known about his brother. I suppose he could have spoken to him back then and not heard from him since, but then why not tell us? Why pretend he didn't know about his birth family?"

Paolo stood up. "That's a good question, Dave, and one I want to ask Matthew Roberts as soon as possible. I suppose he could have been embarrassed about his background. His adopted parents were terrible snobs, so maybe he didn't want to admit to coming from a working class family, or maybe it was the prostitute mother he wanted to hide. There's only one way to find out. Come on, it's visiting time again, but this time we won't let Matthew know we're on our way over."

CHAPTER TWENTY-FOUR

Paolo and Dave reached Matthew's office just after five, but they were already too late to catch him at work. Jennifer, Matthew's secretary, had insisted her boss couldn't be disturbed, but Paolo had stood his ground. She'd been more surprised than any of them when she'd opened the inner door to find Matthew's office empty.

"I can't understand it," she said when back in her own office, re-checking his diary. "He definitely has an appointment marked down with a Mr Gordon. He told me it would run late and he wasn't to be interrupted under any circumstances. If you hadn't insisted on seeing him I would never have opened that door."

As she said the words Paolo got the distinct impression that somehow she blamed him for Matthew's disappearance.

"It's most unlike him," she said. "He always works such long hours. I can't imagine why he didn't tell me his appointment was over."

"Maybe he went to meet someone," Paolo suggested. "Has he ever mentioned his brother to you?"

"He doesn't have one," she said. "I thought you knew that he was an only child."

Paolo nodded. "Yes, he was, but only in the adopted sense. He has a brother by his birth mother and we know that they have been in touch with each other. We've been trying to find him for some time. You might have seen the appeals on television. His name is Sean Andrews."

"Do you mean to tell me that the murderer you're looking for is Mr Roberts' brother?" She shook her head. "I don't believe it. The resemblance is there, I even commented on it to Mr Roberts, but... no, I don't believe it. When I mentioned how much he looked like that man when the picture first appeared, Mr Roberts made a joke of it. He wouldn't have done that if... no... surely not."

She fell back into her chair and looked so close to passing out that Paolo sent Dave to fetch a glass of water to give her. When he came back from the kitchen and handed her the glass her hand shook so badly the water spilled over the papers on her desk. She patted at the mess with a tissue, but so ineffectually that it was clear she was in no fit state to be left alone.

"Is there someone we can call to sit with you for a while?" Paolo asked.

Jennifer nodded. "My sister. I'll... I'll call... I'll..."

"Give me the number and I'll call for you," Dave said.

Paolo waited until Dave had made the call before questioning Jennifer further.

"We need to locate Sean Andrews as soon as we possibly can. You know most of Mr Roberts' business. Other than his penthouse, does he have any other property? Is there somewhere he might have allowed Sean to hide?"

Jennifer shook her head. "He wouldn't do that. I'm sure he wouldn't. You must be mistaken."

Paolo tried hard not to let his irritation show. The woman was clearly distraught, he didn't want to add to her distress, but somehow he had to get over to her that Matthew Roberts had definitely been in touch with Sean, even if it had been a while back.

"It's possible that Mr Roberts is being coerced in some way. Maybe he is hiding Sean Andrews because he's being forced to do so. Jennifer, if you know of somewhere that Matthew goes, maybe a weekend place or something like that, you must tell us. Matthew could be in danger from his brother."

She looked more distressed than ever. "He does have a weekend cottage, but I'm not supposed to tell anyone about it. I've never been out there; I don't even have a telephone number for it. If ever I've needed to get hold of him in an emergency I've always used his mobile number."

"Jennifer, we're going now to his penthouse, but if he isn't there I need to know where the cottage is. We'll go and check that Matthew is safe. You wouldn't want to leave him to Sean Andrew's mercy, now would you?"

She shook her head and reached for a dry piece of paper.

"I don't know exactly how to find it, but this is the address."

Paolo took the piece of paper and slipped it into his pocket. "We have to go now; will you be okay here until your sister arrives?"

"Yes," she said, but so quietly that her voice could barely be heard.

Chapter Twenty-Five

Back in the car after leaving Matthew's office, Paolo and Dave headed to the penthouse. As Dave drove, Paolo checked his voicemail messages and was astounded to find several from Barbara telling him to call her back, each one more agitated than the one before.

He was about to put the phone back in his pocket when it struck him how out of character it was for Barbara to keep calling. He opened the phone and dialled her number. She answered almost immediately.

"Paolo, thank God. I've been going insane thinking I might not be able to reach you. I think Matthew Roberts might be our killer, not Sean."

"But that isn't possible, Barbara. DNA ruled him out. You know that better than anyone."

"Paolo, you'll have to trust me on this one, but it's almost certain that he *is* the killer. I can explain it all to you later, but it seems he might be a chimera. Someone with two separate strands of DNA in different parts of his body."

"Barbara, you're not making sense. This isn't possible, is it?"

"It's not something that happens very often, but yes, it's possible."

"What about Sean Andrews? We're still waiting for his DNA results."

"Not anymore we're not. They came in about ten minutes ago and his DNA is no more a match to the killer's than

Matthew's. We know for sure that a sibling of Andrews and Roberts is definitely our killer and they don't have any other brothers. A chimera is someone who has a dead sibling's DNA in their body as well as their own."

Paolo felt like he was trying to think through treacle. "What? What dead sibling? No, don't answer that. Explain it to me later. Right now I need you to tell me why it can't be Andrews who is a chi... whatever it was you said."

"You're right. That *could* still be the case, Paolo, but I found out earlier today that Matthew was tested years ago and the person who did the testing later became a specialist in the field. It's almost certain that it's Matthew who is a chimera. Jed Lawrence, the Chimera specialist, was, apparently, really excited about Matthew's DNA. The chances of Sean Andrews being the same are too remote to even consider."

"Bloody hell, Barbara, I don't understand any of this."

"I know, but trust me, please. I really believe it's Matthew you need to find. If you bring him in, I can perform a simple test. There's a strange pattern under the skin that only shows up in UV light. Bring him in, Paolo. I'm sure I can give you the proof you need."

"We've just pulled up outside his apartment. I must go. Don't worry, whatever happens we'll find Matthew tonight and bring him to the station. You can explain the science to me when we get there."

Paolo snapped his phone shut and opened the car door. "Dave, I can't explain it, because I don't really understand it myself, but Barbara thinks Matthew's DNA could still be a match with the killer. We need to find him, if only to rule him out."

Dave frowned. "What about the brother?"

Paolo shook his head. "Apparently he isn't a match."

"Well neither was Roberts. Don't tell me there's another one out there?"

"Not exactly. Barbara says Roberts could have two lots of

DNA." He shrugged. "I felt at the time he offered that bloody test that he was playing me, but I thought it was just to drop me in it with the chief. It seems there might have been another reason. Let's find him, shall we? We can worry about understanding the whys and wherefores later."

They entered the building to find the same security man as before guarding access to the foyer and lifts.

"If it's Mr Roberts you're after, he hasn't come in yet."

Paolo stepped up to the desk. "Are you sure? Could he have come in without you seeing him?"

"Nope, not possible. To get to the penthouse you have to come past my desk and he hasn't been in this evening."

Paolo smiled as if it was no big deal. "What time do you come on?"

"I took over at two and I've been here ever since. Some of the tenants are home, but not Mr Roberts."

Paolo thanked the man and signalled for Dave to follow him out. "Jennifer saw Matthew at four-thirty, so if the security guy has been here since two, there's no way Matthew could have come back to his apartment without being spotted. Let's call in the cottage address to the station. I'd like some uniform backup – just in case Barbara is right."

Dave tapped the address into the satnav and followed its directions out into the countryside.

Paolo's phone rang and an unknown number lit the screen. As he flipped the phone open, Katy's voice came through in an urgent whisper.

"Dad, you've got to help me."

"Where are you?"

But the only answer was the sound of a hard slap, someone falling and then a high-pitched scream before the phone went dead.

Chapter Twenty-Six

He'd driven around the corner and received such a shock he'd almost swerved into a lamp post. Regaining control of the car, he'd pulled over to the kerbside, his heart hammering so hard he could barely breathe. My God, could it be true? Talking to one of the older whores, acting for all the world as if she'd belonged there, was Paolo Storey's daughter. She was nothing more than a dirty little whore.

He hadn't known what to do. She looked nothing like the others. Nothing like the photograph of the first. But if he'd left her there, she would tread the same path. He'd closed his eyes in prayer, begging Jesus to guide him. The Lord's words had answered him. Save her.

"Katy, what are you doing here? Does your father know where you are?"

She'd scowled at him in recognition. "No, but he—"

"He doesn't know? What about your mother?"

A man, drunk or drugged, it was hard to tell, had appeared from an empty shop doorway and staggered towards Katy, yelling and swearing. Her eyes flicked between the incoherent man and the car.

"I can't leave you here. Your father would never forgive me. Get in the car."

"I'm fine," she said, but he'd heard the edge of panic in her voice.

The junkie had lurched forward, trying to grab Katy's arm.

She'd pushed the man away, opened the car door and scrambled in. God had delivered her into his keeping.

And now, he had to fulfil the Lord's wishes. He slipped the cassock over his naked body and then dropped to his knees in front of the prie dieu. The Lord had entrusted him with a special soul. He wouldn't let him down. Before dealing with Katy he had to compose himself. The thought of saving this one from the devil's clutches excited him more than he'd believed possible. The lash wouldn't help, he knew that. If anything, it would increase his desire. He rested his head on the prie dieu and begged for the strength to hold back until she was dead. He'd believed her innocent, but she was a whore like all the others.

When he finally had himself under control, he rose and picked up the key to the bedroom where he'd locked up Katy while he prepared for the ritual. His heart pounded as he left the cell and walked along the passage. *Dear Lord, help me to do thy bidding. Help me to remain pure in thy name.*

He slipped the key in the lock and opened the door, astounded to see Katy with a mobile in her hand. The bitch must have searched his things. He rushed across and smacked her across the face. As she fell backwards the phone dropped from her hand and spun across the floor. He grabbed her hair and dragged her to where the phone lay. Stamping down, he ground the phone with his heel until the casing shattered.

He shook her by her hair, wanting to kill her there and then. The bitch was spoiling everything. Still holding her hair in one hand, he slapped her with the other.

"Who did you call?" he yelled. "Was it your father? Did you tell him where you are?"

Katy shook her head. "I couldn't get through. Please let me go. I won't tell anyone you brought me here. I promise."

He smiled at the devious look on her face. The little whore thought she could fool him. Letting go of her hair, he brought his fist back and let fly. As she sailed across the room he felt a surge of blood in his groin. The fucking little bitch was trying to make him come while she was still alive. Anger surged through him. He must calm down.

Walking over to where Katy cowered on the floor, he knelt down next to her.

"Are you ready to repent?" he asked, reaching forward to caress her face.

She scrambled away from him until backed into a corner. "I haven't done anything. Please let me go."

"You were whoring. I found you waiting for customers. Don't try to deny it."

"I wasn't. Honestly. I was looking for Father Gregory."

He laughed. "You expect me to believe that? He's gone. Locked up in rehab where he should be. You were whoring, weren't you?"

Katy shook her head. "No. My dad will come looking for me. You should let me go."

"Your father hasn't a clue where you are. No one knows about this place. Just me and the Lord. I'm going to save you, Katy. I'm going to wash your soul clean. You should say thank you."

"What are you on about? You're not right in the head."

He walked over to her, and pulled her to her feet by her hair. As she screamed, his desire rose.

"You see what you're doing to me, you bitch, but the Lord will keep me pure until the time is right."

Ignoring her cries, he dragged her over to the table where the CD was set up ready to play.

"Katy, sweet Katy, we're going to dance."

***

Dave pulled the car into a lay-by. Paolo's hands shook so badly he could hardly press the keys to get Katy on speed dial. When he did, her phone rang and rang.

"Whose bloody phone was she using, Dave? And why the hell isn't she answering her own?"

He ended the call and keyed in Lydia's number, gasping with relief when she answered.

"Lydia, where's Katy?"

"What do you mean, where is she? She's with you."

"What? No, she isn't. I've just had a call from her on someone else's phone and she sounds like she's in trouble. She's not answering her own phone."

"Paolo, this isn't funny."

"Jesus, you think I'd joke about something like this? Why did you think Katy was with me? Where did she say she was going?"

"She didn't come home from school. She called to say she'd be meeting you at the station and the two of you were going to do something together. Didn't she turn up? Is that it?"

Paolo thought back to Katy's call earlier, when he'd brushed her off. A freight train hit him in the pit of his stomach. Katy was in trouble and it was his fault for not listening to her.

"Lydia, I've got to get off the phone so that I can put a trace on the number Katy called me from and one on her phone as well. Don't worry, I'll find her. I promise."

"You mean you don't even know where she called from? Paolo, I swear to God, if anything happens to Katy I'll never forgive you. Never."

"You think I'll ever forgive myself?"

Before she could answer, he ended the call and scrolled through the menu to find the number Katy had called from. He read it out to Dave who was already on the line to the tracing service.

Paolo was vaguely aware of Dave saying they needed to know the whereabouts of the two signals urgently, but couldn't concentrate on the actual words. He couldn't breathe. His head swam as nausea washed over him in waves. Someone had Katy. His beautiful daughter was in trouble. She needed him and he'd let her down.

They sat in silence until Dave's mobile rang. Paolo wanted to snatch the phone out of Dave's hand, but forced himself not to move. Katy's safety depended on him following procedure. If he did his job, he'd find her. Please God, let that be true.

"Right, yep, got that. Thank you," Dave said, shut his phone and started the engine. "Katy's phone signal is showing as still in town, but..."

"But what?"

Dave pulled out onto the road. "But the coordinates from the phone Katy used are the same as those for Roberts' cottage. It looks like he might have Katy."

The freight train picked up speed and demolished Paolo's insides. This couldn't be happening.

"Drive, Dave. Put your bloody foot down. If that bastard hurts her I'll kill him. Put out a call for all units nearby. Let's hope there's a car closer to the place than we are."

After a nightmare journey, with Paolo's mind painting pictures he couldn't bear, they finally arrived at the GPS coordinates.

"Christ, Dave, this is the back of beyond. No other houses for sodding miles, apart from that tiny building up ahead. Are you sure we're in the right place?"

"It's where the satnav is taking us, so it must be."

Dave pulled up outside the cottage and Paolo jumped out before the car had even stopped moving. As he ran towards the front door, he could hear music playing. Then, overlaying the words of *Bad Moon Rising*, the sound of someone in agony rent the air. Katy, that was Katy screaming. His brain felt like fire as he pounded on the door.

"Open this fucking door," he yelled. "Dave, help me here."

They tried to force the door open, but it wouldn't give an inch. Another scream filled the air and Paolo nearly threw up.

"The windows," Paolo yelled. "You go that side and I'll go this way."

But when he ran to the nearest window, he found burglar bars blocking the way. Dave called out to say the windows on his side were also protected. Then a klaxon sounded, getting closer with each note. A uniform car screeched to a halt and Paolo ran down the path towards it.

"I'm DI Storey," he panted. "The girl screaming is my daughter. Get the fucking door open."

One of the uniformed officers opened his car boot and pulled out a portable battering ram. He and his colleague rammed it against the door, again and again until it flew open and the sound of Katy's screaming intensified. Paolo pushed past the officers and ran inside.

He was halfway down the passage when the music stopped. Katy screamed.

Then the screaming stopped.

Chapter Twenty-Seven

Paolo ran, almost falling over in his haste to reach the first door, but the room was empty. Rushing to the next door, he flung it open and stopped dead on the threshold of a room that looked for all the world like the inside of a chapel – with the exception of the bed in the middle of the room.

Naked and spread-eagled on the bed, tied hand and foot, was Katy, her face a mass of bloodied bruises. Straddled over her was a figure in a monk's robe, his hands round Katy's throat. Paolo flew towards the bed and launched himself at the man, his momentum carrying both of them to the floor.

Pinning the monk to the floor, Paolo lashed out, fists flying.

"You've killed her, you bastard. You've killed my Katy."

Rage such as he'd never known took over. He'd kill the bastard with his bare hands. Taking hold of the hood, he smacked the man's head against the floor. When Dave tried to grab hold of his arm, he turned on him with a snarl.

"Fuck off."

Dave was yelling something, but Paolo couldn't take it in. He tried to get his arms free, but was eventually pulled away by Dave and one of the uniformed officers.

"Let me go. Fuck you, let me go. I'll kill him. Let me go!"

"Sir, she's alive. Katy's alive."

"What? Are you sure?"

Dave nodded. The fight went out of Paolo. The two men freed his arms and he turned towards the bed. Dave had untied

Katy and covered her naked body with his jacket, but she lay unmoving.

Paolo was vaguely aware of a voice in the background, but couldn't seem to grasp the words. Sounds were coming at him in slow motion, as if his brain was working through treacle.

"Uniform have called for an ambulance, sir. She looks bad, but she's still breathing."

Paolo fell to his knees next to the bed and took Katy's hand in his. Her skin felt waxy and at first he thought Dave was wrong, but then he saw a tiny movement as her body struggled to breathe.

He turned back to Dave. "Did uniform say how long before the ambulance would get here? She looks... she looks..." He couldn't finish. The words refused to come. Dropping his head to the mattress, he silently begged Katy to hang on.

By the time he'd pulled himself together, Dave and the uniform guys had handcuffed the monk to a chair. Dave reached down and pulled the hood from Matthew Roberts' head.

The bastard had taken some direct hits and his face showed signs of bruising. Compared to Katy's bloody and swollen face, he hardly bore a mark. Nowhere near enough in Paolo's eyes. Never had he hated anyone as much as he hated this bastard.

Matthew smiled. "You should thank me, Paolo. I was trying to save her. She's a whore, just like all the others."

Paolo jumped to his feet and rushed towards Matthew, but Dave stepped in the way.

"Don't give him that satisfaction, sir."

Paolo leant round Dave. "I'll kill you for this, Matthew. I'll fucking kill you for what you've done to Katy."

Matthew laughed. "I hope all you honest police officers are taking note of his threats."

Paolo tried to shove past, but Dave stood his ground.

"Don't rise to the bait, sir. He's doing it deliberately. Listen, I can hear the ambulance siren."

Paolo nodded. His vengeance could wait. He went back to the bed and looked down at his lovely Katy, battered beyond recognition. If it took Paolo the rest of his life, Matthew would pay for what he'd done.

The paramedics seemed to take forever working on Katy. Not once did she appear to respond and Paolo, watching from the side of the room, too scared to move in case he somehow caused them to lose concentration, had to keep telling himself that she wasn't dead.

Dave tapped his arm and he jumped as if struck by a bolt of lightning.

"Sir, sorry. I didn't mean to startle you, but don't you think you should let Katy's mum know?"

How could he have forgotten Lydia? She must be beside herself with worry. Hands trembling, he dialled her number and she answered within one ring.

"Have you found her? Where is she?"

"Lydia, Katy's been attacked..."

"She's okay, though, isn't she? Tell me she's okay."

He opened his mouth, but couldn't force out the words to tell Lydia just how bad things were.

"Tell me, damn it!"

"She's going to be okay, but..."

"But what?"

"She's in a bad way, Lydia. I'm sorry. It's my fault. All my fault."

"I don't need you to tell me that," she spat. "Where is she?"

"At the moment she's being attended to by paramedics, but they'll be taking her to the hospital soon. Do you want to meet me there?"

"I don't ever want to meet you anywhere ever again, but I want to see my daughter, so yes, I'll be at the hospital. But I warn you, Paolo, I'll never forgive you for this. Never."

The line went dead and Paolo felt again that sense of a freight train out of control running through him. The senior paramedic looked over, his expression grave.

"Her condition is just about stable enough to move her now, but her injuries are very serious. I've already called ahead to let them know she needs immediate surgery. We're ready to go. Will you follow or come in the ambulance with her?"

Dave stepped forward. "Go with them, sir. I'll take care of Roberts."

Paolo felt tears pricking his eyes. "Thanks, Dave."

He nodded to the paramedics and they carefully lifted the stretcher they'd manoeuvred under Katy's body. As Paolo followed them out to the ambulance, Dave called after him.

"Good luck, sir."

An image of his daughter's shattered face came to his mind. "It isn't me needing the luck, Dave, but thanks."

CHAPTER TWENTY-EIGHT

The ambulance ride passed in a blur. Every fibre of Paolo's being was concentrating on willing Katy to keep breathing. The slightest beep from the equipment wired to her body sent him into fresh agonies of fear. He couldn't lose her. Not his Katy.

As soon as the ambulance stopped outside the hospital, the doors flew open and a team of doctors and nurses took over, wheeling Katy out of sight.

Paolo grabbed one of the paramedics who was closing the ambulance doors.

"Where are they taking her?"

"Theatre. She needs urgent surgery on her face. I'm sorry; you must be going through hell."

Hell? It's where I deserve to be for letting this happen.

Inside the hospital he found the information desk and explained who he was. A kindly receptionist directed him to the third floor and told him to go to the waiting room. In a daze, Paolo followed her instructions and found Lydia being comforted by Jack. Paolo knew he should care, but he didn't. Jealousy, regret, anger, anything would be better than this emptiness.

He'd barely stepped into the room when Lydia launched herself at him and slapped his face.

"You bastard! Katy said she'd be with you. Why the hell wasn't she?"

Paolo didn't have the strength to defend himself.

"I'm sorry," he whispered. "I'm so sorry."

"Sorry? You're sorry? If Katy dies..." She broke off and brushed away her tears. "If Katy dies, you and your precious job will have killed both my babies."

Jack stood and put his arm around Lydia. "Come and sit down. You don't mean that, Lydia."

She shrugged him off. "Don't I?" she spat. "Ask him why Sarah died. Ask him who the driver was aiming for. Go on, ask him." She turned back to Paolo. "Your job killed Sarah and we both know it. Now it's going to kill Katy."

Paolo said nothing. There was nothing he could say because he knew Lydia was right. As Jack led her back to the seats on the far side of the room, the sound of her sobbing brought back all too clearly the day he'd had to tell her about Sarah's death. The driver had been aiming for him, but Sarah had seen the car and pushed him clear just in time. As he'd fallen, Paolo had heard the sound of metal hitting flesh. By the time he got to his feet the car had reversed. He shuddered, remembering the way Sarah's body had been dragged along under the car as the driver accelerated away.

Two hours of silence later Paolo looked up as the door opened, praying it was the doctor to say Katy was out of danger, but Dave hovered and waved to Paolo to follow him out.

"I just came by to see how Katy's doing. What have the doctors said?"

"Nothing yet," Paolo said. "She's still in the operating theatre. I keep telling myself she'll be okay, but I'm not sure I believe it."

"How's her mum holding up?"

Paolo shrugged. "About as well as me. Until Katy's out of surgery we won't know what sort of damage that bastard inflicted. Tell me you've got him securely locked up? You haven't come to tell me you've let him go?"

Dave shook his head. "No chance of that. He's locked up tight. Would you like me to stay here with you? You look rough."

Paolo managed a smile. "No, you go on home. I'm fine."

He watched Dave leave and then braced himself to go back into the waiting room, but this time Lydia didn't even look up. She was asleep with her head resting on Jack's shoulder. Jack gave him a questioning look, but Paolo shook his head – still no news on Katy.

He slipped back onto the chair he'd vacated earlier. He had a direct view of the door, and the frosted glass windows filling the upper half of the wall enabled him to see if anyone came down the corridor from the direction of the theatre.

An hour and a half later his vigil was rewarded. The door opened and a tired looking man in a white coat came in. As Paolo leapt to his feet, Jack woke Lydia. She opened her eyes and gave a sleepy smile.

"Mmm, where am... what are we... Oh, God, Katy!"

She jumped up, reaching the doctor seconds after Paolo.

He wanted to ask so many questions, but his throat seemed to be full of cotton wool and the words wouldn't come out. Lydia appeared to have the same affliction, because her lips moved, but she didn't say anything.

"Mr and Mrs Storey?" They nodded. "I'm Doctor Blanchard, Katy's surgeon. The injuries to her face were extensive. We've performed reconstructive surgery on her cheekbones, nose and jaw. She also has several broken ribs and has suffered severe trauma to her upper body, including fractures to the radius and ulna on her left arm."

Paolo finally managed to get his throat working. "She's going to be okay? She's going to live?"

"Yes. She's a healthy young woman and should make a full recovery."

"Can I see her?" Lydia asked.

He nodded. "You won't be able to go into the room, but you can look in from the outside. She's in ICU."

"Intensive care? Why? You said she'll make a full recovery,"

Lydia said.

The doctor gave a sympathetic smile. "She should, but as I said, her injuries were severe. We're keeping her in ICU until her condition stabilises. After you've seen her tonight I suggest you go home and get some rest. You should be able to talk to her tomorrow." He looked at his watch. "Or rather, later today."

Jack came and stood next to Lydia, putting his arm round her. "Let's go to ICU. What's the earliest time we can come back?"

"I suggest phoning after eight. The nurse on duty will let you know how Katy is and tell you when to come in."

Lydia and Jack shook the doctor's hand. She left without saying goodbye or glancing in Paolo's direction, but Jack turned and nodded farewell.

Paolo held his hand out, but the doctor closed the door and pointed to the chairs.

"Do you mind if we sit for a while? I'm exhausted."

Paolo dropped into a chair. "No, not at all. You've got something to say to me? Something you didn't want Katy's mother to hear? Is she worse than you said?"

"No, don't worry; it's nothing to do with Katy's condition. I simply wanted to ask you about the police report. I would normally forward it to you, but as you're also the father of the victim, should it be sent to someone else?"

Paolo thought about having to read in precise detail what Roberts had inflicted on Katy and his stomach heaved. Words from the autopsy reports on the other victims danced in his mind. A few minutes later and Katy's injuries would have been in an autopsy report, not a surgeon's. As much as he didn't want to read it, he knew he had to. Not doing so wasn't fair to Katy.

"Send it to me. Thank you for not asking in front of Lydia."

"No problem," the doctor said. He stood and held out his hand. "I'm off to get some sleep. I strongly advise you to do the same. You look as if just standing upright is more than your body can take."

"It is," Paolo agreed, shaking the doctor's hand. "I have one last question. I know it'll be in your report, but I need to know before I read it. Was she... was Katy... did that bastard..."

"Sexual assault?" Doctor Blanchard finished for him. "No, there was no sign of vaginal trauma."

Relief flooded Paolo's body and his legs gave way. He collapsed onto a chair.

Paolo barely slept. All through the night, images of Katy connected to tubes and support machines had appeared each time he closed his eyes. He looked at the clock for perhaps the hundredth time, only to find that it was only just after six. Realising that he wouldn't sleep regardless of how hard he tried, he got up and showered. That took the time to six-thirty, still an hour and a half too early to call the hospital. Having too much time on his hands and nothing to stop his mind from dwelling on how close Katy came to death, Paolo did what he always did when life became too hard to bear – he went to work.

He had just dialled the hospital's number when Dave came in. Signalling for him to sit, Paolo waited to be put through to the right person and then explained who he was and asked about Katy.

"She's comfortable," the sister said. "Her condition improved during the night."

"Her condition's improved?" he repeated, hardly daring to believe he'd heard correctly. "Can I see her? I mean, actually go in the room?"

"Yes, but not this morning. The doctor's advice is to leave visiting until later today. I'd suggest coming in this afternoon. Say about two?"

Paolo agreed and shut off the call. He felt as if all his bones had turned to liquid. Funny, he'd thought relief would give him strength, instead it seemed to have sapped the little he'd had left.

"Are you okay, sir? You don't look too good. Not bad news

about Katy, I hope."

Paolo forced himself to sit upright. "No, good news, actually. I'm fine, Dave. Just tired. You wanted to see me about something?"

Dave looked so uncomfortable, Paolo's heart dropped. What now?

"It's Roberts, sir. He, er, he wants to see you."

"Does he? Well he can go to hell. I don't think I'd be able to keep my hands off him."

Dave fidgeted with a paperclip he'd picked up from Paolo's desk. "You're not going to like me saying this, but I think you should see him."

Anger closed Paolo's throat, but he forced the words out. "You do, do you? And why's that? So that he can tell me he thinks my daughter's a whore? Fuck that."

Dave didn't answer.

"Okay, spit it out. Why do you think I should see him?"

"Because he's waived his right to legal representation and says he'll explain about Sean Andrews, but only to you. He won't speak to anyone but you."

"Why?"

"He won't say. Just keeps repeating that you are the only one he'll talk to."

"Dave, I'm not sure I can trust myself. You saw what the bastard did to Katy. I bet this is some trick to get me to attack him so that he can claim we beat a confession out of him."

"I know, sir, I thought so too, but I'll be there with you and we can have a couple of uniform in the room as well. I promise I won't let you touch him, no matter what he does."

Paolo nodded and got to his feet. "Come on, then, before I change my mind."

Matthew smiled at Paolo when he entered the interrogation room. Paolo had to put his hands in his pockets to stop himself from lashing out.

He sat down, glad the table was between him and Matthew.

He flicked the switch on the recorder.

"DI Storey interviewing Matthew Roberts, who has waived his right to legal representation. Also present are DS Johnson and constables Beech and Smith."

He finished by giving the date and time, then looked up at Matthew. "Where is Sean Andrews?"

"Don't you want to know about my work," Matthew asked. "God's love covers me. I'm doing his will."

Paolo couldn't tell if Matthew was deliberately goading him, but was determined to keep his temper.

"Tell God you've officially retired. Where's Sean? Are you two in this together?"

"Are you mad?" Matthew spat. "God would never have entrusted his sacred work to someone like Sean. I dealt with him as God wanted."

"What the fuck does that mean?"

Matthew laughed. "It means Sean is dead. There's no need to swear, Paolo. Sean was not worthy of God's love. He tried to blackmail me."

"Where is he?"

"He's in a very peaceful place."

"Skip the riddles, Matthew. Where is he?"

"When you find him, you'll be at peace," Matthew said and laughed again, more of a giggle this time. Paolo wondered how much of an act Matthew was putting on.

"Did you kill your natural mother?"

"I killed a whore. Sean contacted me and told me our so-called mother was a whore. The bitch wanted me to touch her. Can you imagine that? I went to see her and she wanted to fuck. I killed a whore who was so wasted on drugs she didn't even know I was her son. She touched me, Paolo. She made me want to defile my body. Jesus told me to kill her."

"Christ, Matthew, all you had to do was walk away."

Matthew laughed again. "You're so holier than thou, always have been. Even more self-righteous than Greg, and that's saying something. He knew about my work. Did you know that? He kept on at me to stop, but how could I when God Himself told me who to save?"

"Greg knew?"

"Of course, I told him in confession. Not because I wanted forgiveness, I hadn't done anything I needed to confess, but I wanted him to know how close I was to the Lord. You know Greg started hanging out with the prostitutes? Trying to keep them from me. The idiot thought he could stop God's work. But I had him removed."

"What do you mean, removed? He's in rehab."

Matthew laughed again. "Who do you think told his superiors that he was a troubled soul who needed help with his demons? He was back on drugs, Paolo. I did him a favour getting him sent to rehab, but I can't take the credit for the idea. Jesus told me how to get rid of Greg. When you've got the son of God on your side, everything is easy.

"Did you know where I found your daughter, Paolo? On the streets. I wonder how long she'd been a whore. You never guessed, did you? Of course, she said she was only there looking for Greg, but the Lord told me she was a liar."

Paolo didn't trust himself to answer.

"I tried to save her soul for you, Paolo. For old time's sake. I couldn't let your daughter fuck for money, now could I?"

Paolo stood so quickly his chair flew backwards. He had never wanted to kill before, but now he wanted to wipe Matthew from the face of the earth. Dave jumped up and moved in front of him, blocking his view of the scum on the other side of the table. Paolo sidestepped, determined to get to Matthew, but then he saw the bastard smirk. His head pounded, but he couldn't give in to his rage. Don't give him what he wants, the tiny sane part of his brain that was still functioning told him.

Pull yourself together.

Taking a deep breath, he forced his anger under control.

"Sorry, Matthew, that won't work. You're not getting me to lay a finger on you."

Matthew's smile faded, leaving disappointment in its place. The change in Matthew's expression told Paolo he'd guessed correctly.

"This interview is terminated," he said and flipped the switch to stop recording.

CHAPTER TWENTY-NINE

A week later, Paolo sat at his desk staring into space, thinking how strange life could be. Everything seemed to turn on luck in the end. If Leanna hadn't decided to add her name to the genetic trial; if she had never dated Matthew Roberts; if she hadn't been a close friend of Barbara's; if Sean Andrews hadn't tried to blackmail Matthew Roberts – so many ifs. How would things have turned out if even one of those things hadn't happened? But the most important if of all: if only he'd told Katy about Greg's call she would never have gone looking for him. Never have fallen into Matthew's clutches.

Physically she was out of danger, but mentally? She hadn't communicated with anyone since coming round from the operation. Not that she was able to speak with her jaw wired, but she wouldn't even make eye contact. He and Lydia took turns sitting with her, but Katy wouldn't look at either of them. She stared up at the ceiling in her own private world, keeping everyone else out. Even when the nurses came in to check her vital signs, or wash her, she stared at the ceiling. Forcing back the tears that always seemed to be on the verge of falling these days, he picked up the phone and dialled the number Doctor Blanchard had given him.

"Jessica Carter's practice."

"Could I speak to Ms Carter, please? DI Storey speaking. She's expecting my call."

He waited a few seconds and then heard the psychologist's

voice. "Detective Inspector Storey? Doctor Blanchard said you'd be calling. He's filled me in on Katy's recent trauma. I understand you'd like me to assess your daughter."

"I don't want you to assess her; I want you to help her, if you can."

"Yes, of course, but first I need to get some personal background information. Would it be possible for you and Mrs Storey to come to my rooms this afternoon? Say four o'clock?"

Paolo scribbled down the time. "I can make it, but I don't know about my wife. We're separated. Can I find out from her and call you back?"

"Of course. Let my secretary know if either of you are unable to make it. She'll reschedule. If I don't hear from you, I'll assume you can both make the appointment."

Paolo thanked her and cut the call. Dreading it, but knowing he couldn't put it off, he dialled Lydia's number.

"What do you want?" she said as soon as she answered.

"The psychologist Doctor Blanchard recommended wants to meet us this afternoon."

"Fine. What time?"

"Four o'clock. Lydia, I..."

"I don't want to talk. Just give me the address."

He'd barely finished telling her when the line went dead. She hadn't spoken to him since the night Katy had been admitted. He didn't blame her for hating him, but it hurt hearing the loathing in her voice.

Five minutes later a knock on his door brought a welcome end to the thoughts running in circles; he'd been feeling as though his head might explode.

Barbara stood watching him. The compassion on her face almost broke his self-control, but he forced himself to stay focussed on the investigation.

"Come in, Barbara. I hope you've come with some solid information."

She sat down opposite him. "How's Katy? Any change?"

He shook his head and fortunately Barbara seemed to understand how he felt, because she changed the subject, answering the question he'd posed.

"I've got so much information for you," she said. "I hardly know where to start. Firstly, you'll be pleased to know that the hair we took from Matthew Roberts matches the semen DNA found on all the victims."

Paolo sighed. "Barbara, I know you've explained it once already, but can you give me the layman's version so that I can get my head round it? How the hell can Matthew have two sets of DNA? I'm sorry; it just doesn't make sense to me."

Barbara smiled. "I can understand that, Paolo. It's quite rare, or at least we used to think it was, but now we're not so sure. Okay, here's what happens. It comes from something called 'Vanishing Twin Syndrome' and means basically that a mother has two fertilised eggs, which would normally result in non-identical twins. The non-identical part's important because identical twins share the same DNA. You with me so far?"

Paolo nodded. "I understand non-identical twins have different DNA, but not how one person has both."

"I know, this is the technical part. The two non-identical embryos fuse into one early in the pregnancy. One embryo literally absorbs the other and the mother gives birth to only one child. The baby has two different cell types, some of the organs have the living child's set of DNA and the other organs have the missing twin's DNA. Not only that, but hair, for example, can have one set of DNA and saliva the other. Or semen one and blood another. Both sets are spread around the body."

Paolo thought about what he'd just heard. He understood more now, but it still seemed pretty off the wall. "But wouldn't that lead to health issues? I mean, in effect, the living twin has foreign matter in his body. Why isn't it rejected?"

"We assume it's because it happens at embryo stage. Because there are no physical problems, either at birth or later in life, usually the person isn't even aware of it. Matthew might never have found out if he hadn't attended the test that day in university."

Paolo pushed the papers on his desk to one side, searching for a file. When he found it, he flipped quickly through the pages until he found what he needed and passed the file to Barbara.

"I've been doing some checking into the hit and run accident that killed the geneticist. I can't prove it, but the report says he was knocked down by a car very similar to the one Matthew drives. Look at the eyewitness descriptions of the driver."

Barbara read for a few minutes and then looked up. "It does sound remarkably like Matthew. Pity none of the witnesses thought to take down the number plate. Why would he want the guy dead though? I mean, why now after all these years?"

"I've been thinking about that, Barbara. I think Sean getting in touch and telling him about their mother sent Matthew over the edge. His adopted mother, Mrs Roberts, was a first-class bitch. From what I can make out, she instilled one of the great Catholic myths into him from a very early age, which was that sex is wicked. Apparently she lived and died a virgin – refused to have sex even after marriage."

Barbara sat up straighter. "You have got to be joking. You said they were married for decades."

Paolo smiled. "Apparently Mr Roberts senior used to get what he needed from prostitutes and Mrs Roberts eventually found out. Matthew told Dave he used to listen to the arguments, which always ended up with Mrs Roberts screaming about how truly evil prostitutes were. She used to get so worked up she needed to be sedated to stop the hysteria."

"That must have been a difficult house to grow up in," Barbara said. "No wonder he's messed up."

"You're not kidding. From other things Matthew told Dave during their last interview, I have a feeling she might have been completely deranged where sex was concerned. Anyway, it seems that finding out his own birth mother was a prostitute was bad enough, but apparently when he went to see her she was too far gone on drugs to realise who he was and thought he was a trick. It must have been more than his mind could cope with. Add to that his knowledge of being, in effect, two people, plus a lifelong friendship with Azzopardi who treated prostitutes like cattle, it's not surprising he lost his marbles."

"You think he's really off his head?"

Paolo sighed. "I don't know. I think he killed Jed Lawrence, his old university pal, after he'd killed Sean. At that stage he must have been at least partially sane because he wiped out Sean who knew his birth mother and Jed Lawrence, the only person who knew about his genetic makeup."

Barbara nodded. "I suppose that makes sense – as much as anything makes sense with Matthew Roberts. I mean, how do you think he reconciled the good work he did on all those committees and charities with being a killer?"

"His psychologist tried to explain this, but I'm not sure I get it. Apparently Matthew really thinks even now that he's two people. Not a split personality as such, but he believes he has the bad twin inside him, or the good twin, depending on how you look at things. Anyway, the good twin tries to make up for the bad one and the bad one wants to destroy the good one. Not sure if he still does, but apparently he believed that Jesus walked at his side through all this, so he never expected to get caught. On the other hand, I think he left the DNA behind to put the blame on Sean should he ever need to cover his tracks." He forced a smile. "Which begs the question: why would you need to cover your tracks if Jesus was there to protect you with a miracle whenever you needed one?"

"Phew, and I thought I had issues!" Barbara said. "He's sick, sick, sick. Right, on to the next bit of news, although it's not really any surprise. The remains found in the cottage garden under the peace rose are definitely those of Sean Andrews."

Paolo shrugged. "As you say, no big surprise there. We've had feedback from Liverpool. Matthew's fingerprints have matched those found on some of Sean's possessions. We can't be sure, but it seems that he met with Sean, then went on his own to visit his real mother Catherine Andrews, presumably to find out the truth. She came on to him, which freaked him out, and he killed her. Then he called Sean and arranged to meet him. It appears that he brought Sean down to his cottage and strangled him.

"As for Sean Andrews, he must have thought all his Christmases and birthdays had come at once when he spotted Matthew on television and saw how alike they were."

Barbara looked up from the files she'd been studying. "You think Sean contacted Matthew intending to extort money to keep quiet about their birth mother?"

"That's what Matthew claims. If there had been another reason, I don't suppose we'll ever find out what it was."

Barbara rose. "You're most probably right." She walked over to the door, paused and looked back. "Oh, by the way, Sharon called me yesterday. She and Larry are going to marriage guidance counselling and Larry is starting anger management classes. It seems that a visit from an old school friend made him rethink his life. Thank you for stepping in. I'd hoped that you would, but didn't want to push it. What did you say to him, Paolo, or is it a secret?"

Paolo thought back over the threats he'd made to Larry, both spoken and implied, and shrugged. "I just suggested he might like to make a few life changes – and that I'd be dropping by from time to time to see how Sharon was getting on."

"Whatever it was you said, it's worked like a charm. Sharon is convinced he's transformed into Mr Nice Guy. Me, I'm not so sure he's capable of it, but we'll see. If he keeps his fists to himself I can most probably put up with him being a jerk in other ways. Sharon loves him, God knows why. I don't want to lose her friendship, so I'll pretend I don't mind his smutty comments. Men! There isn't one of you who isn't a pain in the proverbial arse," she finished with a grin.

Paolo managed to smile back, but it was an effort. He stood up. He had a meeting with the chief in half an hour and needed a coffee fix before then. Barbara hesitated in the doorway, then closed the door and came back. Standing next to him, she rested her hand on his arm.

"Paolo, if there is anything I can do, anything at all, just call. I know you must be going through hell right now."

Emotion welled up. He couldn't speak, couldn't even see as the tears he'd been holding back flooded. She opened her arms and he walked into them, put his head on her shoulder and wept.

Chapter Thirty

Paolo took a deep breath and nodded to Dave. He was ready. Matthew was brought into the room and made to sit down. Paolo waited until the prisoner's handcuffs were attached to the chair, then flipped the switch on the recorder and stated the date, time and who was in the room. When he'd finished, he looked up and locked eyes with Matthew.

"This interview is taking place at the request of Matthew Roberts, who has, once again, waived his right to legal representation. Mr Roberts, would you please confirm this to be correct?"

"It is. How are you, Paolo? And how is Katy?"

Paolo kept his hands under the desk. He didn't want Matthew to see he'd touched him on the raw.

"Say what you've got to say, Matthew. Let's get it over with."

"Apparently I'm insane, Paolo. My psychologist is going to recommend a spell in a secure psychiatric unit. He seems to think I can be cured. I simply wanted you to know that I wouldn't be averse to receiving a visit from you occasionally."

"Very funny, Matthew. CPS doesn't think the same way about your sanity. I heard this morning they're going to prosecute. They think you're sane. You'd better hope your shrink is up to the job of convincing a jury otherwise."

Matthew's smile faltered, but he recovered. "He's the best money can buy. But let's not talk about the trial and what might happen in the future; let's talk about now and your lovely

Katy. I've heard on the grapevine that she isn't talking. That's going to make it difficult for her to tell her tricks how much she charges."

Paolo's body went rigid. Rage made his head throb. He was on the verge of lashing out when Dave touched his arm. Paolo glanced at Dave and nodded. He waited until he had his emotions back under control. He knew just how to deal with Matthew.

"It's an interesting theory, Matthew, claiming insanity. It might have worked, too, except that you refined your act after killing your birth mother. You see, you made sure you never left any evidence behind apart from the semen which we think you'd known since your university days wouldn't match your saliva or blood."

Matthew shrugged. "You can't prove that."

"No, but we can prove that you killed Sean."

"While my mind was unbalanced due to the shock of finding out about our whore mother."

Paolo allowed a smile to escape. "That might have worked if you'd killed him in a fit in Liverpool and dumped his body up there, but you didn't. You brought him down here, strangled him, and buried his body in the cottage garden."

Paolo tapped the file in front of him. "You did that so Sean would never be found and could always be blamed if you needed a scapegoat – that action alone blows the insanity plea. One other thing, I couldn't figure out for a long time why you gave the voluntary DNA sample. Then I realised it was because you knew it would appear to be a sibling's. Killing Sean was a calculated act, Matthew, whether you admit it or not. A rational, calculated act that is going to get you put away for a very long time. And no, I won't be coming to visit you in prison."

Matthew lunged forward, but the handcuffs prevented him from rising.

"I think we're done here," Paolo said. "This interview is

terminated."

Paolo arrived at the psychologist's rooms nearly twenty minutes early, but the receptionist said Lydia had already been waiting for ten minutes. He wasn't surprised. He also wanted to get this part over with so that Katy could get the help she needed. The receptionist directed him to the waiting room, where he found Lydia, staring into space. She glanced over at him as he entered, but quickly looked away and snatched up a motorsport magazine from a side table next to her chair. She seemed to find the content fascinating, because she didn't look up again.

Knowing how much she hated anything to do with motor racing, Paolo took her interest as a sign that anything was preferable to talking to him. Sighing, he sat on the other side of the room and waited for Jessica Carter to call them in. Not wanting to read about flower arranging, golf or hiking, the only subjects available on the table next to his chair, Paolo looked around the room, trying to get a mental image of the woman they were to meet. Judging from the pastel shades and old-fashioned watercolours on the walls, he imagined someone in their late fifties, maybe wearing tweeds and with a pair of glasses suspended from her neck. Her voice on the phone had been ageless, she could have been any age from twenty to sixty, but if this decor was anything to go by, she'd be closer to the upper age.

Finally the door opened and Paolo realised his guess had been way off. The woman smiling and inviting them to enter her office couldn't have been any older than early thirties. Short dark hair stood up in a spiky style that suited her elfin features. There were a few laugh lines around the most vivid blue eyes Paolo could remember seeing. She was dressed in jeans and a sweatshirt. All in all, she was nowhere near what he'd been expecting, but he could imagine Katy warming to her. No wonder Doctor Blanchard had recommended her.

"Please come in."

Paolo allowed Lydia to go in first, then followed and sat in the chair next to her.

"Doctor Blanchard has given me details on Katy's medical condition, but if I'm to help her, I need some background on how she came to be in hospital."

"Ask him," Lydia said.

Jessica turned her attention to Paolo.

"What she's saying is that it's my fault. What happened to Katy was my fault. She got involved in one of my cases and ended up in hospital. Lydia's right."

Jessica opened a pad. "Okay, let's take things from the beginning. I'd like to start with some insight into Katy's personality before this happened and we'll go on from there."

Paolo went straight from the psychologist's to the hospital, giving Lydia chance to go home for a couple of hours to rest. He sat next to Katy's bed, trying to convince himself that Jessica Carter would be able to help her, but right now he wasn't sure anyone could break through the barrier Katy had erected. She stared at the ceiling, not acknowledging in any way that he was in the room. He forced himself to keep talking, keep telling her about his life, her school, anything that might spark some interest and bring her back from wherever her mind had gone.

"So, let's see, what else can I tell you about? I've finished painting your room, so when you're out of hospital it'll be ready for you any time you want to visit. I expect you'll want to change the colour scheme, but that's fine. We can do that."

He watched her as he spoke, praying for a flicker of interest, but there was none.

"Anyway, most of my boxes are unpacked now..."

He broke off as the door opened and Lydia looked in.

"I want to speak to you," she hissed and then closed the door.

"Your mum's here, Katy. She wants to chat to me, but then

after that I expect she'll be coming to sit with you." He reached down and dropped a gentle kiss on her forehead. "See you tomorrow, kiddo."

Lydia was waiting for him in the corridor. She nodded at him, then walked off to the waiting room. He followed and shut the door behind him. Looking at her face, this was going to be yet another conversation he'd rather not have.

"Paolo, I've gone over and over everything we talked about in the psychologist's today. I know I'm never going to be able to forgive you for what's happened to Katy, but I realised this afternoon that for Katy's sake I've got to find a way to be in the same room with you without wanting to lash out all the time."

She dropped into one of the chairs as if being on her feet was simply too much effort.

"When Sarah died," she continued, "you didn't seem to care about how it affected anyone else. I know you did care, but you shut me out. Your bloody job took over your life completely. You left me. Not physically, but mentally, emotionally, you left me to fend for myself. Katy, too. You have... had... such a great relationship with her, but you didn't deserve it. I was the one that was always there for her, but she didn't want me, she wanted you. Now look where that's left her."

"Lydia, I—"

"No, Paolo, let me finish. I need to get this out without losing my temper, or getting overemotional. Okay?"

"Okay," he said and sat opposite her.

"I loved you, Paolo. I loved everything about you. Had done since the day we met. But then Sarah died and you changed; you wouldn't let me in. Katy loved you, too. I expect she still does. If that woman can help her come back to us then we'll find out. But you're toxic, Paolo, did you know that? Really toxic. People who love you get hurt."

She stood up, staring down at him with an emotion he couldn't figure out. It almost looked like pity.

"For Katy's sake, when we're with her I'll laugh, talk, carry on as if you haven't killed one daughter and turned another into a vegetable, but don't imagine for one moment that I don't despise you, because I do and I always will."

She walked to the door, opened it and left without looking back.

Paolo arrived back at the station still feeling as though his heart had been ripped out. He made straight for his office and closed the door, locking it. He couldn't face talking to anyone right now. He reached up and pulled the blinds down, then turned and rested against the door. How the hell was he going to carry on working as a cop, feeling as he did?

Sarah dead – his fault. Katy catatonic – his fault. Lydia struggling to cope – his fault.

He slid down until he reached the floor and sat without moving, his back against the door. Maybe he should resign, just get out of the force and find something else to do. Something that wouldn't put his loved ones in danger.

He had no idea how long he sat in the dark, but eventually an ache in his spine told him that whatever he did with his life, sitting on a cold floor wasn't going to improve matters. He shook his head. Maybe he should look around for a different career, but until he found one, he had *this* job to do, so he'd better get on with it.

Forcing himself to his feet and ignoring the protests in his knees, he flipped the blinds open and unlocked the door.

Five minutes later it opened and Dave came in.

"Did you know that Azzopardi is off the critical list?"

Paolo nodded. "I heard a whisper, yes. Apparently he's not expected to make a full recovery though. Why do you ask?"

Dave sat down. "Because, sir, the word on the street is that someone else has already picked up the reins and is now running the business. You'll never guess who it's supposed to be."

Paolo smiled. "I can see from your face that it's not going to be obvious, so go on, shock me."

Dave leaned forward. "Oh, I think I'm going to do that, sir. It's Maria."

For the first time in weeks, Paolo felt genuine amusement and laughed. "Maria? She wouldn't say boo to a goose, how the hell is she intending to control Paolo's men? You must have that wrong."

"That's exactly what I thought, sir, so I've been asking around. It seems that gentle Maria has turned into Iron Maiden Maria. One or two who tried to get in her way have found out that she's not afraid to deal out pain – and not just by proxy."

"Bloody hell, that's all we need. At least half of Azzopardi's crew will revolt. One or more of his cousins will try to take over. With a bit of luck they'll wipe each other out. I just hope to God they don't do it on our streets." He sighed. "Oh well, that's a problem for the future and I'll worry about it when it happens. This will be the first weekend in my new flat and I don't intend to spoil it by giving any thinking time to Azzopardi and his successors."

"You all settled in now, sir?"

"Only one box left to unpack. It's still a bit of a mess, but at least it no longer looks like a parcel delivery depot. What are your plans for the weekend, Dave?"

"You know me, sir. I don't make plans. I'll find myself a bird or two tonight and have a good time. Love 'em and leave 'em, that's me."

"Dave," Paolo said, trying not to laugh, "you don't do any such thing and you bloody well know it. You're head over heels in love, but don't want to admit it, least of all to yourself."

Dave shuffled on the chair. "I am not."

"Yes, you are. It shows in your face every time you look at Rebecca. For Christ's sake, give her a call and explain to her that you're a pillock. Ask her to give you another chance. Believe me, letting someone go when you really care about them is stupid." Lydia's face flashed into his mind. "I've done it and now I'm having to live with the consequences."

"But, sir, it's not, she's not ... I don't know if she even likes me."

Paolo smiled to take the sting out of his next words. "She might like you more if you stop pretending to be something you're not. Go on, go away and call her. I can't take the chance on you going all morbid and getting plastered again. The next time you fall down the stairs you might do more than graze your back. You're an idiot much of the time, but a good copper; and I need you around the place."

THE END

Fantastic Books
Great Authors

Meet our authors and discover our exciting range:

- Gripping Thrillers
- Cosy Mysteries
- Romantic Chick-Lit
- Fascinating Historicals
- Exciting Fantasy
- Young Adult and Children's Adventures

Visit us at:
www.crookedcatpublishing.com

Join us on facebook:
www.facebook.com/crookedcatpublishing

Lightning Source UK Ltd.
Milton Keynes UK
UKOW04f1941270815

257676UK00001B/9/P